DESIGNED LIES

Designed Lies

CARMEN ELLE

Dedication

To those who I've lost but still watch over me. To those who never gave up on me. To the two who remind me, I can never give up. And, to the creatives fighting for their dreams.

THE COUPLE'S DINNER

PART ONE

"You stupid bitch!"

"Who are you talking to?"

"You dummy. No one else in this room is the jerk you are."

"What the hell is wrong with you?"

"Act like you don't know."

"You were invited here, back into our lives, and this is how you talk to me?"

"Oh, please, quit trying to play the good Samaritan. We all know you ain't shit Katrina."

"Faith, you're so disrespectful."

I smirked. "You're right." I stood up from the table. "You're absolutely right, Katrina, I am disrespectful. Disrespectful ol' Faith. That's why I slept with Edris."

Stillness surrounded us in the private dining room of Hotel St. Michel, but it didn't last long. Glass crashed into the plant-lined wall behind me. I flipped my feet out of my Gianvito Rossi mirrored slingback heels and climbed onto the table. I lunged my body towards Katrina's, reaching for her 24-inch chestnut brown hair. I kicked plates of mushroom risotto, linguine, and asparagus. Nothing was going to get in my way. She was finished. My fists swung furiously at her head, her hands attempting to cover her face.

Someone wanted to keep us apart, but rage had taken over. I didn't care, and I wasn't letting up. I kept swinging. I heard Chloe's high-pitched screams in the background. I think Jack was screeching for me to stop, and Edris could only drop F-bombs.

JACK

I made my way over to this alluring golden pecan princess sitting in the lounge area. I played it composed and thought of the suitable words I needed as I sat next to her on the black tufted sofa. She made it easy for me by speaking first.

"Hi, handsome, how are you?" She spoke over the smoothness of some Afro-beat vibe the DJ had mixed along with the invisible click-clack of women's heels across the stained concrete floor. I was all too familiar with the sound echoing off the paneled beige walls lined with hanging plants.

Her body language said she was looking for someone to accompany her home, at least that's what I was going to tell myself. Her rounded breasts on display in a black dress, the scent of lavender mixed with Black Love incense lingered around her. Her hair, Neo-soul Angie Stone, to match her crystal jewelry. I guessed her place was eclectically decorated with some sort of exotic fish swimming in a large tank.

"I'm doing well tonight, how about you?"

"The only thing keeping me happy tonight is this cranberry and vodka I'm nursing." She smiled slightly; I could only hope she wasn't missing any teeth under her crimson-stained lips.

"Sounds like you had a hard day at the office."

"Yeah, you could definitely say that. I caught my boyfriend cheating on me in my own bed. You could say I'm nursing more than this drink."

"You have some steam to let out, huh?"

"I sure do." She licked her all-embracing lips and moved closer to me. "And the way I'm feeling right now, anything is possible tonight." She licked her lips again in reassurance.

"Would you like another drink, Beautiful?" I extended the offer.

She nodded yes as she finished the last of the drink she had. Now don't get the wrong idea about me–I wasn't trying to get her drunk so I could have her. I was simply giving her what she wanted. If it worked out to my desire, then so be it.

I went over to the bar to get her drink. Bryant and Edris were standing there shaking their heads. "What?" I shrugged.

"Every time, man, every single time. It's unbelievable," Edris's eyes deadpan, leading down to the sharp tip of his winced nose.

"Hey, don't be upset with me because your women dictate your lives. I'm out having a good time, and this little freak over here is trying to have a good time herself and include me in it." I ordered Little Freak's drink while Bryant and Edris looked at me sideways for my comments about their controlling women. We'd only been there for a few minutes, and I bet their girls will be calling at any moment to ask what they were doing.

"I thought these nights were supposed to be for the fellas. We haven't been here more than ten minutes, and you already got your freak for the night."

"We all up in here, but when we leave, you two will go home, ladies will be waiting for you, dinner hot and ready, but what do I have? Cold, barren bed sheets, no hot and ready meal for me." I turned on the hopeless eyes.

"If you were more like us, you wouldn't have to worry about a hot meal or cold sheets." Bryant decided to speak up, and I knew Edris wasn't too far behind. The two of them always stuck together when it came to bringing me down.

"You think that too, huh?" I said, looking straight at Edris, waiting for the answer I already knew.

"Man, there's nothing like what Katrina and I have. I'm going to marry her real soon. You need to work on building something like that with someone you can trust."

The bartender handed me two drinks, and I gave him a nod. "I'm not trying to get into this right now with you two; I'm having a good time. Alright, now I'll be right over there." I grabbed the drinks and headed back to Little Freak.

"Sorry about that, I hope I didn't keep you waiting long?"

"No, it wasn't long at all. Thank you for the drink. My name is Rayven." She extended her hand to me, her nose ring catching the light.

"I'm Jack."

"It seems like we've met before. Do you come here a lot?"

"Actually, I come here every Thursday with my boys."

"I've been here a couple of times."

"I'm interested to know, but I understand if you have nothing to say on the subject. How did you find your boyfriend cheating on you?"

"I gave that idiot seven years of my life, and he cheats with the woman who was supposed to be the maid of honor in our wedding when he finally asked me to marry him. And to make matters worse, they do the deed in my home, where I've lived with him for the last four years. She loves to sleep with men who don't belong to her. She especially loves married men, but never thought she would be after mine."

"How about I take your mind off the situation for tonight? My place is only around the corner, and I don't mind being the friend you need." Smooth huh? My speech was always slick off the lips and always the precise terminology I needed to get me to where I was trying to go.

"Jack, as a matter of fact, that sounds excellent to me right now." She put her cup down on the small table in front of us, the ice giving its last clink. As she stood up from the sofa, I noticed the way the soft fabric of her hips hugged her thighs.

"Alright, let me get with my boys, let them know I'm out of here." I walked back over to the bar where Bryant and Edris were still standing. "Fellas, I got the green light. I'm going to get up with you two tomorrow. Enjoy those hot and ready meals." I chucked them the deuces.

They shook their heads, knowing how right I was about hot meals and cold bed sheets. I needed warm sheets, too. As much as we went back and forth, they understood me. Bryant and Edris had been my boys forever, since we were kids, and we always looked out for each other. They were content with just one, but I liked variety. But the biggest disagreement we always had was their women. Bryant's girl Chloe wasn't too bad, but Edris's girl Katrina was the absolute worst. The worst of the worst. I didn't want anything to do with her, but I tolerated her for the sake of my friendship with Edris. I wasn't worried, though. One day, he would see her deceitful ways. Hopefully, by then it won't be too late. He was over there talking about marriage. That would be a tragic mistake on his part.

Rayven and I ditched the bar; she followed behind me in her Infinity to my condo, which had been newly renovated. She parked her SUV next to my new Jag F-Pace, which I had purchased a couple of weeks ago.

"You must do well for yourself," she said, eyeing the sedan as she walked around the car to meet me.

"Why do you say that?"

"You live in this high-class building and drive that nice car."

I snickered, "This is South Florida. Doesn't everyone have a nice car?" I winked at her as we crossed the parking lot to the main door to enter the building of my condo. We took a short and quiet elevator ride up to the fifth floor. I unlocked the door and invited her in. "I do alright. You must not be doing too bad yourself; your Infinity is on point."

She looked around, noting the hardwood floors and white walls. She commented on how clean the carpet looked, saying that it was evidence that I must not have children. She settled into the sectional sofa and continued her attempt at getting to know me.

"What do you do, Mr. Jack? I would at least like to know your last name before I lie in your bed."

I sat next to her on the sofa, and she moved closer to me, kissing me with those crimson-stained lips. Her tongue slipped between my lips and filled my mouth with the remnants of cranberry and vodka, but nonetheless, it was a sweet kiss. Once she was completely in my lap, she finally let go of my tongue. I wiped my lips of her wetness and was somewhat surprised by her actions, but she had been willing to follow me here rather easily, and she said herself she wanted to be in my bed.

I quickly regrouped. "I work for Davis & Toule Marketing, I'm the lead executive, and my last name is Spencer. What about you?"

"I'm a nail technician, I own Coral Glam Nail Spa, and my last name is Paul."

"Is there any other information you need to know?"

"Where's your phone in case your girlfriend comes in and tries to cut me, and I need 911?"

"I don't have a girlfriend," I said, kissing her neck.

"What if you're a serial killer?"

"Shouldn't you have asked me that before you came over here?"

"Then I guess I'm getting ready to die tonight!" She smiled through breathy kisses.

I never took women into my bedroom. I guess there was a part of me that cared about what I was really doing. Every time I would lie down, a different memory would come. I ran the risk of the wrong name coming to mind, but I guess that could happen anyway. There was something about my bed that I didn't want to be infiltrated by my bad habit.

Rayven's kisses brought me back to her, and I could tell she had built up sexual tension; she became a ravenous creature with every kiss. She began to rip into my clothes like they were on fire, and she needed to save my dark umber skin from being burnt. She moved gracefully, but still with passionate aggression.

"Come on, Mr. Jack Spencer, show me I didn't make this trip for nothing."

I pulled away from her to go into the kitchen to get a couple of condoms from the drawer–I know, odd place to keep them, but since my bedroom was off-limits, I had to keep them handy somewhere. She was quick to come here–who knows where else she had been tonight–especially with the anger about her boyfriend following her like a hanging cloud. (See, I do have a conscience about certain things!)

When I returned, protection in hand, Rayven's eyes widened. "It's going down like that since you pulled out two?"

"Don't want to jinx it, but you are sexy as fuck."

I dropped my pants and slipped into the rubber confine. I went to her as she hiked up her dress and guided my hands over her smooth, golden lavender-scented skin. I wanted to relax her and work out every stress her boyfriend had given her. She rubbed my chest as she pulled herself to me, giving me more of her sweet taste; she was undeniably ready to release on me.

Now, you may be thinking I'm your average jerk who goes out and patrols for women to sleep with. But that's not me at all. My goal is not to pursue women, but to make them feel as comfortable as possible when they are with me. If my pleasure is delighted along the way, who am I to argue with that?

Rayven left my place at three-thirty in the morning, left me with one last sweet kiss, and told me to keep her number handy so we could go back in time and have dinner first. I wasn't sure if I was going to call her. I knew she needed time to recover from the offense her ex and her best friend had committed against her. If they had been together for seven years, she needed more than one night with me. I wasn't trying to become her fatal attraction story–if I wasn't able to take her pain away–and end up looking like Martin Lawrence at the end of *A Thin Line Between Love and Hate;* water seal wasn't a good look for me.

I met up with my boys for lunch the next afternoon–another ritual of ours to get away from our daily stresses and catch up on what was going on with each other. Our lunch spot was Lidia's, a hole-in-the-wall pizza joint central to all our jobs. Never a big lunchtime crowd, and the food was good; something quick and easy.

"What happened last night, when you took that woman home?" Bryant asked, rubbing his long, bushy beard as we sat down to eat our slices. They didn't even give me time to chew; they went right in with what they wanted to know.

"You know how the story goes," I replied, trying to remain a gentleman.

"Come on, Jack, let's be mature about this. You need to stop running around with these random women." Bryant said.

"One of these women is going to give you something you don't want one day, and by then it's going to be too late. Might be *something* a shot can't cure." Edris chimed in, always ready to give his two cents.

"Come on, man, how long have you known me? You know I got this; all my situations are under control. Let me ask you something, though. If it was meant for us to be with one woman, then why did the Creator of all living things make so many awe-inspiring ones, one after the other? It gives me chills thinking about them and what I can do to them." I licked my lips, having a nostalgic moment of how Rayven tasted.

"You're gross. Will you ever stop trolling?"

"Hey, they come to me and tell me what they want. It's my duty to give them what they want when they ask. I can't tell the ladies no, don't make me say it." I pleaded with the guys, throwing my hands up in surrender.

"But do you have to say yes to every single one you come in contact with?"

"Alright, let's change the subject, please." Bryant turned his attention to Edris. "What's up with this weekend?"

"Katrina wants to redecorate after seeing Jack's new place. She wants to drag me to damn Home Goods, but you know me, I'm all about football this weekend, and I am not trying to miss a thing." Edris answered.

"I'm trying to get on that too, but Chloe is on some lunch with her mom stuff. I told her she should use the time to bond with her mom, but she wasn't trying to hear it."

"See, that's exactly what I'm talking about, you both have these women that you let dictate your lives and tell you what you are going to do with all your time. That's why I'm a free man, and I do what I want to do when I want to do it. Believe the Tigers will be on my screen with nobody in the background asking me, '*baby, what you doin'?*" I mimicked.

"So, they a lotta nosy, but they love us, and they are sent from God." Bryant had to laugh at himself for that comment. Edris and I joined in.

"Listen, the next time you talk to God, ask him if there's a money-back guarantee or a warranty agreement or something because your women have made a down payment on you and are close to paying you off."

"If any of us need to talk to God, it would be you," Edris said.

"He's too busy drinking from the devil's goblet." Bryant's voice erupted into laughter.

I was done with them laughing at me for today. "Well, fellas, it's been real nice talking about controlling women and sin, but I've got to get back to work." I wiped my mouth and threw my napkin back on the table.

Edris looked down at his watch. "I'll catch up with y'all this weekend." He pointed at me. "You won't be the only one watching those Tigers!"

We all dapped each other up and told each other peace to go our separate ways. These were simple, everyday gestures, but for us, it was as if saying no hard feelings. They got one on me, I got on them, but at the end of the day, we were brothers.

Out of the three of us, Bryant was the most mature; he had this relationship thing down and wasn't giving it up, no matter how much I picked on him, but Chloe was alright with me. Not enough to make me only want one woman, but it worked for them. I remember when they met while we were out having dinner, and she was cute but not quite for me. All night, he had been staring at he,r and when I caught him, he still didn't take his eyes off her.

She was an exquisite honey-toned woman, her dark hair in loose waves down to her shoulders that night. Her eyes shone a luminous chestnut. She wore a pink body-clinging dress, no doubt a mix of rayon and nylon that hugged the curves of her womanly figure.

"Who are you staring at?" I asked.

"That beautiful girl over there, excuse me." He said, licking his lips and walking over to her. They exchanged words, and I saw her typing on his phone. He returned to the table with a huge grin on his face. I'll admit, Chloe was the right type of woman, but Edris's girl, Katrina. Pure wickedness. Wicked beyond Satan's measure would be my hypothesis.

KATRINA

I couldn't stand when Edris stayed out with Jack and Bryant at night. Here I was, another Thursday night, waiting for my man to come home. I paced back and forth in front of the window of our apartment, looking through the thin blue curtains. I especially hated Jack; he was the definition of a bad influence. All he wanted to do was sleep with whatever woman would let him, and every time Edris came home, he had a new story to tell about Jack's bad habits and freaks of the evening. He needed to be more like Edris and find a real woman like me; even Bryant had Chloe. We both ensured that our men had anything and everything they wanted, most often, before they even knew what they wanted.

I thought about Jack's last girlfriend, Celeste, the aspiring model. She was tall, yes, stunningly beautiful with newly hand-crafted 36D's to complete the physical package. Thin waist, curvaceous bottom, and the longest legs I'd ever seen on a woman. No one could deny she was jaw-dropping.

Jack met her at that stupid bar they go to every Thursday; that had always been his place to find victims. From Edris's recount of the story, she approached Jack and asked him to buy her a drink. Bold if you ask me, but she must have known she was stepping to the right one to give her what she was asking for. He probably looked her body up and down and couldn't refuse. No doubt, rubbing his chin as I'd seen him do before when he was sizing someone up.

They sat and talked, he invited her to dinner, and the following evening, he picked her up, took her to her favorite restaurant, and enjoyed her company. To my surprise, he dated her for about four months. Even introduced her to Chloe and me. She wasted no time telling us how he sexed her crazy, and they were doing shit she'd never experienced before and that she had only thought of. She said his reputation was well deserved, so much so that she would pop up at his office because she was missing him. Personally, I thought the woman was delusional.

I thought that the women Jack always chose were just plain dim-witted, and Celeste was no different in my mind. But I guess I really shouldn't be too hard on her. I'm a woman, and I knew all too well that sometimes we just didn't read the blaring signs. Come on, ladies, sometimes we just downright ignore them.

What would have been the last straw for me was the night she found a bra between the pillows of the man's bed. When Edris told me about it, I couldn't help but literally roll on the floor laughing. Because that's what his sneaky ass gets. If Edris had pulled something like that on me, you better believe I wouldn't still be there having a conversation, let alone an argument with him about it, as Celeste did with Jack.

But apparently, even though she knew he was lying, they still stayed together, and there she was at our next cookout like absolutely nothing was wrong. I remembered covering my giggles the entire afternoon to keep from laughing in her face. She probably didn't know that my man was telling me everything, but that wasn't her problem. Her problem was her man.

I never understood, if you find hardcore evidence that your man is seeing other women, why continue to give him the time of day? Oh, I had many theories on this crisis that seemed to be raging through the feminine population.

Maybe it was a self-esteem issue, or that we're afraid to be alone, and wouldn't be able to find another man, so we're willing to put up with the unnecessary. Or maybe it was a daddy issue that was never resolved. Abusive fathers that you never outgrow, you grow up thinking that all these demeaning things are normal and supposed to happen. No matter the reason, my answer is, don't let these men run all over you.

That was two years ago, and Jack hadn't changed since. I was quickly getting agitated that Edris had asked me to cook dinner for him, and he was an hour late because he was with Jack and Bryant. I liked Bryant, but Jack was a jackass, and I didn't like him around Edris.

"What's up, babe?" He said when he finally decided to come home.

"What do you mean? *What's up*? You are an hour late, and your dinner is cold."

"Katrina, you know I was out with the fellas."

"Yes, I know that, but did you forget that you asked me to cook dinner this morning when you left? I'm sorry for taking that statement as a fact that you would be home to eat it. Anyway, don't you think it's about time you guys give up hanging out so late? Especially you and Bryant, you two are not on the prowl anymore like Night Howlin' Jack."

"My night out with the fellas is not about being on the prowl."

"Then what is it about? You guys see each other all the time. I'm just saying you should be spending more time with me."

"How much more time do you want, Katrina? We live to-gether? You see me more than they do." He got that ugly, con-fused look on his face that I hated.

"That is not true, you work late, then you go out, while I'm here alone waiting on you. What about us? Remember the time we used to spend together?"

"Come on, you know things at work are crazy right now. I'm seeing twice as many patients as I was just a few weeks ago. So, when I go out with the fellas, it's my chance to unwind and re-lax, especially after listening to other people's problems all day."

As much as I admired Edris for what he did, this excuse was getting overused. He was a great rehabilitation counselor, but what about the parts of our relationship that needed rehabilita-tion? And what do I do to unwind and relax? That used to be what we did for each other, but now I guess Jack and Bryant were the remedy. My services were no longer needed.

"I used to be the one to relax you," I approached him, throw-ing my arms up around his neck. "Remember me, your woman. I can do things that your boys can't do, and those women at the bar, you know, they don't compare."

He tittered, "No, I haven't forgotten about you, how could I? Listen, how about tomorrow night I finish up work early, we check into a suite downtown, and it's me and you for the night."

I backed away. "I'm only worth one night to you? I mean, come on, Edris. I can't even get a whole weekend?" I liked the idea, but I wasn't in love with it.

"It's not even like that."

"No wait, let me guess, you are going over Jack's to meet up with him and Bryant to watch football this weekend, and that's why we can't have an entire weekend to ourselves. Is that about right?"

"Babe, football doesn't last that long. I'll be back before you even miss me." He kissed my forehead and went to the bedroom.

"Did I call it or did I call it? Edris, I'm not crazy. I've watched football before; two minutes is really forty-five." He was always picking them over me. "You know what, go ahead and watch football all weekend, I'll call Chloe, and we can make it a football party." I went into the kitchen to grab my phone off the charger.

"I'm pretty sure when Jack invited me over, he wasn't planning a party."

"Oh, maybe Chloe can make that crab and shrimp dip everyone likes so much."

He followed me to the kitchen, but I ignored his protest. If he wasn't going to make room for me, I was going to make it myself. I had given him plenty of chances.

***

While the guys had their own tradition of Thursday nights, Chloe and I never missed an opportunity to meet up for some dinner and cocktails whenever we could. I loved my best friend; she was always trying to keep me straight, and I appreciated it even when I didn't want to hear it.

"What were you and Edris arguing about last night anyway?" Chloe asked as we sat down to order margaritas and nachos at Los Playas. The food was always great here, but damn the decor. Someone had gone overboard with beach balls, fish nets, and the plastic shovels that littered the walls. Yes, we were a stones through from the beach, but damn.

I told Chloe. "It was more of a disagreement, but I'm sick of being down on the bottom of his list of priorities. He doesn't understand why I'm over him, Bryant, and Jack going out so much and hanging out so late."

"I don't like Bryant coming home late either, but the guys deserve to have some time to themselves just as much as we do. I need a break too; Bryant and I don't need to be up under each other all of the time."

"But Edris acts as though there is a limit to how much time we can spend together. He had the nerve to tell me that for just one night we can check into a suite downtown."

"You've been reduced to a night?" Chloe scoffed. Maybe now she was seeing my point.

"I've been thinking, maybe it was a mistake for us to move in together. He never misses me because he knows I'll always be there. I feel silly for thinking we should live together before getting married."

"You were expecting him to propose by now, right?"

"Exactly, he was supposed to propose shortly after I moved in with him, but as you can see, things aren't going according to plan. It's been over a year since we moved in together." I held up my left hand to show her my empty ring finger.

"It might be time to play that ultimatum card, either he proposes, or he no longer gets his milk for free. But, if you tell him that you have to be prepared for what his response may be, especially if it's not to your liking."

"I was so mad at him last night, I spoiled his plans for this weekend," I said with a smirk.

"Oh yeah, Bryant told me he wanted to go over Jack's for the game."

"And you didn't object?" I said, shaking my head from side to side and lowering my neck.

"No, I knew I wouldn't have to since you would. What did you say to Edris?"

"That you and I were coming too, we are making it a party." I snapped my fingers.

"You're always dragging me into your mess," she squinted her eyes at me. "You know I can't stand football. And I'm supposed to be having lunch with my mother on Saturday anyway."

"Hey, this weekend is crucial if we want to get our men to spend more time with us. Forget your mother, she's had you for almost 30 years."

Chloe rolled her eyes and tipped her drink up to her lips.

My phone rang out, vibrating against the wooden butcher block top table; it jolted me. Even more to my surprise, I saw 'DO NOT ANSWER' flashing across the screen, and I knew immediately who it was. Why would she be calling me?

"Who is that?" Chloe asked.

"You won't believe it, but I only have one contact saved as that."

"What are you talking about? Who?"

"Faith."

"Faith Watson?"

"Do you know any other Faiths?"

"What could she want? Probably haven't spoken to her in at least three or four years."

I shuddered a little bit thinking about what she could possibly be calling for. Chloe was right; neither one of us had spoken to her in so long that I thought she would have taken the hint and realized that we were no longer friends.

"Anyway," I continued.

"We need to do something about our men now, or we'll be stuck with this crap forever. You know Jack ain't never settling down, and he's determined to keep Edris and Bryant right by his side."

Chloe rolled her eyes.

But, you know what we should do?"

"What bright idea do you have now?" Her tone was annoyed.

Chloe always wanted to play it so safe. She was much quieter than me and didn't speak up much when it came to Bryant, but I knew she wanted her man around just as much as I wanted Edris with me. She didn't have to say it; I knew it.

As I drove home from dinner, I thought about putting on something sexy for Edris once he got home, but I quickly changed my mind, thinking that he didn't deserve the show. Why should I do anything for him when he couldn't even set aside a weekend for me?

I needed to think about something else. My mind wandered back to that phone call from Faith. As much as I wanted to forget about it, I still wanted to know why call now? She must be in some sort of trouble; that was all she used to call for.

I met Chloe and Faith during our freshman year in college, while Chloe had proved to be a tried-and-true friend, Faith made our lives a real reality show that we used to only like to watch in between classes.

There were four of us. Me, Chloe, Faith, and Rayven. I thought I had found my sisterhood for life, but Faith ruined that when she spiraled out of control during our junior year. Chloe and I were well on our way to becoming teachers, studying our way to degrees in Education at FAU. While Rayven was doing her thing in the International Business program. And Faith had been our Nina Mosley, giving us all the feels and vibes we needed at the student center's poetry nights. We knew back then that the girl had talent for all things creative, but writing was her favorite. When she would get up on open mic nights and read her work out loud, it was soul-stirring. Shit, I'd never heard before. We all had been pretty focused, but Faith switched up on us in ways I just hadn't been prepared for.

It all started when she began dating Quinton. One day, he just popped up at our lunch table, and he proclaimed himself to be Faith's boyfriend. I didn't have a problem with the guy. Who was I to say who she could and couldn't date? But what I didn't like was his humdrum attitude. Whenever he was around, he brought everybody down.

All he ever wanted to talk about was famine, war, politics, and whatever building was getting torn down that week. Yes, these things needed to be talked about, but all the damn time. I remember asking him how his day was going, and he said, "Have you eaten today, Katrina?"

"Yes, of course."

"See how you have that option? Did you know that 55% of Haiti's population is below the poverty line?"

Did he really expect me to answer that? I never knew what to say when Quinton was around, and no matter how uncomfortable he made us, Faith never noticed. Her rose-colored glasses smeared as hell. Although Chloe and Rayven agreed with me that Quinton wasn't about much besides spewing statistics he had probably only just learned in his Social Sciences program, we never tried to pull him and Faith apart.

Faith would confide in us that sometimes, she didn't think Quinton was well mentally, but she admired his ability to think about the world's problems, and stood by his side and listened to his theories on solving the world's most complicated issues.

But things had gone too far when Quinton had a complete mental breakdown and barricaded himself and Faith in his dorm room. That was a day I knew I'd never forget, even as much as I tried to forget Faith.

The air that night was salty, but crisp as light winds came up from the Atlantic. As I walked across the large, landscaped campus yard with Chloe and Rayven, I knew something was wrong. Rayven had been calling Faith for a couple of hours but hadn't been able to reach her. We were all supposed to be meeting up to buy tickets to the upcoming basketball game, so Chloe suggested we go over to Quinton's dorm to see if Faith was there.

As we walked across the yard towards the boys' dorm, my skin prickled under the spurts of salty wind. We hadn't gotten fully across the palm tree-lined sidewalks when I knew something dreadful was going on; I just couldn't imagine what.

The closer we got to Quinton's dorm; we saw the blaring lights of an ambulance outside the entrance of the four-story building. My heart sank to the soles of my flip flops at the sight. Simultaneously, all three of us took off into a sprint to join the onlookers that had already gathered. Chloe spotted Faith first.

"There she is," she pointed to Faith.

Faith was sitting on the sidewalk, a blue police blanket wrapped around her shoulders. Her mocha honey cheeks were splattered with running mascara that had pooled underneath her eyes before dripping down her pointed chin.

The officer she was talking to sprang into top-flight action. "Excuse me, ladies." He said gruffly. Inspecting all of us in an up and down motion with his eyes.

Faith spoke up for herself, "No, it's ok, these are my friends."

The brute, square-shouldered officer backed away after releasing his pursed thin lips.

Rayven said. "We've been calling you. What the hell is going on?"

She spoke slowly, almost methodically, trying to hold back tears. "Quinton...is...dead."

"What do you mean, dead?" I had just seen him that same morning.

Chloe's eyes darted at me. I knew she was telling me to shut up. She turned her attention to Faith as she sat next to her on the sidewalk. "Tell us what happened."

Before Faith could part her full lips, two men in black neoprene jackets came down the steps of the dorm with a gurney and a black body bag. Faith's eyes slammed shut as tears rolled down her already wet face. She turned, looking away as Rayven joined her and Chloe down the sidewalk. She began to sob into Rayven's shoulder.

Our friend was never the same after that night, and I couldn't blame her. I also couldn't imagine what she had experienced while being kept in that room with Quinton, watching him fall completely apart until he decided to end his own life with a gun he had taken from his brother's house while visiting home. Neither of us knew what to say or how to console Faith. As much as we wanted to be there for her, she pushed everyone away.

Thinking back to those moments made me feel bad for not speaking to Faith in such a long time because I knew everything she had gone through, but it also brought back the memories of what led to the demise of my group of friends, which I thought would last long past college.

I couldn't think of what she could possibly want after nearly four years. I didn't keep up with everything about her, but I knew she was still doing her thing in the writing world. She had two books on the *New York Times Best Sellers* list, so I figured life wasn't going too badly for her. But a phone call from her after all this time was concerning. I knew my curiosity would get the best of me. I had to call her back to see what was going on. If I didn't, I would spend much more time thinking about the phone call I had ignored.

I pulled into the parking lot of the low-rise blue and ocean white condo I shared with Edris. Putting the car in park, I cautiously dialed Faith back and waited.

Sound from the other end of the phone rustled through my ear. "Hey." Her voice was light, unsure.

"You called me?"

"Yes, I did. How are you doing?"

"I'm fine. I won't pretend that I'm wondering why you've decided to reach out to me."

"I know it's been a while. I wasn't sure if I should call or not, but I decided to try."

"Why? What do you want?"

She exhaled. "Look, Katrina, I know I did some things in the past, but come on, we were good friends at one point, and it would be nice to reconnect. I'd love to see you and Chloe."

"Reconnect, huh?"

"Absolutely. I just moved back from New York, and I want to see both of you."

"I don't know Faith."

"Just give me a chance. I promise you I've changed."

Oh, so you're not sleeping with married men you have no business being with anymore? That was my question, but I decided to keep it to myself.

"I'll tell you what. Saturday, Chloe and I are getting together at a friend's house for a football party. Why don't you come?"

"Are you sure that's going to be cool?"

"Yea, maybe I can even introduce you to my boyfriend's single friend. Are you seeing anyone special these days?"

She chuckled. "Not at all."

"Are you positive?"

"Katrina," she scoffed. "I told you, I've changed."

I finished the phone call, giving Faith Jack's address and telling her to bring a side dish. She didn't know it just yet, but she was going to help me. Help me by becoming a wonderful distraction.

FAITH

I couldn't believe that chick, asking me if I was sure. I rolled my eyes as I hung up the phone. She was making it obvious her standing grudge against me was well intact. I guess I couldn't blame her; I expected that to be the case when I decided to call her in the first place. We hadn't spoken in quite some time, and I knew an old stubborn mule like her never forgot a damn thing. But that was fine, because neither did I.

Katrina and Chloe had been two of my closest friends throughout college; unfortunately, that made them, along with our other friend Rayven, the main targets in the downward spiral that were my tortured years of higher education.

I made my way up the carpeted stairs of my two-story North Gordon home, still thinking of Katrina's reaction to my attempt to reconnect with her. I had worked hard to regain control of my life, and I did want to make amends to the people I knew I had hurt the most, but not if they wanted to rub the past in my face. Katrina hadn't always been the most graceful in expressing her negative feelings, but when she was disgusted with you, she made sure you knew it.

Chloe had always been the more down-to-earth and more understanding friend. That had been her role in our group of comrades, and I truly appreciated her for that back then. I could only

25

hope the energy would be the same if we did reconnect and she hadn't been sullied by Katrina's judgmental rain clouds. But, as understanding and compassionate as Chloe was, she still followed behind Katrina as if the two of them shared a brain.

I believed that if Chloe had been able to separate her own feelings from Katrina's, we still would have been friends. Chloe was the one who tried to keep me going once I fell into depression after the death of my boyfriend in college, but I allowed depression and self-hate to take over too much, and I was only a shell of myself back then.

Too many memories of the past were coming back to me. Without realizing it, my fists clenched so hard the pointed tips of my acrylic nails dug into my skin, leaving small pricks of red on my palm. I'd done a lot to better myself and my life over the past four years, but Katrina remained on my shit list. The one imperfect spot I knew wouldn't be washed away until I made her feel half of what she had made me feel for abandoning me in college.

I never thought I'd be able to back then, but even without the support of my one-time friends, I did return to college, finish my English degree, and managed to land a major book deal. Most of my dreams had come true. But I had created a lonely life for myself. Giving myself too much time to think. Allowing my mind to replay old situations and purposes that no longer served me.

I slid my body into my oversized king bed. I spread out across the isolated mass of 600-thread-count white sheets, pulling the white down comforter over my head to black out the rest of the world and the last sliver of light showing through my window from the yard lamp. It would be nice to have someone to cuddle up to, I thought as I closed my eyes.

I envisioned a man lying next to me. Holding me in his brawny arms, my cares, worries, and anger drifted off as I fell asleep in his naked arms. I reached for one of the overstuffed pillows that filled the top of the bed, quickly stuffing it between my legs. The cotton of my nightshirt rose over my thigh and up to my bottom as I pushed the thick material where heat was rising from my second pair of lips.

My storybook man would sense what I needed, moving to reposition my body, spreading and lifting my legs to quench both of our thirst. He would push my thighs to my stomach, his rugged hands squeezing my thighs as he kissed down my naked triangle mound. He would stop to savor the aroma of my flower that was budding just for him. His tongue slowly, methodically teasing my lips before he moved his fingers down my thighs to spread open the flower that bloomed just for him.

His tongue searching, his fingers rubbing the delicateness of my inside petals. My moans growing, my nipples hardening, anticipation replaced with passionate desire. His search returned results, but he wasn't satisfied. He would sense that I needed him to keep searching. Keep licking, keep rubbing, keep letting me feel the hotness from his own moans against the folds of my petals. He would sense that I never wanted him to stop, even after he found the pathway to make my legs shake, make me call his storybook name, have me scream so loud from release that I didn't care about trying to control the volume of my moans.

I sat straight up in my bed. My fingers sticky and wet. My chest heaved in excitement. I looked down at the pillow that had been my storybook man. What would he say to me?

***

As I walked down the hall of the high-rise condo in Playa del Sol, I didn't know what to expect. I wondered if I would have the chance to catch up with Katrina and Chloe. Katrina said this was a friend's place, but I didn't know who all was involved when she said party. And by the looks of this building, I wanted to know who could possibly be Katrina's friend who lived here. I knew these places started at half a mil.

I knocked on the door, and Chloe answered.

"Hey, I didn't think you were going to actually come." She extended her arms to hug me.

"It's so good to see you."

She eyed me for a moment, then stepped back to let me through the door. "I was surprised when Katrina said that you were coming, but I'm glad you're here."

Chloe looked great. Her smile still radiant, her chestnut eyes shone brightly with genuine happiness, and I relaxed a little. Not too much, still had to face Katrina.

"Come in."

I followed her into the open living room, where a huddle of men was seated in a semi-circle in front of what looked like a 75" LED TV. Only one bothered to pull his eyes away from the game to look in my direction. Our eyes connected for a moment; his deep cognac stare led the way to his broad nose, brimful lips, and cleanly shaped goatee and mustache. Since his eyes weren't letting up, I took in his charcoal heather V-neck t-shirt and dark stonewashed jeans. He was fine.

Chloe said. "Let me introduce you to everyone." She started farthest away from the cutie who still had his eyes on me. "This is Jack, my boyfriend, Bryant, and this is Edris, Katrina's boyfriend."

Of course he was! I stretched my hand to all the guys, "Hi, nice to meet you, I'm Faith."

Jack and Bryant gave hollow salutations and returned their attention to the enhanced TV screen. Edris's eyes returned to me, but his pace said that he wanted to linger again. Katrina must have known that our eye contact had been just a little too long as she made her way from the kitchen, cozied up in the corner to the left of the TV, and the living room area.

She stopped to size me up. Her cocoa-colored eyes did the same up and down look her man had just given me, but I knew what she was doing.

"Hi Katrina, it's been a long time."

Chloe patted me on the shoulder as comfort.

"Yes, it has been." A slight sneer was on her face.

"Thanks for the invite."

"Sure," she took a sip from the canned margarita she had been cradling between her red acrylic manicured fingers. "So, you've met the guys?"

"I did, Chloe was nice enough to introduce me. I'm surprised, though, when you said football party, I was expecting something else."

"Well, did you bring something?" Katrina's neck snapped from side to side. I could see her attitude hasn't changed much.

"I did." I presented the bag of chips and dip. I know she wasn't expecting me to actually cook something.

Katrina didn't even blink or flinch to grab the bag.

She wanted to have a staring contest, and I was all for it, little did she know. Still eyeing me, she called out to one of the guys. "Hey, Jack, why don't you come over here?"

The medium-built, earth-toned man stood up straight from his bent position over the couch, elongating his 6-foot, about 2, I'd say, frame as the game went to commercial. His face crunched as he approached Katrina. "What is it?"

"You met my old college friend Faith, right? Faith, this is Jack."

He turned his attention to me. Licking his thin upper lip, he said, "Yes, I did. Faith, it's nice to meet you. Here, you can put your purse down. Since Katrina doesn't seem to be helpful at the moment." He showed me the console table near the front door.

"Thank you." I chuckled. His digs at Katrina brought joy to me.

I followed behind Jack, his rounded shoulders moving back and forth as he walked in his black high-top sneakers. He wore black denim jeans with just the right amount of loose swag. His white round-neck t-shirt hugged the soft veins in his neck. I couldn't quite decide if he was more attractive than Katrina's boyfriend. He showed me a mostly empty room to put my purse on a dresser.

"So, has Katrina always been the joy we've come to know her as today?"

"Katrina is Katrina," I stated, following him back to the kitchen.

"You went to college with her and Chloe?" He glanced at the TV.

"Yes, that's right."

"Are you a teacher as well?"

"No," I snickered. "I'm an author, actually."

"Wait, Faith, Faith Watson?" he said, handing me a soda from the stainless-steel fridge. "I've read your book; I like your style."

I stepped back in astonishment. "You read, *Can You Hear Me Calling?*"

"I sure did."

"Wow, I'm surprised."

"Why, because brothas don't read?" he shrugged his shoulders.

I smiled, "No, they absolutely do."

Silence ruled us for a moment. I could tell he was still sizing me up, and now I was intrigued. Jack was pretty easy on the eyes, now that I had a chance to take him in. His haircut was freshly tapered near the ears. His auburn brown eyes held a glint of light; he had a kissable, rounded bottom lip, accented by a trimmed mustache and goatee.

"This is your place, right?" I decided to comment.

"Yes. Got it for a great steal a few months ago."

"Good for you. Mind giving me a tour?" I decided to take him for a spin.

He looked back towards the living room as if he needed permission from his other guests. I glanced at Katrina, who had turned to watch us through the open half wall that separated the living room and kitchen. She smiled as if her plan for 'hooking me up' was falling into the perfect place.

Jack hadn't done very much to his place yet. All the walls were still freshly painted white, no marks; I hoped that meant no kids.

I followed him down the short, narrow hallway that led right to a bathroom and split into two additional hallways, one left, one right, leading to separate bedrooms.

"Nothing much on that end," Jack pointed to the right, noting the bedroom was empty and unused. He hoped to turn it into his home office. "This side is the master where I've taken a bit more initiative."

More white walls held a large custom beige quilted headboard and a California king-sized bed. Set next to the bed were two light pine two- drawer nightstands. The room was rather empty but opened to a great view of neighboring condos. We were close to the ocean, but not quite close enough.

"This is a great space."

"It is. Never thought too much about what to fill the space with, but this has been serving me just fine."

"I'm sure you'll find something to make it your own." My voice almost echoed up to the sixteen-foot pitched ceiling. "So, what do you do?"

"I'm a lead executive of market research at a marketing company."

"No wonder you have this awesome place." I smiled, looking back at him.

He returned the intrigue, "Are you working on another book right now?"

"I have a poetry collection I'm working on."

"I'll be reading," he flashed a bright grin towards me.

I thought, ok Mr. Jack, let's see what you're about. Jack and I swapped numbers, and he didn't hold back the grin that he had plastered across his face. I needed to stay close anyway I could, and if that meant taking Katrina's hookup, then so be it.

JACK

"Did y'all know Katrina and Chloe knew Faith Watson?"

"No." Bryant was clueless, shrugging his shoulders.

Edris asked. "What's so special about her? You spent the entire end of the fourth quarter talking to her and showing her your place. Your place ain't that big."

"She's Faith Watson, the author of *Can You Hear Me Calling?*"

"Never heard of it," Edris said, watching a waitress walk past. "It's probably one of those man-hating books, and you read it."

"She's a Terry McMillan mini-me, huh?" Bryant co-signed.

"No, she's not. I read her book, and I thought it was good. She talks about some real stuff that goes down in relationships. You two need to read it and take notes from her characters, it might help the two of you put a leash around them two wild, giant poodles you're trying to domesticate."

"How are you going to tell us to take notes and you are the only one here at the table without somebody?"

"I'm getting ready to have Faith if I play this thing right."

Bryant chuckled. "Now, Jack, you know, you are in dangerous territory, trying to fool around with someone Katrina and Chloe are friends with. That could blow up in your face so quick."

Edris said, "Who is this chick anyway? Since when do the girls even have a friend named Faith?"

"She said they all went to college together and she even said she could tell Katrina ain't changed a bit."

"Aye, you gonna get enough of always baggin' on my girl."

I looked at Bryant, and we shared a laugh this time. Edris knew damn well Katrina was a handful. "Either way, I know Katrina and Chloe invited her over on purpose, just like they invited themselves. I see right through those two. You hadn't stopped to think that your women followed you to watch football to force the two of you to spend more time with them? And they invited Faith on purpose to get me to chill with her so they could have even more time with the two of you."

"I swear, man, the stuff you come up with. You swear up and down you know women so well." Edris exclaimed. "Instead of worrying about our women, maybe you should focus on finding one woman for yourself. The keyword in that sentence being one!"

"I already told you Faith is about to be mine. Y'all didn't see the rhythm she was giving me while she was all up in my bedroom. I probably could have taken her down right then and there."

"You nasty for that." Edris scrunched up his face.

"Okay, keep playing around, watch Faith be the one who comes along and teaches your goofy butt a lesson." Bryant pointed his finger at me.

"Bryant, you know it's no use, this man ain't never going to change."

"I might for the right one."

"And you think the right one is going to be Faith?"

"I don't know about all that, but what I am going to do is take her out."

"Alright, the warning has already been put out there, and if this all goes bad, I do not feel like hearing Chloe's mouth. And I'm sure Edris feels the same way about Katrina. You'd better not do your usual thing. You'd better think it through before you dial that number."

"What do you mean, my usual thing?"

"You know exactly what he's talking about. You play the shit out of these women that fall into your web. Please don't pull that crap on Faith."

"Look, if I found a woman who was worth my time, then maybe I would consider chillin' with just her."

"Look, man, if you want to take Faith out, I say do it because that was Katrina and Chloe's motive for inviting her anyway. I say go ahead and give them what they want, and if things turn out badly, Katrina and Chloe will learn their own lesson." Edris stated his opinion.

Bryant spoke up, "You better be careful with this woman. It doesn't make sense that she would turn up so randomly. The girls have never mentioned her before as more than a past college friend. Now, they randomly invite her to hang out with us. Something is definitely up here."

I had to get back to work, but Bryant and Edris's thoughts on Faith stuck with me as I made my way back to my office. Their soapbox preaching about my love life got old a lot of times, but even that wasn't going to stop me from calling Faith and asking her to have dinner with me.

Before I was back in my office, my date with Faith was a done deal. She chose the restaurant, and I promised to be on time. No matter what my boys were saying, I was going to enjoy myself tonight and let things with Faith fall as they may.

***

I met Faith right outside of the beach restaurant on E. Ocean Ave. at 8 p.m. on the dot as promised. I opened the door for her and followed behind into the neutrally decorated glass-encased restaurant. The large glass paneled ceiling-to-floor windows were accented with fake candle lighting, perfect for couples wanting to keep their business to themselves.

"I'm glad we had a chance to do this, Jack." Faith smiled at me as we were seated in a half-moon booth in a quiet back corner.

"Listen, I hope this isn't too forward, but this weekend there's a play showing at Olympia, would you like to join me?"

"We haven't gotten through the first date, and you're already on to the second?" She giggled, and it was adorable.

"You don't feel the vibrations between us?"

She smiled. "Alright, why not? It sounds like fun. I haven't been to a show in a long time."

Faith was different, I could see it already. Typically, I'd be ready to invite her to my place, but she already agreed to a second date, and that was enough for me.

I took care of the wine order. And Faith took control of the food ordering for both of us. I would have protested, but it seemed that she had read my mind, ordering exactly what I had been eyeing on the menu.

We talked as we enjoyed our food and wine. Faith even offered to share with me if I shared with her. We scooted closer to each other, meeting in the middle of the booth. She smelled so good. Her long, tousled dark brown curls wrapped me in the scent of vanilla and raspberries. Her cinnamon skin glowed with radiance.

I was fighting all temptations to take her to the men's restroom. She looked so good dressed in black slacks with a matching jacket, the lace of her yellow top winking at me, the perfect accent to her skin. The lace gave me a slight peek into the curvature of her chest.

I had to bring myself out of my growing fantasy. "What type of men do you ordinarily date?"

"I've pretty much had them all, from the playas to the I still live at home with mom to the 'I can't clean my own apartment' to the 'I can't bring myself to commit'. Which one are you?"

"I'm none of the above. I hope you haven't been listening to any of Katrina's stories about me."

"Katrina didn't tell me anything about you, honestly. She doesn't even know we're out tonight."

"Are you going to tell her?"

"You sound worried. Are you trying to impress her or get on her good side by taking her dear old friend out or something?"

"No, I'm not trying to hear her mouth about this little rendezvous between us, especially if you end up giving me a bad report."

"Listen, Jack, we are both adults, and we do not have to sneak around Katrina or Chloe or your boys for that fact. I'm having a good time with you; I'm not going to let them ruin what's clearly going on between us."

She was speaking my language and all too well. I had to be careful with this one; she could back me into unfamiliar territory and have me thinking about her all day and night. I had to protect myself. And her audience was too wide for me not to be concerned about becoming her latest shelf-filler.

CHLOE

The smell of sweet blueberries brought me out of my sleep. I knew Bryant was in the kitchen cooking breakfast. Bacon and maple syrup soon joined my senses and pulled me out of the orange cotton sheets of our queen bed.

Bryant knew I was always a sucka for bacon, so I followed the direction of the smoky scent to find him in the kitchen. He was barely dressed, his gray sweatpants hung on his hips right at his Calvin Klein underwear. I admired his muscular back and mocha skin that was only covered in the front by the red apron he was wearing.

"Hey, I thought you were going to stay in bed all day." He said as I entered the kitchen of our one-bedroom apartment. I had to squeeze my body past his tall frame to get to the fridge.

"I could have. I was sleeping so well. This would be the perfect day to stay in bed: it's cloudy and raining, but I smelled something good, so I had to come check it out." I hugged him from behind, kissing his shoulder just where my 5'4 frame met his 6'1 stature.

"Sit your beautiful self down, and I'll fix you a plate." He soon handed me a plate with pancakes, eggs, and bacon. "I hope you're not on any type of diet."

"Do I need to be?" I questioned him.

"No, you could gain three little people, and I would love you the same, honey. If you walked around here eating nothing but salads and started hanging out at the gym, I would be worried I'd have to follow you to school every day."

"I still have to stay in shape for you."

"You don't have to stay in shape for me, I'll love you forever no matter what, but I do appreciate the consideration." He flashed a pearly smile. His lips, sexy and seductive, as they pulled away from his perfect teeth framed by his thick, curly beard.

"Baby, I was thinking." He sat across from me at the table. "Edris had the right idea about spending the weekend at a hotel, but his approach was all wrong. I think next weekend, we should check into the InterContinental, turn our phones off, and create our own world. I think it's been a while since we got away from everything and everyone."

I couldn't help but smile, "I like that. And I wouldn't mind having you all to myself."

"Is that right?" his words drawn out as he leaned across the table to kiss me. "Perfect then. I'll make a reservation. You want some more food, baby? I made plenty."

"You spoil me." I beamed.

He stood up and leaned down to be closer to me, "I love you so much," he whispered into my cheek.

Our eyes met, "I love you, too."

He kissed my neck, "I know this isn't the InterContinental, but I was hoping to spend this rainy day with you. We can take this breakfast to the bedroom, you know."

"Now you know I have papers to grade today."

"Come on, you're a teacher five out of seven days a week, it's the weekend, and you know you hate grading papers anyway. So why not let me distract you?"

He wasn't going to leave me alone, but I figured a little play was okay to go along with work. "How about this, you go and work on those papers while I clean up, and then you can work on me?" Bryant continued to place benevolent kisses on my skin. I loved it when he kissed my collarbone. He knew what he was doing.

"I might be able to play along for a while." I teased back.

We sneaked back into bed, turning the TV on, knowing we weren't going to watch it. Bryant held me close to him. He always had a way of holding my body just right to make me feel the love that poured from his soul to mine. I loved him, and I knew he loved me; Bryant gave me security, and that was irreplaceable.

He was absolutely nothing like what I was used to. The way he spoke to me was always warm-hearted and thoughtful. His actions followed suit, and he was always so considerate. Bryant was a dream guy. He allowed me to be soft, independent, and completely myself. I didn't have to worry about much of anything. He mostly took care of everything. I never had to question the bills being paid; he cooked for me, did our laundry, and he was never too busy for me.

Bryant was the opposite of my previous situation, Michael. I was naïve back then; I would have done anything for Michael to keep him in my life and keep him happy. In the beginning, it was something about his confidence that had attracted me to him. Everything was alright the first couple of years, but soon he began to drink excessively. Don't get me wrong, there's nothing wrong with a grown man having an occasional drink, but he became an alcoholic right in front of my eyes. Even now, I can't pinpoint when I saw the man I had fallen in love with completely disappear.

Shortly into our third year together, he began to physically abuse me anytime he felt like it. Once, he even bruised my cheek so badly I couldn't go to school for a few days. I had ignorantly criticized women who said they couldn't leave men who treated them like they weren't human, but I didn't leave right away, either.

Katrina was my saving grace. She showed up at the townhouse and helped me pack all my stuff up. She even paid for me to stay in a hotel in Coral Gables while I got Michael off my back. For a long time, I still lived in fear, but a few months later, I saw that he had been arrested and given a 10-year prison sentence for assaulting a female officer.

I was relieved knowing he would be away and unable to put his hands on me or any other woman. Hopefully, he could get some help for his problem with alcohol as well. After that, I vowed never have another man in my life that wasn't my father or Jesus. I never thought I'd be able to handle another relationship until I met Bryant two years ago.

During the time I spent alone, trying to get over my fear of Michael, I reevaluated my life and thought about what I truly needed to do to make sure I didn't keep attracting men who were no good for me or who only wanted to hurt me. I wanted true love, although, at that time, I didn't think it existed, but I didn't want to be jaded or bitter.

I focused on what I wanted in my next relationship instead of harboring what had happened to me. This wasn't something I did in just a few weeks; it truly took some time, and even when Bryant and I first started dating, I wasn't completely over all my triggers, but I'm thankful for the patient man that Bryant is. He helped me through all of it. Within a few months of our budding relationship, I no longer feared saying what I perceived to be the wrong things or not sharing how I felt at times for fear of confrontation.

I've been in a euphoric state ever since with Bryant. He's just a cool type of dude, and most importantly treated me like an absolute queen from day one to now. His love was unconditional, and he'd spent every day proving that to me.

Sometimes, I wished Katrina would take the time to do as I did and evaluate herself and her relationship with Edris. I love Katrina like a sister at this point. We've been through so much together, and I'm grateful for what she has done for me, but I definitely knew when she was trippin'.

I know how much she loves Edris and wants a happy relationship with him, but she could be downright ridiculous trying to make everything perfect relationship goals. As if she wasn't bright enough to see that was a social media ploy. To me, Katrina was insecure in her relationship, but of course, I would never tell her that. The backlash would be so ugly it wasn't worth it, especially when it wasn't my relationship. I always tried to give Katrina the best advice I could, but at the end of the day, I knew my breath was being wasted, and Katrina would do what she deemed best. She was just that difficult and controlling, I was surprised Edris even dealt with her aggressive nature, to be honest.

She had this dependence on Edris that was unnatural. I always thought Edris was a fool for the way he spoiled that girl. I mean, we were broke college students together. I wasn't sure when she had become so materialistic. Edris may have brought this terrorism on himself by fulfilling her every request. If he ever smartened up and left her, I wondered if she would be able to survive. We were modest teachers, but because of Edris, Katrina wore Balenciaga, Derek Lam, Moncler, and Saint Laurent. Edris had even sprung for a brand new, fully equipped Lexus for her, but she still gave the man hell at every chance.

Katrina was always plotting; she had been that way since college, and I had no doubt that her invitation to Faith was another plot. I was sure it wasn't because she wanted to mend fences.

As nice as cuddling time with Bryant was, it was getting late in the day, and as much as I didn't want to leave, I had agreed to meet up with Katrina for dinner. Edris and Katrina showed up right on time. The guys were going to watch the game while we opted for the Chinese restaurant around the corner in Hollywood Beach Gardens.

Katrina wasted no time jumping into the topic of her relationship. "Edris was in a big rush to get to your place today."

"He just wanted to watch the game with Bryant, so what?"

"Why doesn't he rush to see me like that anymore?"

I chuckled as a plump waitress balancing on black wedge heels brought us a large platter of orange chicken and fried rice to share. "Will you let that man live his life. So what?"

"I just don't understand him. I feel like I do so much for Edris, and he doesn't even care."

"What are you expecting from him? You act as if he doesn't take care of you as well."

"Seriously? You know exactly what I want. I want the man to marry me already."

"I know that, but you can't force him. Have you had this conversation, calmly, with Edris?"

"What do you mean, calmly?" Her neck snapped around like a fair ride.

"Katrina, come on; you know you can be a bit abrasive."

"Oh, please, I'm just me." She flipped her twisted extensions.

"Yea, but some men don't want that."

"He didn't have a problem with it when he met me. He knew what he was getting into, and if he didn't like it, then why was he still here?"

"You should be asking yourself that question. Apparently, the man loves you because he's still here. Maybe he's not ready to take that step yet. You can't rush into a commitment like marriage."

"It's Jack's fault Edris hasn't asked me to marry him. He's too distracting. Telling Edris and your man all his nasty stories about the women he chases behind. Edris is probably going back and forth in his mind, thinking he should be telling stories like Jack."

I was so confused. "How do you come up with this stuff? Jack has nothing to do with your relationship, and you know that. Stop trying to place blame on other people."

"Then where should I look to place the blame, Chloe?"

See what I mean, can't tell the woman anything. These conversations with Katrina were getting more and more bothersome. She couldn't see how controlling she was, and that was the real problem in her relationship. If Edris was doing what she wanted, peace reigned, but as soon as he decided to use his own brain, it was World War XII.

I was the complete opposite. I didn't need Bryant up under me all the time, and I didn't need to know or control his every move. I needed and loved having my own space. Edris and Katrina were just like us. They lived together and saw each other every day. How much more time could you spend with a person?

"Just talk to Edris," I said flatly, hoping the topic would change.

"We both know how that will turn out."

Since she didn't want to let it go. "You can't get upset at whatever his reaction may be to what you have to say. You need to let him express his feelings and make him feel safe in doing so, not make him fear your retaliation."

"Oh, is that what he tells Bryant?" she said in a mocking tone, her eyes squinted.

I put my hands up and shook my head. This was where I receded into my corner. Again, it wasn't my relationship. "So, how about seeing Faith again?"

Katrina shoveled rice into her mouth, taking a few seconds to chew and then take a sip of her soda.

"What made you invite her to Jack's anyway?"

"What difference does it make? I told you before the party that she was coming. You were still surprised to see her?"

"I honestly didn't think she would show up."

"Oh, please, I mentioned a single man, and there she was."

"Stop it."

"You know I'm right."

"Shut up. We haven't spoken to Faith in some time; she could have changed. And if you suspected she was the same person, why even invite her?"

Katrina's eyes turned dark. I knew that look. This was not good.

"Katrina, what are you planning?"

"You didn't see it?"

"What?"

"How much time Faith spent with Jack? Asking him for a tour of his place."

"And?"

"I have to explain everything to you."

I sat back in my seat; I was losing my appetite.

"Faith hooks up with Jack, leaving Edris and Bryant to spend more time with us." She threw her napkin down as if she had just cured world hunger.

"Katrina, no."

"What do you mean, no?"

"Don't do this. Don't try to play matchmaker."

"I don't need to try; it's already done. You know Jack will sniff around anything with a new scent he's never experienced before. And we both know how Faith is. I wouldn't be surprised if they were out right now together."

"You wrong, you know you wrong for this. Even if Jack is interested in Faith, it's none of your business."

"Hey, I just put things in motion."

"Alright, well, your *motion* is going to get you in trouble if you don't stop getting into other people's business."

We grew quiet, and I could see the proverbial hamster running on the wheel that controlled her brain cells. I contemplated whether I should tell her about Bryant taking me to the InterContinental, but I figured that would only be poking the bear and not a good idea either.

"Do you and Bryant have plans for the weekend?"

Of course, she would ask me that.

"Yes, actually, but nothing fancy."

"Oh, come on, spill, what is it?"

"Nothing, just headed to the InterContinental."

Her jaw nearly disconnected from her head as her mouth flew open. "What?"

"I knew I shouldn't have told you."

"Bryant is taking you to a hotel for the entire weekend?"

"That's what he said."

She threw her napkin over her plate and started digging in her doctor's bag-shaped purse. She frantically pulled cash from her wallet and threw it on the table. "C'mon," she demanded.

Oh crap! What had I unleashed?

I only lived about 10 minutes from the restaurant, so in no time flat, Katrina had beaten me to my place and was headed up the winding concrete steps, her heels echoing through the open corridor. She was about to knock like Broward County PD until she realized I was right behind her with my key.

I had tried calling Bryant as I left the restaurant, but he didn't answer. Unfortunately, Hurricane Katrina part two was already in full swing. I knew her running up on Edris dropping torrential rain and blowing unnatural winds wasn't going to get the time with her man she was begging for, and it definitely wasn't going to get her down the aisle of marriage any faster, but when Katrina was like this, it was best to move out of the way.

I backed her away from the door so I could open it and enter my apartment first. "Hey, fellas." I greeted them and headed to the sofa, leaning down to kiss Bryant on the cheek.

"Hey, baby," Bryant responded with a bright smile.

Snacks were spread out all over my coffee table, the boys' feet propped up on my furniture, but it didn't bother me as much as it clearly bothered Katrina. I could see steam blustering from her nose like a bull about to take off on a rampage.

Katrina didn't waste any more time. "What are you doing, Edris?"

"What do you mean, what am I doing? I'm chillin' watching the game. What are you doing storming up in here like this? I'm very sure Bryant and Chloe don't want you tearing up their stuff."

"Oh shut up."

"What is your problem?"

"I'm about to tell you what my problem is. How the hell is it, Bryant can take Chloe to a hotel for the weekend, but you can barely give me one damn night?"

"Are you serious?"

"No, are you serious? It was your own idea, and you can't even get it right."

I could see Bryant eyeing me from my peripherals and I was sure he was blaming me for this assault on our typically quiet home.

"That's why you're storming in here like a maniac? Going to a hotel in the same city we already live in is that important to you?"

Damn, Edris. I sighed in my head for the man. Wrong response, brotha. I rubbed my eyebrows and bowed my head.

"It's not about the hotel, Edris." Her voice was escalating. "What you don't seem to understand is the time I'm trying to spend with your dumbass. And really, I don't even know why I'm trying. Forget you."

She sharply turned on the stiletto of her sandals and flew back out of the front door. Edris stood up, exhaustion and irritation rang out of his windpipes as he grabbed his wallet from the table.

"I'm sorry, y'all, let me go deal with this woman. Bryant, I'll hit you up later." He shuffled out of the room like a kid who knew his mom was going to have her belt waiting for him when he got home.

"Wow!" I couldn't formulate any other words.

Bryant stared at me. "What was that?"

"Katrina," I answered, grabbing the small white trash can from the kitchen to start cleaning up Bryant and Edris's snack buffet.

"Was that necessary? Why would you even tell her about our weekend plans?"

"She asked, and it just sort of slipped out."

"Slipped out?" Bryant wasn't going for it. "You always think before you speak; nothing just *slips out*."

"She asked if we had plans for the weekend, so I told her."

"So, you were trying to start something between the two of them?"

"Come on, Bryant, you know that's not my style. Besides, I'm always playing the peacemaker when it comes to Katrina."

"But you know the dynamic between the two of them only needs the smallest spark, and it's on."

"Well, maybe you should have told your boy not to try and shortchange his woman on spending time with her."

"You know, if it were up to Katrina, that man would never leave the house. She'd have his ass chained to her 24/7."

"Katrina wants to feel like she's a priority in Edris's life. She's his woman, what's wrong with that? I don't blame her for not wanting some half-thought-out weekend."

"It doesn't even matter. All of this is none of our business, and you should have kept your mouth shut."

I didn't like where this conversation was going, and I truly didn't appreciate Bryant's tone. "Now you're mad at me?"

"I just wish you would stop sticking up for your girl when you know she's wrong. Dead wrong."

"You say that as if I can control Katrina's actions."

"You can, by keeping our business to yourself. I'm telling you, do yourself a favor and let our friends deal with their own disasters."

JACK

When we arrived at the theater, many eyes went to Faith's stylish white suit that showed off her curves in a classy and sexy way. Her dark brown hair pulled back into a tight bun accented the look. Being the first time I'd seen her with her hair pulled back, I noticed the small beauty mark on her right jawbone close to her ear. She was stunning, her skin radiant without unnecessary enhancement. Her makeup, natural and unfiltered, instead of that caked-on stuff that makes women look like extras in *Thriller*. And I wasn't the only one to notice.

A dark-skinned, thick, chunky brother about 6 feet tall turned from his post outside the men's bathroom to watch as Faith and I walked by. She slipped her hand into mine, shooting a wink my way. I didn't mind when men admired what I had. The nosy brother shook his head and turned back around.

We found our seats in the center aisle and settled in to enjoy the show. Faith caught me by surprise when she kept her fingers laced through mine. I was perfectly comfortable and didn't mind if she never let go.

I should have been watching the show on stage, but Faith held my attention. She laughed and cried all through the drama happening on stage, but my mind was elsewhere. I had so many questions running through my mind, I wanted to ask her, but didn't want to cross any lines too soon.

She leaned over and whispered in my ear. "Are you enjoying the show?"

"Yes," I whispered close to her earlobe. Her signature scent of vanilla filled my nostrils.

She smiled at me and squeezed my hand as she continued to cradle it in hers. "Do you have anything planned after this?"

I pushed my neck down to catch her whispered question. She came closer to my ear, enough to allow her glossed lips to graze my lobe as she spoke.

I replied. "Anything you want. Just let me know."

"We could go back to your place and talk for a while." She countered, moving her hand from mine to placing it on my knee.

I was fighting all urges to grab her by her face and kiss her lips until she pushed me away, but I had a feeling she wouldn't. My mind couldn't help itself as it began to race. Sex with Faith was probably electrifying. I was sure she had some tricks that would make me curl my toes and say her name all at the same time. I was willing to bet on it from the way she wrote those steamy sex scenes in her book.

When the show ended, we left the theater hand in hand again. I had to admit that she was making me nervous, which was something I rarely experienced. I wasn't going to admit this to anyone, but Faith Watson was doing something to me. Something I was unsure of, something I couldn't name. This something I'd spent so much time avoiding, but somehow Faith was making it easy. But I was still on guard, after all, she was Katrina's friend.

I agreed to take Faith back to my place. Rain poured as we rushed from the car to the entrance of my building. Faith giggled like a little girl as we walked to the elevator. Her hair was starting to curl at the roots of her bun from the wetness, but she didn't seem to mind. She was still smiling as I unlocked the door, and she followed me inside.

"You can use any towel in the closet," I pointed her to the closet in the hall and to the bathroom. "I'm sure you remember where it is."

"Okay, thanks. I'll be right back."

She only took a few moments in the bathroom before she returned to the living room to join me. She'd released her hair from its tie and allowed her curls to free form, perfectly framing her face. She hung up her white suit jacket on the back of the bathroom door and put a towel around her shoulders. I asked her if everything was alright and if I could get her anything.

"I didn't know rain was in the forecast."

"When isn't it?" I joked.

"Jack, can I ask you a question?"

"Sure, anything you want."

"Do you want to kiss me?" Her voice turned low and soft; I could bury my head in it.

"Um, of course, what man wouldn't?"

"You've thought about it, pictured it in your mind?" She asked.

"I've pictured a lot of things in my mind, honestly."

"Can I ask you something else?" She sat close to me on the sofa.

"Sure?"

"What turns you on?"

"An intelligent, beautiful woman would suit me. What about you?"

Faith was like no other I had encountered before. It's like she had already read my playbook before we met. She had all the right words to say, like I usually did; she wasn't new to this.

She began to search me, the raw umber of her eyes piercing and drawing me into a game I didn't want to play. I needed to clear my thoughts in case she was trying to infiltrate them. I didn't want her to know that I was restraining myself from taking her down right here on this sofa.

I cleared my throat. "I'm curious to know why you became a writer." I decided to lead us down another street.

"I'm a thinker. I started out writing all my thoughts down, found them kind of interesting and universal, so I ended up making them into a story. Didn't happen overnight, by any means, it took me a while, but I sent a few manuscripts out, and almost two years later, I got a call that changed my life forever."

"Your family must be very proud of you."

"Funny enough, they don't care until they want to borrow money. Most of them have never read any of my books."

"Family can be that way." I paused to take in her beauty as she continued to make searching and piercing eye contact with me. "You are one of a kind, you know that? You amaze me."

"Why, I'm a regular woman?"

"I've never met a woman like you before. Women like you seem to be extinct. Are you sure you're real?" I gave her a little pinch on the arm.

"I'm sitting here with you, aren't I?" She giggled again.

I couldn't resist, "Have you been thinking about kissing me?"

"Jack, can I kiss you?"

She moved even closer to me, the palm of her right hand reaching to touch my face. She leaned in, giving me her tongue passionately. Her kiss was slow and deliberate, filled with infatuation and craving as our tongues wrestled. She moved into my lap; her damp hair became a sheet for my face, but I didn't mind because all I could think of was feeling her thighs straddling my thighs as she continued to position herself on top of me.

I pushed away the urge to feel her ass and kept my hands on her lower back. She allowed the towel to fall from her shoulders and revealed to me her satin bra peeking through her damp shirt. I pulled away first, and we stared at each other. At this point, I was ready to get to the business, but tonight I felt different.

This beautiful woman was in my lap, but I wanted to wait to see what her bra contained. I didn't want to take her right here on this couch or to my bedroom. As curious as I was to know how she sounded and what her moans of glee and gratification were, I wasn't going to make that move. She had to have put a spell on me!

"What's wrong? Why are you stopping?" Her breath was short as she licked her lips.

"This feels too weird to me for some reason."

Her voice was low but sweet, "Do I make you uncomfortable? I'm not trying to." She placed her hands on my chest. "I'm trying to make you as comfortable as possible."

"I know, and it's working…" My voice trailed off as I carefully chose my next words, "Maybe we should hold off on the intimacy, you know what I mean?"

"Are you really denying me right now?"

"I'm not denying you, I'm just slowing things down, showing a bit of respect."

"Maybe I should go." She quickly moved from my lap and went back into the bathroom with a heavy, disappointed slam to the door.

What the hell was I doing? I had Faith Watson in my lap, and I was sounding like an inexperienced punk. *Maybe we should slow things down.* Dumb move! Now would be a good time to punch my damn self in the face.

I knocked on the door, calling out to her. "Faith."

There was no answer.

"Faith, come on, baby, I'm sorry I didn't mean it, like I don't want you. Trust me, I want you, but I respect you. I don't want to move too fast." I simulated hitting my head on the door frame.

She opened the door with her hair pulled back into a tight bun again. "It's cool, you know you're probably right. I'll call you tomorrow." She kissed me on the cheek, walking right past me and out of the front door.

"Man, what did you do to Faith last night?" Edris slammed his fist on the table at our usual time and spot.

"She, Chloe, and Katrina were on the phone all night talking about the two of you," Bryant joined in on the assault towards me.

"It was a conference call, man," Edris said.

I threw my hands up. "I'm convinced this woman is not normal. I can't even explain to myself, let alone y'all, what happened last night."

"You are crazy. She's no different." Edris said.

"She's definitely different from those birds you two call girlfriend."

"Ok, hold on, you won't be calling my precious Chloe a bird. She's far from that."

"Alright, I apologize. You're right, but seriously, I don't know what happened last night."

"Just tell us what went down?" Bryant pushed me to relive the incident.

"I took her to see the play, and we had a great time. She suggests we go back to my place, no problem. We get caught in the rain, but she's cool about it, no big deal. We get inside the crib; she gets a towel, and we chillin' on the sofa. She starts asking me what turns me on and shit, so I'm feeling the conversation, but I'm also thinking, damn, I don't even want to take her to the bedroom just yet. I'm actually trying to take my time."

"Okay, so where did it go wrong?" Bryant asked impatiently. "That sounds like a regular night for you."

I ignored Bryant and continued. "She climbs into my lap and starts laying it on me, kissing on me, feeling on my chest. You know me, I'm usually ready to go, but last night, I don't know, I just thought we should slow things down."

Edris's eyes popped out like an old Tex Avery cartoon. "You stopped a beautiful woman from kissing you? Why? Seemed like she was ready? You didn't even have to work for it."

"I do have a conscience."

They looked at each other and laughed right in my face. Oh my god, with friends like these. "For real, y'all gonna laugh at me? That's cool." I had to pause to laugh at myself. "She was right there, and I actually told her and myself no."

"Maybe you did it because there is something about her that makes you want to be with her and not play her off like you usually would. You said yourself you think she's different. Wouldn't a woman who was different and made you stop to think make you realize nothing good can come out of the way you've been operating?"

Edris said. "Look, just kick it with her, don't screw her over like you usually would."

"I just wonder if she's playing a game with me."

"Oh, please," Bryant said. "And what if she is, you don't deserve it?"

Edris chimed in. "We are creeping into our thirties, it's time for us to settle down, have wives and families. You don't feel that way?"

"You mean to tell me, in thinking that it's time for us to settle down, Katrina is the woman you want to spend the rest of your life with?" The thought of that chilled me to the bone.

Edris's demeanor changed. "I thought that was where we were headed, but ever since we moved in together, that woman has been almost intolerable."

"Seriously," my eyes hung low, "since you moved in together, that's when the problems started?"

"Be quiet." Edris snapped back. "You've never been with a woman long enough to have a real problem."

"My question is," Bryant finished slurping his water. "When are you going to tell Katrina she can't act however she wants and expect you to deal with it? And the better question is, why *are you* just dealing with it?"

"You know good and damn well, there's no controlling Katrina. She brings the spice wherever she goes. That shit used to be cute, but now…"

"But now you see what I've been saying."

"Jack, get the hell outta here. If it were up to you, Katrina would have been out the door."

"And she can still be out the door. Why even deal with the headache?"

"Listen, I know how things look from the outside, but it's not like my entire relationship with Katrina has been all bad. She can be sweet when she wants, but those days have become few and far between."

"That's exactly what I'm saying," I shook my head. "Why even deal with her if the majority of the time she's acting like her brain isn't attached?"

"It's complicated."

"Yea, okay." I chuckled.

"Jack, are you going to see Faith again or what?" Bryant decided to bring my situation back to the forefront.

"I haven't spoken to her, I'm not sure."

"You sound like you are scared of the woman."

"She could have called me if she wanted to talk."

Edris smacked his lips, "You know damn well a woman is not about to make the first call."

"Listen," Bryant said. "The bottom line is you shouldn't shy away from this woman. You never know what this could lead to; you should give it an honest try."

I hesitated, "I'll think about it. I had to fall for this woman."

As I headed to my office, I couldn't get Faith off my mind or Bryant's parting words. He was right, I didn't know where this could lead, and that was exactly what scared me. Did I really want to live the rest of my life in a relationship Katrina could take credit for? That sounded like a bullshit headache. But I couldn't deny that I wanted to see Faith again. She was so damn sexy, I wanted her in my lap again. I could bash my head against the side of my office building for pushing her away.

The chemistry I was feeling with Faith was disparate. It was natural and unforced. Typically, I had one thing on my mind, and with her, that just wasn't the case. With her, everything seemed genuine.

Maybe this is what I had been missing in the other women I had dated; I could sense how special Faith was. When I was with her, I didn't think about her being Katrina's friend; I had honestly forgotten about that tidbit. If I could forget that, maybe we could be cool.

I decided to call her once I was in my office, "Hey, what's going on? I was calling to check in on you."

"Oh, I'm working on a few storylines. How about you? Have you been busy today?"

"No, I'm only working on a few projects. It's sort of slow for us right now."

"Listen, Jack, I'm sorry about last night," she rushed right in, "I overreacted, I was caught off guard about how you pushed me away. I mean, I thought we were getting closer, but I was moving way too fast, you were right to slow things down, and I'm grateful that you respected me enough to."

Damn, another one of my lines, "Why don't we get together tonight? No pressure. Leave last night behind us, no need to dwell on it."

"That would be nice, but this time let me play hostess. Dinner at my place, 7:30? I'll shoot you my address."

"Okay, I'll see you then."

I was sure I looked like an idiot, unable to control the grin on my face. Yes, I was excited to see her and happy that we could get past what could have been awkward. Although I was excited, the thought still lingered in the back of my mind that I wasn't trying to get caught up, especially on the first woman I decided was worth my time. But I knew that for this to even have a chance, I would have to let that go. I wanted to enjoy myself.

After work, I headed straight home to shower and get dressed to go to Faith's house. The doorbell rang, catching me off guard, especially when I recognized through the peephole who was invading my privacy, and like an idiot, I opened the door.

"Hey, Jack, miss me?"

"Rayven, what are you doing here?"

"You're supposed to say, yes, you missed me." She tittered in amusement, but I wasn't amused at all. "I decided to drive on over and see you for myself since you seem to have lost my number."

"Now you've seen me, and it's time to go!"

"Wait, you're not happy to see me?"

"This is not a good time. I was on my way out." I pointed down the hall. "I'm sorry, but we'll have to catch up later. How about this, I'll give you a call."

"Oh no, you're not getting away from me that easily." She forced herself in, pulling me into the living room.

"Okay, see this is where I have to stop you, my girlfriend won't go for this," I said, resisting her aggressive pursuit. She looked at me as if I had just told her I had an STD.

"You have a girlfriend, since when?"

"It doesn't matter, but you should go; she's expecting me."

"You're not getting rid of me that easily, Boo." She continued until she was able to kiss my lips; she did so like she had been in the desert, and I was the cool drink she had been thirsting for.

A couple of days ago, I would have taken her on and given her exactly what she was looking for, but in light of my trying to figure out my situation with Faith, I wasn't trying to give in so quickly, but I was still Jack Spencer, and I couldn't change in a matter of minutes. I kissed Rayven back.

"Come on, let's go to our spot." She said, leading me to the couch where only a few weeks ago I had lain her down and only a night ago I was sitting with Faith in my lap.

Giving in to her seduction, I followed her over to the couch, ready to undress her and relive our one-night stand. I figured this would be a good way to end my bachelor days, I mean, really, was this wrong? Faith and I had not committed to anything; we were still on the friend level, and there was no exclusivity.

I got on top of Rayven as she started to unbutton my shirt and feel my chest. I saw the clock out of the corner of my eye, and I was supposed to be meeting Faith at her place in fifteen minutes, and it would take me at least 20 to get there.

"Okay, no, I can't do this with you, I can't do this to Faith."

"So that's her name, pretend I'm her." She said, pulling me back to her.

"No, you have to go. Get out!" I pulled her up from the couch and rushed her to the door. I guess she realized how serious I was and didn't put up any more of a fight. I slammed the door behind her and waited a few minutes.

I went to the bedroom and grabbed another dark blue button-up shirt to change into, as nervous sweat had started to ruin the one I was wearing. I poked my head out into the hallway and started to make my way to my car. Once I was safely in my car, I called Faith to let her know I was on my way and apologize for running late.

"Hey, I'm sorry I left the office a little late, but I'm on the Sunrise right now."

She spoke sweetly. "Sure, no worries. I'm here, no rush, be careful, and I'll see you in a few."

I loved the sound of her voice. I hadn't noticed it much before, but maybe because I had just called her my girlfriend to keep me from sleeping with Rayven again, or maybe my hearing was impaired. The term of endearment came out so easily, like it was true. A lie could be your savior and demon at the same time. It hadn't crossed my mind yet if I even wanted to have a title with her; I was still trying to grasp the idea of exploring the thought of committing to one woman. She was changing me without knowing it.

I pulled up to the address she texted me in North Victoria Park. Running up to the door and looking behind me before disappearing behind the tall hedges that hid the driveway. I wanted to make sure Rayven hadn't followed me. I straightened my clothes and wiped my forehead before I rang the glowing doorbell.

I could see Faith's lovely curvy figure approaching the door through the glazed glass laced between an intricate semi-circle pattern design of the heavy double mahogany doors.

Faith beamed when she opened the door. "I'm glad you're here, come in, I made something I'm sure you'll like." She reached to hug me, she smelled as sweet as she sounded. I believe it was verbena that was giving her such a charming scent.

As I followed her down the tan-painted entryway, I noticed the plentiful African artifacts that decorated the walls. But I quickly turned my attention to what was in front of me. I watched her body switch back and forth in a sexy, body-gripping sapphire blue dress. She wore matching peep-toe stilettos, and I couldn't help but wonder if she was wearing underwear to match, but it wasn't my mission to find out, not tonight at least, but believe it was on my mind.

"You got here pretty quickly from your house. Were you speeding?"

Still trying to catch my breath, I said. "I was trying to get to you as quickly as I could."

"You were that excited to see me?"

"I was eager to see what you had planned for me."

"I told you something you would like. Come on to the kitchen, I got it all set up for us."

Her house was more beautiful the farther she took me in. It was open and spacious with hardwood floors and crown-molded ceilings. I noticed the living room was painted in a light lilac, and the room was accented with fresh white flowers. The Calcutta grayish-brown kitchen counters were laced with glowing candles that mixed with what I hoped was a delicious dinner.

"It smells good in here; you must be able to throw down in the kitchen unless you're tricking me with some takeout." I took in the surroundings of dark trim cabinetry and top-of-the-line stainless steel appliances; it was very gourmet.

"Oh no, baby, this is all me!" She flashed me the brightest smile.

I thought I wouldn't mind waking up to that smile tomorrow morning. I followed her over to the large island situated between the kitchen and the living room. She began to uncover the food, the savory scent enticing my taste buds. Pot roast, vegetables, and rice enticed my senses, and Faith sent me over the edge with a chocolate cake for dessert. She made sure to mention she baked it herself earlier in the day.

"Do I deserve all of this?"

"I guess you've been a pretty good boy." She teased.

Faith guided me to sit at the intimate round eat-in kitchen table as she prepared our plates. I wanted to tell her how I felt about her, but my mouth was frozen, and I took that as a sign I was getting ahead of myself. I wasn't sure of what to say, and if rejection was in the forecast, I wasn't sure of how to counteract.

"What's up?" she asked, setting the plates on the table.

"Nothing," I tried to hide what I wanted to say.

"You seem like you have something on your mind."

"No, what makes you say that?"

"It's written all over your face. Come on, tell me what's up, what are you thinking?" She prodded.

"Well, I guess I'll come right out with it." Here I was turning right onto Rejection Row. "We've been spending a lot of time together, and I'm really feeling you."

"I know. I feel the same way."

"I know, but I'm feeling you to the point where I want you with me."

"I am with you."

"No, baby, I mean *with me*, I want you to be my woman."

Her face was puzzled, like I was someone she hadn't invited into her house.

"You look surprised. I can't read whether that's good or bad."

"I am surprised. I didn't know what to expect from tonight just because of what happened between us the other night."

"I wasn't trying to blow you off. I didn't want to move too fast with you because of how much I want you beyond something physical."

"I didn't think you were looking for something beyond physical. I didn't peg that as your style."

"Would you like to explore what something on a deeper level with me would be like?"

She stopped picking at the cut of meat on her plate but avoided eye contact with me. "I'm not sure at this point in my life, I kind of feel like a relationship would be a distraction, and I'm completely committed to writing right now."

"Career over love?" I asked, astonished.

"Love," she snickered, "I'm saying with where my career is right now and the other ventures I want to take on, I can't be distracted."

I had no choice but to accept her turning me down.

She exhaled, "Listen, let me think on it and I will get back with you."

CHLOE

Katrina called me early in the morning and convinced me to have dinner with her and Faith tonight. Exam week for my fifth graders was coming up, so I had been in prep mode all day. I wasn't in the mood for whatever trick Katrina was trying to play today. I knew all she wanted to do was see if anything was going on between Jack and Faith. And I knew Katrina strategically chose the restaurant on Poinciana St. that had my favorite spring roll appetizer to lure me to show up.

As soon as we sat down at the stark white table and chrome polished chairs with our food, Katrina didn't waste any time getting into Jack and Faith's potential hook-up.

"So, a little birdie told me you've been hanging out with Mr. Jack Spencer." Katrina snickered to cover her intentions.

"Act like you didn't plan on me meeting Jack when you first invited me to hang out with you guys?" Faith threw back a verbal jab.

"I may have mentioned he was single."

"He may not be for long." Faith's right eyebrow raised independently in mischief.

"What does that mean?" I was intrigued.

"Jack and I have been out only a few times, and he asked me to be his woman the other night when we had dinner at my place."

I nearly spit out my lemonade tea mix while Katrina's eyes bugged out of her head. "The two of you had dinner at your place?"

"Forget that," Katrina exclaimed. "He asked you to be his woman?"

"Yes, no lie," Faith responded. "He asked if I would like to explore something with him on a deeper level and have a relationship with him beyond just something physical."

"What did you tell him?" I asked.

"That I'd think about it and get back to him."

Stunned, I said, "Get back to him?"

"Ooh, that's good." Katrina's mouth turned into an evil grin.

"How is that good?"

"She should leave his ass hanging, just like he's done to probably countless women."

Faith's face twisted, "What are you talking about?"

I looked away at the oversized bowl of pho that had been turned into artwork on the wall next to our table. Katrina's plan wasn't off to a great start.

"Chloe, what is she talking about?" Faith questioned me.

"Tell her, Katrina."

"Ok, so Jack doesn't have the best reputation, but I've never seen him ask a woman to be his girlfriend, let alone so fast like with you. You should see what's good."

Faith turned to look at me, "What is she not telling me?"

I didn't know what to say. "Jack just needs the right woman."

"To what, fix him?"

"I mean, we all could use a little Jesus."

"So, what, he's a hot potato?"

Katrina and I looked at each other.

"You know a pass around."

Katrina slapped the table with laughter. "Yes! That's the perfect way of putting it."

"And you thought this would be the man to hook me up with?"

"Don't worry about that, Faith, you like him, right? You said the two of you have been seeing each other and you were feeling him before you knew this minuscule bit of info, so why not see where things could go?" I tried to lighten the mood.

"Yes, what she said. Besides, you could be the woman to change his entire life and help me get my man off Jack's wagon."

"What does Jack have to do with your man? Edris, right?"

"Oh God, please don't ask her that." I pleaded.

"Edris and I are in a rough patch, that's all."

"But what does that have to do with Jack?" Faith questioned.

"I think Edris and even Bryant spend way too much time with Jack instead of with us, and I know he loves to fill their heads with BS about his dating shenanigans. That's why if you join our happy little group, then Jack can be occupied, and I can have my man back."

Faith rolled her eyes and dropped her fork with a piece of sesame chicken still stuck to it on her plate. "Katrina, I don't know what your plan was, but don't include me in your shit." Her voice flexed.

"Hold on. You just sat here and said you were feelin' the man, so what's the problem?"

"Why would you try to play me like this?"

"Are you seriously mad at me over this?"

"I reached out to you to make amends because I wanted my friend back, but you pull some bullshit like this." She stood up, grabbing her messenger bag.

"Now hold on, Faith," I reached for her forearm. I didn't want her to leave. I gave Katrina a sharp look; she needed to say something. "Katrina."

"Okay, I'm sorry, come on, Faith, sit down."

"Why would you do this? To get back at me?"

"Get back at you for what?"

"Oh, please, what's the real reason you haven't spoken to me in almost four years?"

Katrina was quiet for once. Maybe Faith should have come back into our lives sooner if this is what it took to shut Katrina down.

"Come on, tell the truth, I'm sure Chloe has the same question."

"You know good, and damn well you spun out of control once you left college, and you left us behind to clean up your mess."

"I've been waiting for you to throw my past mistakes back in my face."

"Don't talk like what you did was minor, Faith. You put yourself and us in danger."

"You're so dramatic."

"Okay! So getting hooked on drugs, stealing money from Chloe and me, bringing known dealers on campus, and getting expelled for having affairs with multiple professors were all baby mistakes, huh?"

Tears began to well up in Faith's eyes. Katrina didn't have to bring all of that old dirt up. We could clearly see Faith wasn't the same young girl who made questionable decisions, but we had all witnessed firsthand the hurt and trauma she had gone through. No one could be the same and just move on with life after watching someone they loved take their own life.

"Okay, ladies, come on." I needed to make peace. "Faith, you're right, we all haven't seen each other in quite some time, so we were bound to still be harboring ill will, but none of us are the same little girls we were in college. We're grown women now, and we should act like it. Let's squash this right now."

The two past grown women looked away from each other like teenage girls fighting over the varsity football player. These two were still as stubborn with each other as they were in college. Tug of war had always been the game between the two of them, while Rayven and I sat back and watched.

"Katrina, listen to me." Faith began. "I didn't reach out to you to have you throw the worst part of my life back in my face. I know I hurt you, I know I hurt Chloe, and Rayven, but I'm here now to apologize, and I wanted us to try to be friends again."

We were quiet for a moment. Enough time for me to realize we had slowed down all other activity in the restaurant, and apparently, everyone was waiting with bated breath to see if these two could let the past be the past.

Faith sat back down. "I didn't come back around with any type of malicious intent, but I feel like that's why you let me back in. If that's the way it's going to be, tell me now so I can go about my way."

I looked at Katrina, I willed through telepathy that she would show Faith some compassion and empathy.

"Both of you are right. A lot of time has passed, and we were all so close at one point. Maybe we can get there again."

I wanted to cry, but I knew they would laugh at me. For years, I wanted to say something about Faith, but I knew Katrina would fly off the rails. I hoped for this day because I had missed Faith. Yes, she had done terrible things, but she had gotten the help she needed to get back on the right track, and that was all that mattered now.

Faith shared about her time in rehab and all the emotional and mental work she had done to reach the place of stability she is in now. She told us how she was required as part of her ongoing therapy to keep a journal of her thoughts. She started this back when she was in rehab, and from there, she wrote her first book.

I looked over at Katrina, and she hadn't taken her eyes off Faith as she spoke. I could only hope this meant that she was willing to stop bringing up the past and move on. I thought about bringing up Rayven, but I figured we had done enough unveiling for today. But I did find it curious that Faith didn't bring up wanting to reconnect with Rayven. I suppose after Rayven found out Faith had also been seeing a guy she was getting close to, Rayven wasn't willing to be so forgiving.

What should have been a quiet dinner turned out to be emotionally draining, and I was run down by the time I got back home. I wanted to crawl back into bed with Bryant and create our own cocoon away from the outside world. I missed my man.

As I opened the front door, Bryant peered his head from the kitchen. He was shirtless, but this time, no apron. This was typical for him, especially when his boys weren't around, and I'd be lying if I said I didn't enjoy the show. I loved his muscular body, his broad shoulders, rippling abs, and stocky arms. He was strong, and every time he picked me up when we would play, it turned me on.

"What's up, babe? What are you doing in there?" I tossed my purse on the sofa as I headed to the kitchen to lay a kiss on my sexy man.

"Making myself a little turkey sandwich." He stopped spreading the mayo on his whole wheat bread to give me a peck on the lips. "How was dinner?"

I plopped down at my seat at the ash pine kitchen table. "Dramatic."

"Isn't that always the case with Katrina?"

He joined me at the table with his sandwich.

"This time I had the luxury of Katrina and Faith's dramatics together."

"Oh yea, how did that go?"

"I guess it was bound to happen, but they got into it about everything from college."

"What happened between all of you? You never really told me."

"Baby, it's not even important, honestly."

"Then what happened after Katrina and Faith got into it?"

"They squashed it for now, but you know how Katrina is. I wouldn't be surprised at all if all of this came back up again."

"Well, that's your Petty Betty friend, sweetheart."

"I know, but I hope we can start to rebuild our friendship and even more, that Katrina will calm down. Especially when it comes to Edris."

Bryant shook his head, biting into his stacked sandwich of turkey, lettuce, tomato, and knowing him at least three pieces of cheese. "Now that is the truth."

"I know, baby, trust me. I'm always trying to tell her she needs to treat Edris better, but you know how she is."

"I'm hoping Faith is nothing like Katrina."

"Why do you say that?"

"Act like you don't know."

I chuckled. "What?"

"You know her and Jack have been hanging out. I know she told you.

"She did."

"She's actually into my boy?"

"She is."

He nodded his head in agreement as he finished off his sand-wich.

"Katrina almost ruined that, too."

"What are you talking about? Katrina invited her into the circle."

"I know, but it was weird. I know Katrina already had her mind wrapped around hooking Faith and Jack up, but as soon as Faith mentioned how much time they've been spending together, Katrina started bad-mouthing Jack and blaming him as the reason Edris hasn't proposed to her."

"That doesn't even make sense."

"It does in Katrina's head and in her world that's all that matters."

"Baby girl, listen to me." Bryant stood up to wash his plate and clean up. "I know Katrina is your girl, but stay out of whatever mess she's cooking up. I already warned you before getting into people's relationship mess."

"I'm not involved in anything."

"But if she's plotting something by using Faith and Jack, you can't be too far behind. I'm just saying, don't get wrapped up in her."

I knew Bryant was looking out for me, but I didn't need to be told what to do when it came to my friends. And if I were telling him that I wasn't involved, he should believe me instead of trying to be macho and order me to take his unsolicited advice. I was already tired enough from playing peacemaker between Katrina and Faith; I didn't have the energy to voice my opinion about Bryant's butch mood, so I remained quiet.

"Don't sulk on me, okay? You know I'm only looking out for you. I don't want you stressin' over things that don't matter."

"I know," I said sullenly.

"Come here." Bryant reached for my hand, guiding me to stand up and come to his side of the table.

I wrapped my arms around his neck. He pulled me closer to him, grabbing my hips.

"Chloe, I love you."

"I love you too."

"I'm going to marry you."

I couldn't help but smile.

"I'm going to be your one and only husband, you will be my one and only wife, we're going to have beautiful babies, and live our lives for them and each other. Nothing else matters."

"That sounds like a plan."

JACK

I was surprised to receive a call from Faith at my office, saying she wanted to talk to me, and she couldn't wait until I got off. As much as I was still taken aback by her response to me putting myself out there to have a relationship with her, I couldn't resist; I wanted to see her. I told her to stop by. I imagined she would be wearing some kind of dress with heels that made her lovely backside look just right, giving me something to daydream about this afternoon as I tried to get some work done. She was always dressed in a way that heightened my senses.

When she arrived and was escorted into my office, she had a look on her face I had never seen before, but her emotions were too wide a spectrum for me to try to read. This woman was truly a challenge, but still, I wanted her.

"I'm sorry, I know I'm intruding on you while you're working, but I needed to get this off my chest."

"Tell me what's up, please, before my heart comes out of my chest."

"Jack, I do like you and want to get to know you. I wanted to know if the offer still stood?"

"I guess you've checked into your schedule and you what, can squeeze me in?" I was confused.

"It's not like that, believe me. I was trying to make sure everything would be good before we took further steps. I don't want to get into something with you, then throw it on the back burner. You understand, right?"

"Not really. If someone is important to you, then you make time to see them, no matter what is going on in life."

"I will. You promise to do the same for me?"

"Of course I will. But listen, you must do something else for me." I reached out to take her hands into mine. "If we are going to do this, we have to remember that this is us, and what happens between us will stay between us. You have to keep our business as just that: our business."

"Who are you worried about me talking to? Katrina and Chloe?"

"Absolutely, especially Katrina. Me and that woman have never gotten along."

"I can tell."

"What?"

"I had dinner with her and Chloe the other night, and Katrina made sure to tell me about your reputation."

"The truth is, Katrina doesn't know a damn thing about me and has no room to talk about me or what she thinks I've done in my past relationships."

"You loving the company of multiple women at a time isn't true?"

"I'm a grown man, obviously, I've dated my share of women."

"Can you be exclusive to me?"

Lifting each of her hands to my lips, I planted soft kisses on her cinnamon skin. "Yes, I promise."

She inclined her body to meet mine and gently pressed her lips into mine. The warmth and softness of her kiss were electrifying. I kept my hands contained to hers and resisted the urge to grasp her backside, which I'd been dreaming about. I knew I had to show that the preconceived notion of me being a jerk to women wasn't deserved.

She pulled away from me, looking into my eyes, "Don't play me."

"I promise."

We made plans to meet later for dinner after I finished work. She wanted to talk more about us, and I wasn't sure what else there was to talk about. I hope she didn't think there was going to be a whole line of questioning to find answers regarding my past or so-called reputation that Katrina was trying to convince her I had. I wasn't all up in her business about who she was with before Katrina brought her through my front door.

Neither one of our pasts had anything to do with now. I was willing to put all my past carelessness behind me, but now the question was, if she was willing to do the same, whatever her past may be? She probably had a past just as lengthy to be able to write that book the way she did; she had to have gotten her ideas from somewhere, her imagination couldn't be that un-tamed.

I was well aware of who I was dealing with. In her book, the main character was a woman who hated all men and vowed vengeance on any man who crossed her path by basically using him for anything he was willing to give up. I wasn't trying to be one of her case studies.

I would be staying close to Faith and getting to know every-thing about her, hopefully uninhibited by her friends. I was al-ready on guard with her, and I could see that I wouldn't be able to put my guard down anytime soon. She was so worried about me playing her, what if she was trying to play me? I was the one taking a risk to change my ways.

***

Faith sent me a text asking me to meet her at a cafe in Hol-lywood by Young Circle Park, and I wondered what was up her sleeve. This wasn't what I imagined when we made plans earlier. But I was down for whatever, as long as Faith and I were together.

I arrived at the cafe, pulling the door open for a honey-toned young lady in cut-off shorts. A tall, dark-skinned guy must have thought I wanted what was his, he rushed over to grab her hand as if I wasn't just being polite.

I brushed off the awkward encounter and looked around for Faith. She suggested this place and begged me to be on time, so why wasn't she here?

I headed to the elongated tile and grout bar to order a drink while I waited. I heard the echoing tap of a microphone and turned around to see Faith on the barely raised, gray carpeted, makeshift stage. I looked at her in confusion as she cleared her throat and spoke over the mic, sending me a wink.

"Good evening, everyone, and welcome to Poetry Night." Her smooth voice floated over the crowd.

The crowd of mixed browns and cool dark skin tones snapped their fingers in rhythm, and I thought I was back in a 90's coffeehouse. My lips curled into a tight smile in anticipation of seeing what my woman was about to do on this small stage in front of this thrilled but laid-back crowd.

"To start us off tonight, we have the beautiful and gorgeous Lena." Faith's voice was sultry over the mic.

The crowd erupted into finger snaps again as the honey-colored girl I had opened the door for took to the mini stage.

Faith rushed through the crowd over to me. She planted a soft kiss on my lips. "I'm glad you could make it." She beamed, turning around to lean her back into me as Honey Colored Lena raved into the microphone.

I wrapped my right arm around Faith's waist; her arms overlapped mine. We were falling in sync, and it was nice.

I babysat a strong mix of honey whiskey, ginger ale, and lemon as I watched Faith sashay on and off the stage doing her hosting duties. I never would have guessed she did this in her spare time. Business seemed to be poppin' too, as soon enough all the small tables were full and people were happy to stand and listen to the various poets share their art.

One brotha raged on stage about the system's setup to remove black men from their households. I was sure he was speaking from personal experience; nonetheless, he was telling the truth.

Soon after he was done explaining things that had been known for generations, Faith thanked everyone for coming and closed the festivities. She returned to our spot, grinning and giving me a massive hug, a gigantic smile plastered across her face.

She whispered in my ear, "I have a little hideaway in the back. Would you like to join me?"

I whispered back, "Of course."

She took me by the hand and led me to the smallest corner in the joint where the only booth existed. I stood back to allow her to slide in first, then I sat next to her, wrapping my arm around her neck.

"You were great at hosting."

"Aww, thank you. I love doing it. The owner, Mr. Tower, let me start doing this a few months ago, and every time the crowd gets a little bigger."

"What made you start doing this?"

"Love of poetry, I guess. I know I'm known for my novel work, but poetry is my passion. Once I found my rhythm with it, I joined some groups online and realized how many people wanted a place to go for some great performance art, so I had the idea to start this. It's been inspirational to me."

"You mentioned you were working on a collection, right?"

"Yes. I don't think my publisher is happy about it, but unfortunately for them, my contract doesn't stipulate what I can and can't write, so poetry is what they are going to get."

"Hey, I say go for it. Besides, I know whatever you write from the heart will be awesome."

"Thank you, I appreciate you saying that."

"I'm glad I got to witness your greatness. Do you ever perform your own work?"

"Oddly enough, no. Haven't gotten the courage to do so."

"Why not? I'm sure it's amazing. And you've sold millions of copies of your book; people are already familiar with your writing. What's the difference?"

She paused, looking away from me. "It's just different. Fiction is easy compared to my poetry. It's nothing to make up a story, but to face what's in my heart like I do in my poetry is raw. Not sure I want people to see that side of me."

I nodded in understanding.

We were silent for a moment, but the silence was comfortable and peaceful. I liked it. Time with Faith was getting easier and congenial. I wanted to know where this could go; for once, my mind wasn't just on the short-term. Could we have a future?

"How was work after I left?"

"Pretty good. I got a new acquisition I'm excited about. It's a tech company, and they are dropping a ton on marketing, hoping to compete with the Big Three."

"That's awesome. Good for you."

I smiled, happy to have her praise.

"I did want to ask you something. How is it that your friends ended up dating Katrina and Chloe, who are also friends?"

I chuckled. "Well, Bryant met Chloe first, and once Edris laid eyes on Katrina, it was a wrap. We all just happened to be out at the same bar the same night. Maybe if you had been there, we would have connected that night as well."

"Maybe."

"What is the deal with your friendship with Katrina and Chloe? Did y'all lose contact or something?"

She exhaled. "It's complicated. That's the best way I can put it."

"Do you want to talk about it?"

"Meh, not really."

"Oh, okay." Now I had ruined the mood. I should have known that the subject of Katrina was a mood killer.

"Hey, listen." I touched her chin with my index finger to bring her attention directly to me. "Why don't we get some takeout, and we can relax at my place?"

"That sounds good." The bright smile returned to her face, and that was all I wanted.

We grabbed some Chinese food from the hole-in-the-wall on the other end of the plaza from the coffee house. Faith followed me in her stylish Ibis white Audi, parking right next to me once we pulled into the lot of my condo. I quickly hopped out of the car to open her car door and help her grab the food.

I couldn't help but continue to admire her figure, which tempted me every time I had the chance to take in the view. We entered the lobby, Faith hitting the elevator button with comfort. She took care to stand in front of me as the doors closed us into the tiny steel box. Faith turned to press her lips against mine. I wanted to place my hands all over her, but I remembered I was carrying hot food.

As much as I wanted to take things slow with Faith and not act on my typical sexual instincts, if she kept acting like this, I wouldn't have a choice. She had already been tempting me all night; she looked so damn good.

I clicked on the light and told Faith to make herself comfortable as I grabbed some forks and plates for us to eat.

I joined her on the sofa.

"Here we are again, at least this time I'm not all wet from the rain."

"I didn't mind you being wet." I joked.

"I'm sure you didn't."

I grinned at her. "I'm glad you're here, though. I love spending time with you."

"I'm glad I came." She said with a wink in her voice.

KATRINA

I rushed around the apartment cleaning up random things. I couldn't believe it, but I had invited Faith over to my place. I wasn't happy about the way things had gone during our dinner. I never stopped to realize how much Faith had been through and what she had been doing in the years since the last time we saw each other. I thought, if she was in fact into Jack, then I didn't need to make her my enemy; she would be doing exactly what I needed.

A knock came to the door, and I opened it without looking through the peephole. Faith waved at me and mouthed hello as she was on the phone.

"Ok, baby, I'm here. I'll give you a call a little later." She threw her phone into her purse and came inside.

"Was that Mr. Jack Spencer?"

"It was."

"He's graduated to baby? Look at that."

"I know, I know, but things are going well."

I turned my lips down, mocking her behind her back as she came inside. "Good, good for you," I said, switching to a faux smile as she turned around to face me.

"Thanks for inviting me over. I'm glad that we could put the past aside. I hope this is our first step to maybe getting our friendship back on track."

"I'm open to it, and it sounds like you'll be joining our little group anyway since you and Jack have seemingly gotten pretty close."

I offered Faith a drink, but she declined before sitting on the sofa.

"Well, I would hope even if I wasn't getting close to Jack that we could still repair, I mean, we were close friends at one point, Katrina."

"You're right, we were."

"So, you don't think we could ever get that back?"

"I don't believe it would be the same. I mean, we are grown women now. Back in college, we were kids trying to become women, right?"

"Exactly. I'm sure you even made some mistakes in life you aren't the proudest of."

"What is that supposed to mean?"

"I'm just saying. We've all done things we aren't proud of; it's important that we can see past them all. You've changed, I've changed."

"You're right."

"Then catch me up, tell me everything."

"Everything like what?"

I didn't know what Faith was digging for with this question, but I wasn't so sure that I wanted to spill my post-college life story just because. I wasn't going to rush into being cool with her. We hadn't grown our friendship back then overnight; why should now be different?

"I'm not sure what to tell you. Work is good, I like the school I'm teaching at. Nothing else is really going on."

"What about you and the boyfriend?"

I exhaled, hard. "Edris and I are Edris and I."

"What does that mean?"

"I don't know. Things with him are difficult; I don't want it to be that way, but that seems to be just how we are. We are always at each other's throats."

"Why is that, though?"

"It's like Edris's common sense doesn't exist when it comes to me. He used to be the picture-perfect boyfriend, but somewhere down the line, after we moved in together, everything changed. I can't even get his attention anymore. I told Chloe, I think, if it were up to him, we would continue dating for the next thirty years. He'll probably never marry me."

"Maybe he's not ready yet. You know you can't rush something like marriage."

"But we've been together for three years, and we already live together. These are relatively permanent things for him to be questioning if he wants to spend the rest of his life with me."

"Well, maybe it's not as simple to him. Have you tried talking to him about it?"

I waved off her suggestion. "Every time I bring up the word marriage or even wedding, he jumps stupid, saying, 'Why rush?' I can't force him to be with me forever, but I also can't wait."

"What are you going to do?"

"I was thinking of giving him an ultimatum. Either propose or go away."

"Oh, so, you're serious about this walk down the aisle, huh?"

"I'm starting to think he's too comfortable with the way we are; he doesn't want to buy the cow now."

"Maybe you should talk to him calmly and take a different approach."

"I'm cool, calm, and collected when I talk to him. It doesn't matter how many different ways I say it, the commitment is still the same."

"Now I know we are trying to get back cool and rebuild our friendship, but the Katrina I knew wasn't always so calm and collected. And you just said the two of you are always at each other's throats. Are you sure your delivery when talking to him is loving and compassionate?"

I knew what she was getting at. "You're talking about Mark, aren't you?" I looked at her through squinted eyes. Mark was my college boyfriend, whom I hadn't given much thought to before now.

"I didn't say anything about him."

"I think you hated Mark just as much as I hated..." Damn, I hadn't meant to bring him up.

Faith reached to touch my arm. "It's okay, you can say his name."

"No need to."

"Yes, I do remember not liking Mark too much, but honestly, it was more about who you were when you were with him. You were so mean and controlling. I'm sorry to say, I'm just being honest."

I rubbed my palms together; the moisture of my agitation was apparent. "You're right. I did always want all his attention."

"Do you think you are unfairly doing the same thing to Edris?"

"No way!"

"Remember the time Mark was going to a party at the Alpha house and you..." she held her hand up to her lips to laugh.

I already knew the story. "Yes, I crashed the party looking for him, but y'all followed me there."

"Yea, to make sure you didn't kill the man."

"I was making sure what was mine was safe."

"Overprotective Katrina." She shook her white, polished finger at me. "Are you doing the same thing to Edris?"

"I'm all for Edris doing his own thing, but not into the late-night hours. I figured when we got together, and we had a real commitment, all of that would slow down. But that damn Jack of yours, you'll see soon."

"What's wrong with the guys hanging out? It's not like it's every night. They work hard, they should be able to get their guy time in."

"Let's see if you're saying that in a couple of months."

"Ok, listen to me, try this. Cook him a nice meal, wear something sexy, speak slowly and lovingly about everything that's bothering you. Remain calm, but make sure you shut your trap and listen when he responds."

I crossed my arms, sliding back into the couch. "I hate cooking for his non-appreciative ass. I stopped doing that a long time ago. And he doesn't even notice when I wear anything remotely sexy anymore."

"Well then, there you go, that's why he spends so much time out eating with his boys."

I sighed, knowing she was on to something, but I wasn't going to admit to her.

"What does Chloe say? I saw her and her boyfriend cozy up on the couch at Jack's; they seem to be in good standing."

"Those two make me so sick sometimes. Bryant would do anything for Chloe, and he takes her places that don't involve chicken wings or TV."

"Is that jealousy I hear?"

"That's easy for you to say; you have Jack eating out of the palm of your hand after only a few weeks. My man is the only one who can't get it through his unmindful brain; I'm soup with no spoon."

"I gave you my advice. It will work out with Edris; you have to give him the chance to catch up to you, and if he can't, then you already know what to do."

"Why do I have to explain this to him, though?"

"I'm sorry, but I have to ask, if you're so sure he won't ever get it, then why are you still in the relationship?"

I understood her question, but I hadn't thought about it. I couldn't see myself without Edris. What if he did, in fact, decide he didn't want to marry me? What would my next step be? Could I walk away? I wasn't sure I was ready to face the possibility that we had grown apart. And I was even more unsure if I wanted to take advice from Faith. She had only been back around for a minute, and I was already letting her into my business. I didn't know if Faith had ever even had a successful relationship. Last I knew, she had been cuddling up with someone else's man instead of her own.

Keys jingled outside the door as Edris turned the knob to come inside. His eyes went straight to Faith and then quickly back to me.

"Oh, I didn't know you were stopping by."

"Edris, you remember Faith."

"Of course." He extended his hand to shake hers. "It's nice to see you again."

They held their shake for a moment before Faith cleared her throat and dropped her hand away.

"Maybe I should be going." She turned around to grab her purse from the sofa. "Katrina, I appreciate the invitation. Next time you can come to my place. Chloe, too."

"Yea, that would be cool."

I moved past Edris to walk Faith to the door. We hugged, and I thought maybe we could be okay. Pending, she didn't pull anything ridiculous like back in college.

I turned back to Edris, who was still standing in the same place. "What's up with you?"

"Nothing." He shook his head. "How was hanging out with Faith?"

"It was alright." I headed to the kitchen to get more to drink. Edris followed behind. "So, what's the deal with her?"

"What do you mean?"

"Seems like she kind of popped up out of nowhere. I don't remember you mentioning you knew her before."

I grabbed a soda from the bottom drawer of the black fridge, then reached for a glass from the cherry wood cabinet next to the fridge. I always split my soda with Edris, so I poured half into the glass and handed him the can. "I hadn't spoken to her since we've been together, didn't think she was important to tell you about."

"Well, she's gotten Jack's attention."

"What's wrong with that?"

"Nothing, I guess. I mean, you didn't try to hook them up on purpose, did you? Are you setting Jack up for something?"

I rolled my eyes. "Seriously?"

"Hey, it's a valid question. It's no secret you're not the biggest Jack fan, so I'm trying to figure out why you would care to set him up with anyone."

"Look, I don't have an ulterior motive in introducing the two of them. And, if you really want to split hairs, I didn't even introduce them. They started talking to each other."

He tipped the can up to his lips.

"Can we talk about something else?"

"Like what?"

I didn't even want to talk. Truthfully, I was tired of talking, and I wasn't in the mood for one of our talks to turn into an argument. All I wanted from my man was for him to hug me, kiss me, take me to our bedroom, and make love to me. "Baby, come here."

Edris's face twisted, his eyes and eyebrows lifted in sync.

"Seriously, come over here."

He took the three short steps across the hardwood kitchen floor to me. I lifted my arms to wrap them around his neck. He gave me soft kisses to my lips. This was all I was asking for, a little intimacy. Edris grabbed my hand and led me around the wall that separated the kitchen and the living room, and gave way to the hall to our bedroom.

"Edris, sit down, I want to talk to you about something."

He sat on the edge of the bed. "What is it?"

"Us."

"What about us?"

I quietly exhaled, remembering the advice of Chloe and Faith. I remained calm.

"I hope this isn't the marriage talk again." He slumped down.

"Damn, really? I haven't even said anything yet."

"Is that what you wanted to say?"

"Since you already know what I want, why don't you tell me what's up then?"

"Katrina, come on. I don't know why we keep having the same conversation over and over."

"Because you sidestep it and never explain to me what's going on with us." Be calm, Katrina, be calm, I reminded myself. I slid my hips between his arms to make room for me to sit on his lap. "Baby, I'm basically already your wife. Why not make it official?"

"There are a lot of responsibilities that come with marriage. I don't think either one of us is ready for what marriage truly means."

"You're deciding for both of us?"

"See that right there. I gave you my answer, but you want to flip it into something else."

"Well, I didn't like your answer," I said, folding my arms.

"Excuse me, please." He stood up, forcing me to my feet. "You don't get it. This is supposed to be a partnership, mutual respect. You can't even try to understand what I'm saying to you. You're not getting your way, so you respond like a child. Do you think that's the type of woman I want to make my wife?"

"Now I'm a 'type' of woman?"

"Katrina, please," Edris exclaimed with his hands.

He walked over to the dresser, taking the silver watch from his waist and laying it out flat.

"Be straight with me. Do you want to marry me at all?"

He blew his breath aggressively. "I've told you multiple times that I do. What I'm telling you right now is, you need to seriously evaluate what you think marriage is and how you will treat your husband."

"How do I treat you, Edris, because you seem to always have a complaint no matter what I say or do." The intensity in my voice was rising. All mantras of calm were quickly eluding me.

He shook his head, "See, you get upset because I'm not giving you the answers you want."

"Tell me, what's so bad about being with me?"

He smirked. "Baby girl, listen to me." He joined me again, this time bowing to his knees and taking my hands in his. "Everything doesn't have to be a tug of war. Everything doesn't have to be who's right and who's wrong. And everything doesn't have to be now or never."

"I just want some security."

"What have I done that makes you feel you don't have security with me? I come home to you every night, and that's without the commitment of a marriage."

Calm down, Katrina, calm down. Be calm, Katrina, be calm. Dammit, he was right.

"Katrina, I don't know what else you want from me. I do everything you ask me to do, and you still always want to pick fights."

Now I was ready to yell. "I wasn't even trying to fight with you, but since you want to, it's on." I stepped back, pulling my hands from his. "You want all the benefits of a wife without actually giving me the title."

"You know marriage is just a piece of paper."

"Then if it's just a piece of paper, why don't we have one?"

"You believe that two people who can't speak to each other without yelling should be getting married?"

"I came to you calmly, and that wasn't good enough. You never respond to me unless I'm yelling." I huffed. "You know what, you're right, why should I marry someone that I have to constantly yell at to even get some attention from?"

"What are you saying?"

I looked away. Tears building in my eyes. It was apparent we weren't headed towards any more of a commitment any time soon. And I hadn't heeded Chloe's words at all; I hadn't prepared myself for this response. I didn't know what to say. For once, I was at a loss for words.

FAITH

Sitting in my car outside of Katrina's place, I wondered what Edris was thinking, holding my hand for so long. The man was fine, but why, just why did he have to be with Katrina? But this could be my in. By the way he held onto my hand, he didn't seem too concerned about his woman standing right there. I wondered if Katrina had even noticed. She probably did from the way she hawks the man.

The crack in Katrina's relationship could be my opening, but I needed to plan. I needed to see Jack. My mind circled. Did I rush into things with him since my mind was wandering to Edris so much? But everything between Jack and me had been going fine. He was kind, sweet, and always the perfect gentleman. Made dinner reservations, sent me flowers, sent thoughtful text messages throughout the day, and sent goofy memes. He was Prince Charming. Nothing like the aloof jerk Katrina had tried to paint him to be. At this point, I wondered if Jack was really the one Katrina wanted because he was doing everything she wanted Edris to do for her. I pressed the call button on my steering wheel and navigated to call Jack's phone number.

He picked up swiftly, "What's up? I was waiting on you to call."

"I was calling to see if you were home."

"Yeah, I'm at home," he took a long pause. "I'm glad you reached out. I wanted to ask you if you would spend the night with me tonight?"

I didn't know what to say. I was willing to bet that I knew what Jack wanted and why he was asking me to spend the night with him.

"I'm sorry, I don't mean to pressure you if I'm being too forward. Please don't feel like you have to say yes."

To hell with it, "I'm on my way right now."

I couldn't blow him off, not in trying to ensure that I stayed close to Jack, and essentially, my only way to get close to Edris. So I made my way to Jack's and quickly hopped on the elevator and up to Jack's place. When the elevator doors opened, Jack was there ready to greet me with a kiss.

"Please come in." He looked at me longingly.

"You look like you were busy." I noticed paperwork all over the counter height bar that enclosed the kitchen.

"The tech company project is giving my brain cells a run for their money, but it's time for a break."

He invited me to sit down on the sofa. I kicked my pumps off and positioned myself on my knees, motioning for him to sit down in front of me. I whispered in his ear to relax and to let me take care of him as I began to massage his shoulders.

Jack spoke. "You're coming from Katrina's, right?"

"Yes, I did."

"How did that go?"

"I got my glimpse into her relationship with Edris."

"And you made it out alive?" He laughed.

"Yea," I chuckled. "You know what, though, I can't say that I'm surprised. I've only been back around for a short time, but Katrina hasn't changed."

"What do you mean?"

I continued to rub his shoulders and down his back. "Katrina is treating Edris the exact same way she treated her boyfriend in college."

"Did you tell her that?"

"I did."

"Damn, I know she didn't take that well."

"It doesn't matter, Katrina will be Katrina regardless of whatever anyone says."

"I've been trying to tell my boy that since he met her, but since I haven't been in a serious relationship in some time, he doesn't want to take what I say seriously. He acts as if I have no clue how things work."

"You don't think Edris should be with Katrina?"

"Hell no. Dealing with Katrina is nothing but stress for my boy. I'm tired of seeing it and hearing about it."

"Maybe he loves her, and at the end of the day, it's up to him what he wants to deal with."

Jack turned, repositioning himself to face me. "You're absolutely right. I don't have to deal with it. I'm concerned about what's right here," he gently placed his hand on my thigh.

"Tell me what you're concerned about."

"I've been thinking about you, well us, all day."

"What about us?"

"I was thinking about how we've only known each other for a short time, and you've changed my entire outlook on relationships. I don't know why or how you are doing this to me, but I'm down for the ride."

I cheesed like a kid with a new toy. "First of all, I haven't done anything to you, and second, is changing all that bad?"

"I'm not saying change is bad, you're the first woman to come along that I've connected with. I'm not going to lie; it freaked me out at first, but I'm willing to see what this could be."

"I'm glad you feel that way."

"Does that mean you're down to ride with me?"

"Of course I am."

I swallowed hard. My mouth had moved faster than my brain. But maybe I was overthinking this. I was in the right place for exactly what I needed to do. If getting back at Katrina meant that I had to play extremely close with Jack, then so be it. Besides, he could keep me warm at night and squelch my ever-present desire to be sexually satisfied.

"It's you and me and me and you only, correct?"

"Yes, and I can ask you the same question?"

"It's only you, baby." He gave me a silken kiss on the lips.

"I do want to ask you something, though."

"And what's that?"

"You mentioned that you haven't been in a serious relationship for some time. Why is that?"

He hung his head, "Somehow I knew you were going there." He quickly got up and walked to the kitchen, grabbing a bottle of wine and a couple of glasses.

"It's a fair question, right? We're getting to know each other, and your reasons are a part of who you are. Don't get scared of me now."

"I don't fear anything, let's get that straight right now."

"Tell me what's up. Listen, this is a judgment-free zone. You can tell me anything."

"This is a give-and-take conversation, right?"

"How about this, we'll both share. Whatever I ask, I'll answer as well." I extended my hand for a handshake of agreement.

"Alright, but you start." He agreed, reluctantly shaking my hand.

"Alright," I rolled my eyes. "Well, my last serious relationship was almost two years ago. What about you?"

"Four years ago."

"His name was Nic."

"Celeste."

His short, quick answers let me know this was a strategy game to him rather than a tell session. He could be giving me whatever answers to satisfy my questioning, but he would have to eventually open up to me. But I couldn't blame him too much, I also had to be careful how much information I revealed, especially concerning people that should be in my past.

"I met Nic while I was out to dinner with some friends. What about you and Celeste?"

"I met her at the airport. I was coming back from a business trip, and we had a layover together in Phoenix. She was beautiful, sitting there reading a World Religions book."

"Oh, was she in school?"

"No," he chuckled. "She always used to say that knowledge was everywhere, we didn't need college to teach us anything, just pick up a book. She always liked to read. And she would read just about anything."

"Good for her. That's commendable."

"Brains and beauty, she was an aspiring actress/model, but I always thought she should be a teacher."

"I can't say the same for Nic. Well, I guess I shouldn't say that. Nic was smart, but he's smart when it comes to getting his own way by any means."

"What do you mean by that?"

"If it benefits him, he will find a way to make it work, no matter how much it may hurt other people."

"Sounds toxic." Jack was quiet for a moment. I hoped he didn't feel crushed about what I was saying, especially since I was lying. "What made you finally walk away?"

Shit. "He didn't help the bad mind state I was already in."

"What do you mean by that?"

Shit. I should have taken his approach of keeping my answers short and sweet.

Jack sensed my recoil. "You don't have to say if you don't want to."

"I'll just say, I've faced a lot of emotional traumas in my life and have done my best to heal from them. Nic happened to be during a time when I didn't see the worth in myself that I see now."

"I understand." He reached up to caress my face. "Please don't ever think I'm going to treat you as less than the bright, intelligent, sexy woman you are."

My lips curled slowly, "Thank you, I appreciate you saying that." I exhaled. "What about you and Celeste? Why did you walk away?"

He dropped his hand. "I'm not going to lie to you. I asked her to marry me, and I thought I was ready for that commitment, but I cheated on her."

"So do you have a problem being faithful?"

"No. I promise all of that is behind me."

I wanted to believe him, but did I really have room to ask that question? I was already playing a dangerous enough game, and so far, Jack had been an innocent bystander, but if he kept talking to me like this, I could have more than a couple of problems on my hands.

"I'm sorry, but I must ask. Is what happened between you and Celeste the reason why you have been reluctant to get into a relationship?"

"No, that has nothing to do with it. I don't believe I've found a woman who has been worth my time."

"Until now, right?" I poked.

"Yeah, you're right about that." He grinned and rubbed his chin.

"You're a man dating multiple women, *were* dating multiple women, were you bedding all of these women too?"

"I thought this was a give-*then*-take conversation, you give a little, I give a little? It's starting to feel like an interrogation."

I laughed. "I'm sorry, you're right. I'm not trying to interrogate you. But there's nothing else to tell about Nic, and I wanted to make sure we are on the same page when it comes to the exclusivity of our new relationship." Time to lay it on thick.

Jack repositioned to sit next to me on the couch. "Listen to me." His auburn-colored eyes seared into me. "I'm not here to play any games with you. I've done my share of that, and I see you differently than the other women I did play around with and have my fun with. I'm willing to be exclusive with you as long as we are true and honest with each other."

This definitely wasn't the man Katrina painted a repellent picture of. I wasn't sure what to make of her attempt to push us together, whether it was genuine or part of a larger diabolical scheme. Either way, Jack and I were together now, and I couldn't back out without raising a million eyebrows.

I changed the subject before the relationship talk could go any deeper. "Tell me about your family?"

"That's the dark trauma for me."

"Oh, I'm sorry, don't mean to pry too much."

He held up his hand. "It's okay, I'll say that my mother raised me as best she could. She was either high or drunk whenever I needed her, and my father was the one supporting her habits. I left on my eighteenth birthday and never looked back."

"Sorry to hear that. That must have been tough to get through. You didn't have any siblings?"

"Nope, just me. But I don't dwell on it; my life has turned out just fine and better without them. I always told myself I would never pick up their habits, and I've stuck to that."

I took him in slowly as my eyes watched the expression on his face change.

"Why are you watching me like that?"

My face turned hot. "It's off the subject."

"Tell me what you're thinking."

"You are tempting, sexy, even when you do the simplest things. Do you know that?"

"Thank you." He returned to the same searing intensity with his eyes. "What should we do now? I think we've done enough sharing for one sitting."

I didn't have a chance to answer before Jack's lips were tasting mine; he was arousing every sensual sensation in me with only his lips. The reputation was revealing itself to me; I could see how any woman could want to be close to him. This kiss alone was making me want to explore more.

Our eyes met as our lips unhurriedly retreated. He looked at me with a salacious look, deciding to move his kisses to my neck. Damn, he knew exactly how to get to me. His kisses strong and sure. Speech barely escaped my mouth. "We should go to your bedroom."

"Are you sure that's what you want?" Jack whispered, nuzzling right below my earlobe. His voice breezy and spirited.

"I said it."

He stood up, taking my hand in his. Leading me to the bedroom, my brain was going miles per millisecond. But I didn't want to slow down. I wanted to know why women were clamoring to his bedroom. Seemed an eternity had passed since someone touched me in a way that made me feel like I was more than an object, and I could only hope Jack was capable of taking me out of reality for a few moments. Mixing sexual satisfaction and escape from reality was always an option I'd spring for.

I entered the still ill-decorated but expansive master bedroom.

"You mind if I light some candles?"

I smirked. "You're already going to get it, Jack. You don't have to play romance games with me."

"Oh wow." He laughed. "Trust me, sweetheart, this ain't a game. And you'll always get the romantic treatment."

"I like that."

"Make yourself comfortable. Can I get you anything?"

I sat on the large, framed bed. "Just you." I motioned for him to come and sit next to me.

"We don't have to do anything you're not ready for. We can just lie down and relax if you like."

I leaned into him, planting a soft kiss on his lips, "I'm ready for whatever." I didn't want to slow down. I was attracted to Jack, and for a while, I wanted to forget everything going on around me.

He was slow and gentle, methodical. Kissing my neck, working his way down to my collarbone. The sacred collarbone kiss always sent chills up and down my spine. His hands caressed my body. One spent time connected to my face while the other felt the lace of my bra underneath my plaid button-up shirt. As far as I was concerned, Jack could put his hands wherever he wanted.

His lips rejoined mine this time with the intensity of passion growing. My body and mind ready to get lost in physical heat. Our eyes met, and I knew I wanted him inside of me as soon as possible.

He stood up in front of me, taking off his navy-blue V-neck tee. I reached to unbutton my jeans, but Jack quickly grabbed my hand. He pushed it out of the way, undoing the button and zipper himself as he stared at me. He firmly placed his hands on my thighs, pulling at my jeans. I slid my body up towards the headboard of the bed, loosening my denim confines for him, revealing the matching lace panties to my bra.

I reached to unbutton my shirt so it could follow the same suit, but Jack stopped me again. "You will learn to let me take care of you." He spoke in a hushed tone that echoed down and quivered my lady *V*, who was fully awake. I lay back as his hands and lips continued to explore my body. He kissed his way from my thighs up to where the lace of my panties held my secret. She was ready to be released and share how wet she had gotten from his affection and attention.

But Jack moved away.

"You leaving me?"

"Never. Come here." He pulled me up from the bed.

I stood there as he stared into my eyes, his fingers quickly moving to completely unbutton my shirt, and he threw it to the side to join my discarded jeans.

"You're so beautiful, Faith."

I was sure he could see me blushing in the slip of city lights that covered the bedroom.

"I want to take my time."

I inhaled. "You can have all the time you need."

"We've got all night, right?"

I smiled. "Absolutely.

JACK

I could barely concentrate at work. During the morning meeting, I was telling my team about a new client contract we had landed, and I completely went blank on handing out assignments. My thoughts couldn't stay off Faith. I found myself licking my lips every time I thought back on kissing her. Her lips velvety and plush. The last time I kissed her, she tasted like pineapple.

After losing control of our bodies, we lay in bed eating fruit and drinking wine, laughing under the covers and enjoying more rounds of lovemaking. In between, we would steal kisses and talk. She was easy to talk to, and I was opening up without realizing it. I don't know how, but she managed to get my guard to be almost nonexistent.

It scared me, but felt good at the same time. I could only hope Faith wasn't playing a game with me. I'd be a fool not to think that all the wrong I've done to women in my past wouldn't come back to haunt me. I could wish all I wanted, but I knew what reality was. But, for the moment, I was going to enjoy what Faith and I were doing.

I always said I'd never settle down unless I found the right woman, and from what Faith was showing me, I may have found her. I didn't want to speak too soon, but if she kept showing me this type of relationship, I could fall in love. I kind of shivered at the thought, but I was interested in seeing where our relationship would go.

Being with one woman wasn't completely a foreign concept to me. I knew exactly how I wanted things with Faith to be. Honestly, I wanted to spoil her. Make her feel like no one else mattered to me but her.

Even with all the women I dated in the past, there wasn't anyone I could have seen myself falling for in the way I was with Faith. Celeste was the closest, and I'd messed that all up. I wasn't ready at the time. I still wanted to play, but I was done with that now. I was completely under Faith's spell.

Her vulnerability was making me see her in a different light, and someone I could see myself with. She told me about her college days and how tough that time had been for her. She even made me think a little differently about Katrina. Just a little, not much. And it sounded like Chloe was the same sweet angel she was now. I crossed my fingers and eyes that Faith was closer to the Chloe side of the spectrum than the Katrina side.

As Faith shared her college experience with me, I was intrigued when she mentioned a fourth member of their crew who hadn't been invited to this friend's reunion they seemed to be having. She didn't mention her name, and I figured I'd better leave well enough alone. I was just happy she felt comfortable enough to start having deeper conversations with me. I didn't want to push her too far.

Since I didn't have any other meetings for the day, I decided to pack up my laptop and head home. I'd rather be heading to Faith's place, but I didn't want to bother her. I knew she was working on her poetry collection, and we had plans to meet up later tonight anyway.

As soon as I got home, I set my laptop up on the bar in the kitchen, thinking that maybe I could refocus and get some work done, but a knock came to the front door. I looked at my watch. I wasn't expecting Faith, and my boys were still at work. I didn't know who else would even knock on my door, especially at this time of day.

I got up, and like an idiot, without even checking the peep-hole, I opened the door.

"Well, hey." Rayven's carnal voice greeted me.

Her breasts were on their classic display, this time peeking through an orange t-shirt dress. Her brown braided wedge heels were walking through my door before I could stop her.

"Rayven, what are you doing here, again?"

"Why are you acting like you don't want to see me?"

"Look, I already told you. I didn't mean to make you think we had more than we do, but you can't keep popping up over here like this."

"Oh, right, because you have a girlfriend now. Where was she when you hooked up with me?"

"It wasn't even like that. I didn't meet her until after the night you and I spent together."

"Where is she now?"

"Why?"

"I'd love to meet her." She invited herself in to get comfortable on the sofa.

"Rayven, I'm sorry, but you have to go."

"Are you expecting her?"

"Yes, actually, I am. Could you please leave? I'm asking nicely."

She blew her breath and stood up. Her tiny purse followed the gold chain strapped around her shoulder. She slowly approached me, her face coming within what felt like centimeters of mine.

"I don't know that I can let you go so easily."

Her breath was pungent of alcohol, and I wondered if she was drunk.

"Rayven, did you drive here?"

"I'm not drunk, if that's what you're implying."

"But I can smell it on you, and it's the middle of the day."

"Do you see me falling everywhere and being sloppy? I'm fine."

I didn't need Faith showing up early, unexpectedly. I didn't want to have to explain my innocence and hope that she would understand. It was much too early in our relationship for her to think she couldn't trust me, especially after the night we'd spent together.

With the least amount of force possible, I led Rayven to the door. "I hope you're okay, but seriously, you have to go, and I'd greatly appreciate it if you did not come back over here."

"Fine, I'm going." She passed back through the front door and turned back to face me. "Tell your girlfriend, I said hey." She winked before flouncing back down the hallway, using the wall to hold her up.

I swiftly slammed the door, leaning my back against it as my heart started to pick up speed. I've got to start using my peephole. Shit! Why did she keep showing up here?

***

I dapped up my boys as we met at our usual spot. "What's going on? Good to see y'all."

"What's up with you? You're hard to track down nowadays." Edris laughed as our palms echoed through the half-empty hole in the wall joint.

"What are you talking about?"

Bryant joined in. "You hooked up with Faith, and we ain't seen you since."

"Aw, man, please."

Our favorite ample-waisted server stopped at the table, all smiles to ask if we all wanted our usuals, and we told her she already knew.

"How's that going?" Edris questioned.

"This faithful thing isn't as bad as I thought; things are good. Faith is a pretty cool chick."

Bryant and Edris gave each other *yea right* looks and started giggling like school children.

"Just what the hell is so funny?"

"Nothing, man, nothing at all." Edris continued to laugh. "It's just crazy that you fall for the one chick that my girl brings around."

I rolled my eyes as Ample Waist returned with our drinks. "Yea, yea, I know, but I'm not trying to dwell on that shit. As I said, Faith is cool."

"I know you," Edris said. "She spent the night yet? Spill it."

"I'm not kissing and telling."

Bryant exclaimed. "Since when? The Jack I know would be bursting to tell us how great the sex is."

I chuckled. "Yea, I know, I know. But I have more respect for Faith than that. Besides, I meant what I said, I'm not playing the same old games this time."

My two supposed friends exploded into laughter. I didn't see what was so funny. "What are you two fools laughing at?"

"Alright, alright, our fault, man. We just busting yo' chops." Bryant wiped artificial tears from his eyes. "This is good, man, I'm glad you're taking things with Faith seriously."

"Thank you, can a brotha get some credit? Y'all have been busting my chops for years to chill with one woman, and now that I'm doing just that, y'all think y'all comics of the year."

Edris said. "It ain't that. I'm honestly surprised, but if you're happy, we're happy."

"Thank you," I said, a little jaded.

"But you should still keep your eyes, ears, and brain open," Edris said.

I shook my head. I swear, for as long as we've been friends, I'll never understand these two. What the hell did they want from me? I knew I should have kept my mouth shut. Faith was right that everything should stay between the two of us.

I was in new territory, attempting to revise my relationship history and my relationship reputation, and I wasn't feeling the love from my friends. Here I was trying to make a change, and they wanted to joke on me.

As much as Bryant wanted to preach to me about his loving and committed relationship, one thing I had been that my friends had never been was engaged, and they didn't know how that status upgrade brought changes to relationships. I'd played off my breakup with Celeste for a long time, but Faith's excavation into the past made me think of Celeste. I still denied that she had anything to do with my one woman after the other mentality, but that situation did change me. I told Faith I hadn't found a woman who was worth my time, and I did feel that way, but that wasn't the entire story.

I lived in relationship fear. I watched my parents, and from an early age, I always thought that in some way I would destroy a woman in the same way I saw my father ruin my mother. I couldn't process it as a kid, but with the clarity of an adult, I could see how my father derailed my mother's entire life.

My parents met in college; my mother was set on becoming a lawyer, my father had no direction, but was forced to attend college by his mother. Instead of focusing on studying, he liked the access to drugs that college provided, and once he looped in with the right people, drugs became his subject of choice instead of finding a major.

Thinking that he was helping my mother stay up to study or give her an extra boost for a test, he opened a door to a dark place that she never found her way out of.

Once she became pregnant with me during their sophomore year, she couldn't control her want for any type of drug she could get her hands on; her life was pretty much over. Sometimes I wondered how I was even born healthy or made it to my 18th birthday under their care.

This was part of my life Edris and Bryant didn't know about, despite our decade-long friendship. And I would more than likely keep it this way. I did my best every day to forget where I came from. It helped that both of my parents were gone from drug overdose and heart attack, and since I was an only child, there wasn't much for me to go back to.

Bryant brought me back to the present. "Well, now that Jack has completed our little couple's circle, what do y'all think about this dinner the girls want to have?'

"Katrina hasn't mentioned anything to me. What are you talking about?"

"Wow, that's interesting because it was her idea, according to Chloe."

I spoke up. "Can you really be surprised? Katrina is always plotting."

"Did Faith say anything to you about it?" Bryant turned his attention to me.

I shook my head no. "I'll see her tonight, but if she mentions it, I'm telling you right now I'll probably try and talk my way out of it."

Edris reached across the table to dap me. He scoffed, "Same here."

"Nobody agree to anything. It's already bad enough I took a hook-up from your women, and now they want to smile in my face about it, no thank you; that doesn't sound fun. Anyway, I gotta get out of here, I'll see y'all later."

"Oh, you running to those hot sheets and warm meals now, huh?" Edris poked fun at me.

I waved him off and headed towards the door.

***

As I pulled up to Faith's home, I got a quick flashback to Rayven and her surprise visits. I contemplated whether I should tell Faith, so there would be no surprise later if Rayven decided to continue her pop-ups. At least then, Faith would be fully aware, and I wasn't responsible for keeping a secret. But on the other hand, I didn't want to scare Faith off by giving her the impression that she would always have to deal with my past. I wasn't sure what the right call was in this moment.

I took a deep breath and rang the doorbell. Faith promptly opened the door; all smiles and instant relief fell over me.

"You're early." She said, kissing me on the cheek and grabbing my hand.

"I missed you. I wanted to see you."

"That's so sweet."

I followed her into the open living room. Her usually dressed-to-impress clothing had been replaced with chill wear, and she looked just as sexy. Her black t-shirt was just long enough to cover the bowing crescent of her backside, which was cradled by gray leggings. Her feet were bare, with orange toenail polish expertly applied, more than likely by a pedicurist.

We settled in on the couch. "What's up? How was your day?" I asked her as I moved the loose curly hairs from her ponytail away from her face.

"It was good. Got a lot of work done. What about you? You comin' from meeting up with the guys, right?"

"Yea, same old with them."

I wanted to tell her I couldn't get her off my mind, but I wasn't up for a deep sharing moment.

"Oh, um, Katrina did call me today, she mentioned maybe having a couple's dinner for everyone."

"Oh yea?"

"Yea, I thought maybe it would be nice. Give me a chance to get to know your friends better."

I smiled even though I wanted to scream. So much for playing dumb and not agreeing to anything.

"But, unfortunately, I won't be able to. I forgot to tell you. I have to go out of town, and I leave in a couple of days."

"Damn, you runnin' from me already."

She smirked, "No, I have meetings with my publisher. I'm sorry, I should have told you sooner because the plans were made before we met; it just slipped my mind."

"You don't need to apologize, baby. Go handle your business. I'll be right here."

She snuggled up closer to me, finessing her body for me to wrap my arm around her. "Are you going to be a good boy while I'm gone?"

Damn, didn't she trust me? "Of course."

She continued. "I'm glad we've been able to spend so much time together."

"How long are you going to be gone?"

"Just a couple of days. It will be quick."

"Alright, baby, well, as I said, handle your business. I'll be here waiting for you. I'm not going anywhere."

"And what about being my good boy?" she raised an eyebrow.

Dammit, I had to tell her about Rayven.

"Of course, that goes without saying, but I do need to tell you something."

"Oh god." Her body flew up from my embrace.

"Hold on. Let me explain first before you jump to conclusions."

"You're right." She put her hands up.

"I want to be up front with you and truthful. There's a woman from my past that keeps popping up on me, and I don't want it to happen again, and you think that I've been dealing with her when I haven't been."

Faith moved back a bit. She re-positioned herself to sit on her right leg, her left dangling off the side of the couch. "Obviously, you've dealt with her because she's lightweight stalking you."

"Yea, but you know what I mean. I'm not seeing her anymore. I've asked her to leave me alone, but she showed up to place today completely unexpectedly."

"She knows where you live?"

I thought telling the truth would make this easier, but I felt Faith's intensity growing, and I got the feeling I had only just begun to answer questions. "I'm hoping I never see her again. I even told her I had a girlfriend."

She twisted her lips. "Ok, babe." She leaned into me to kiss my cheek.

My eyes circled back and forth. "That's it? You don't have anything else to say?"

"Jack, what are you expecting me to say? You set her straight. What else could I ask for?"

"You sure we're good? I promise you I want nothing to do with that woman."

"Can I ask you a *real* question?"

Shit, I should have stayed quiet. "Of course."

"Are you sure this is what you want?"

"Yes, haven't I shown you that?"

"I need to be sure, Jack."

"I know I've done women wrong in my past, but I want to change that, and I want to change that with you. I want to start fresh."

"We both could use a fresh start, trust me, it's not just you."

FAITH

I stepped into the lobby of an upscale high-rise hotel. The strong flow of water from the indoor water fountain filled the air, engulfing the sound of my heels against the black and white mirrored and stone floor. At about 6'2, he was standing there waiting on me, his caramel-colored skin smooth with not a blemish in sight, his demeanor sure and confident. I could tell his suit was custom, fitting in the right places. He always had to show that he wasn't the average. I hadn't seen him in a couple of months, but he hadn't changed, I could tell.

My stomach was in knots the entire flight across the country to the Pacific. After spending so much time getting to know Jack over the past few weeks, here I was, lying about where I was, what I was doing, and who I was with. Jack was more than likely being sincere with me, but I needed to close this open-ended chapter that was hanging over my head.

"You're late." He was always impatient, his voice gruff and smoky.

"Nice to see you, too. Yes, my flight was delayed, but I'm okay."

"It's cool, I guess. Come on, I got us the best suite on the top floor."

He didn't hug me or even reach for my hand, not even an offer to take my bag. He only turned on his heels and headed for the ornate steel elevators. As we stepped into the steel box, we stood on opposite sides of the enclosed space as if to keep people who didn't even know us from thinking that we were together. He pressed the button for the 12th floor, then stood back from the door, crossing his hands in front of what appeared to be a bulging crotch. I smiled a little, thinking that better be because of me. He could pretend all he wanted, but we both knew the deal.

When the doors opened again, he hopped off with no regard for me and still no help with my bag. I bent slightly to pick up my duffel, which I had laid on the floor, then exited, hoping the doors wouldn't betray me and try to snap me inside.

I followed behind his tall frame to a door marked 'PRIVATE'. He swiped a black and gold key card with the same ornate design from the elevator doors and swung the handle-barred door open. A short flight of five steps led up to a long hallway. I continued to follow, wondering what kind of suite this would be, or if I was walking into some other sort of trap. Finally, he led me through a set of double doors and into a suite I'd only seen in movies. Fully equipped, it was more like a condo. State-of-the-art stainless steel appliances, a pearl granite top island filled the airy space of the kitchen, which led to a living room area with a bleached white sectional sofa and lounge chairs. The living area blended seamlessly into the most thrilling view of the other hotels, with the beach nestled right in between.

"Check this out." He finally reached for my hand. I followed him to the large balcony. He slid the large glass doors open, and there was a Jacuzzi built into the floor of the balcony. "Is this good enough for you?"

I turned around to face him. "All for me?"

"Of course. I knew I had to show out or you wouldn't come."

"Oh, please, we've been in much less luxurious places. All that matters is that I'm here, you're here." I looked down at our southern regions, surely growing in anticipation of what we came here for. "She's here, he's here."

"You're speaking my language." He took one step closer, grabbing me by the arm and pulling me into him. His lips met mine in a macho way. He knew I didn't mind, and I liked his aggressive approach. Much different than Jack's slow, romantic manner. He broke our kiss, "Think your boyfriend will hate that I kiss you better than he does?"

"I didn't come here to talk about him. And how do you know about him anyway?"

"Rayven."

"Why does she know my business?"

"She said she's seen you around the city with the same guy you stole from her. Why is it you always seem to steal what belongs to her?"

I looked down at the city below us. My mind started to churn; my hands gripped the silver balcony railing. Shit! Was Rayven the sleaze showing up on Jack's doorstep? Damn Jack. Of all the women in the city, he had to have dipped his stick in the one woman who probably hated me the most. The woman popping up at his place could be anyone, but damn, this would be just my luck.

I remained cool. "I'm surprised she's talking to you at all."

"She's still in love with me and most definitely still hates you."

I rolled my eyes. "Then why am I here instead of her?"

He smugly smirked. "I could have both of you here, and I bet you'd get along."

"You're such a pig!"

Before I could turn around again, he was right behind me, grabbing my waist and spinning me around, forcing our faces to meet, leaning me back into the railing. "But here you are."

He was right. Somehow, I had a weak spot for Nic Camden. I knew our relationship was purely lustful and meant absolutely nothing; we used each other. But there was something about this man that kept me drawn to him. Possibly because he had a hand in making my dream of being a published author come true, but I knew that I still allowed myself to be misused.

I had been self-publishing my early writing, but I needed a publishing house for the benefit of my career, and Nic had placed me in the very room I had only dreamed about. To Rayven's detriment, it had been her push for Nic to look at my writing as he was making his way as an agent after working many years in the magazine world. Nic wasted no time securing a publishing deal for me and shooting my writing career up multiple bestseller lists.

Every time Nic and I met, as we worked together, sexual sparks always flew. From our first encounter, we broke the Richter scale, yet he claimed Rayven publicly as his girlfriend.

Rayven and I had been out having dinner when Nic confidently approached our table and made small talk. He spoke to Rayven, but his eyes lingered on me. At first, I thought he was playing a game, but he asked for Rayven's number, and soon after, the two of them started dating. I'd be lying if I said I wasn't annoyed by his choice, but from the first time he kissed me behind Rayven's back at a party, I knew the dynamics had changed, and I was the one he wanted from the jump.

We continued to fool around behind Rayven's back even after they moved in together. I knew I was risking a friendship, but what could I say? The man had taken me from weekend writer with big dreams to full-time writer with multiple deals and advances that netted me a bank account that had also been a former dream.

Although Rayven had been my only friend, especially after Katrina and Chloe parted from our little group, I was deep in my addiction of being selfish and fulfilling what I deemed to be a need for carnal pleasure; I didn't care about the risk of losing the only friendship I had left. I wanted what I wanted, and in my demented mind, it was as simple as that. I never considered how valuable it was that Rayven had stayed by my side even when I had done wrong.

Sneaking around with Nic only fed my addiction to what wasn't right. The secret was sexy, and the rush every time I knew I was going to see him or sneak away to a hotel was thrilling, and I never wanted it to end. I was selfish and never stopped to consider what it would do to my friend. And Nic was no different. He could have pulled away and been faithful to his woman, but he was just as salacious, caught up in a whirlwind of desire.

Our inability to control ourselves took a toll on Rayven that neither one of us had expected. Soon, I started to pull back from Rayven, spending less and less time hanging out with her. Imagine having to look your friend in the eye after spending the night pleasuring her man while she asked you if you believed he was cheating on her. For whatever reason, she didn't connect the dots sooner, maybe out of not wanting to accept the truth, but the more time I spent with Nic, the less time he and I spent with Rayven, and she pacified being alone with bottle after bottle of alcohol.

I already had my own bout with not being able to control my drinking, so I could see the dangerous path Rayven was on, but that still didn't stop me or change my mind about having shrouded trysts with Nic.

I never thought things would get out of hand, but a few weeks ago, both Nic and I lost our damn minds and committed the ultimate betrayal. I thought for sure Rayven was going to kill me that night she found Nic and me together in her bed, but she simply looked at us, shook her head, and left. A quiet woman is an angry woman. We hadn't spoken since then, but apparently, she hadn't lost track of me if she knew about Jack and felt the need to tell Nic about him. She had to be the woman who was popping up at his place just to get back at me.

I was slapped back into reality when Nic's palm struck my bottom.

"Come on, we've been talking for way too long." He walked back through the glass door and headed through the double doors to the bedroom of the suite. He loosened his tie as his Dolce & Gabbana dress shoes flew across the lush tan carpet as he tossed them aside.

He plopped down on the oversized king bed adorned in all-white bedding. I joined him in the bedroom, and the scent of fresh-cut flowers greeted me. Orange cremon mums were next to the bed on each side. Matching orange abstract paintings hung on the wall.

Nic stood up, removing his pants, that bulge saying hello again through his dark gray boxer briefs. He started to unbutton his black dress shirt, his eyes connecting with mine. Just as he reached the top, he headed for the en suite bathroom. "Lose the clothes and meet me in the shower."

***

I stretched in between the sheets, not wanting to open my eyes. That had been some of the best sleep of my life; this posh bed was worth dealing with Nic's pushy attitude. I came here with the intention of this being our last fling, and I was unsure that I'd be able to stick to my guns, but this trip hadn't been worth it. Nic couldn't put aside his ego to satisfy me. He made me think that Jack's reputation in the bedroom was well deserved compared to the bullshit Nic thought he had served me in the shower last night.

I slid my arm to the other side of the bed to find Nic's body, but the bed was empty. I slowly sat up, rubbing my eyes like a confused child woken up for school.

I walked to the door of the bedroom. Nic was on his phone, but he seemed to be concentrating on whispering. He didn't have a problem taking calls around me any other time. Why was he hiding now? I walked up behind him, placing my hands on his back. He put his finger to his lips, telling me to be quiet.

"I'll be back in a couple of days, promise."

I exhaled. No doubt some chick he was keeping behind Rayven's back, as well as me. There was no need for me to be jealous, after all, look at where he was and who he sneaked off to see. I never asked about any female he was entertaining. These hotel weekends were supposed to be about one thing only.

"Another one of your multi-city flings?" I asked once he was off the phone.

"Why are you asking me that?"

"You asked me about what was reported to you. But the better question I'd like to know is why Rayven is following me and divulging back to you what I'm doing? Maybe she should be more focused on the other women you're keeping around."

"Trust me, you're a passing conversation, my dear."

I ignored his downplay of my position in his eyes.

"Don't play jealous, Faith, it's not attractive. And don't act like you didn't know that Rayven and I were back together."

"What the hell is wrong with you? Are you out to destroy this girl?"

"I could ask you the same question."

"No, actually, you can't. It's barely been a month since she caught the two of us together. What slick shit did you say to get her to be back with you?"

"It's not always about words."

"Yes, you're right. Then what did you buy her?"

He remained silent.

"I take it she has no clue that you're here with me now."

"Of course not."

"Then you are the one with devastation on the agenda."

"Act like you care, Faith. You've never given a fuck about Rayven, even when y'all were in college together. You fucked her over back then, too."

I sneered. "You have no right to comment on that. You weren't even there."

"I didn't need to be there. Rayven told me what a sloppy mess you were and how you stole money from all of your friends to feed your habit. Not to mention letting anything between your legs you thought you could gain something from."

My knees buckled as he hurled insults about my past my way.

"You want to spout how much you've changed your life around, you ain't shit. You may not be taking scripts anymore and finishing off full bottles of wine, but you're still a damn wreck." His voice was gruff again, tone rising.

"Then why are you here, Nic?" I yelled back. "You ain't shit just as much as I ain't. You're so worried about my past as if yours is squeaky clean. Yes, I may have stolen money from Rayven back in the day, and yes, I fucked up messing around with you, but at least I cut ties with her instead of continuing to smile in her face like the snake and pig you are."

I turned on bare heels, rushing back to the bedroom to gather my things up. I needed to high tail it out of here as speedily as possible and find a red eye back home to the Atlantic. I never should have come here in the first place.

"Faith, what are you doing?" he followed behind me.

"I'm leaving." I didn't bother folding anything; I threw items back in my duffel bag. "I don't know why I came here with you. I'm going back home."

"Nobody forced you to come here. Go ahead and go home to your boyfriend. That's perfectly fine with me because this little thing is over anyway. Know that this is the last time we will ever meet up."

"Oh, please, trust me, I never want to see you again. You are a snake. You and Rayven can have a great life together."

I should crush his soul right here and tell him Rayven was just as sneaky as him, stalking a man who wanted nothing to do with her and everything to do with me, but I didn't want to stoop to his level. I had come here to close this bullshit chapter between the two of us, and that clearly had been accomplished.

"Whoever this man is, you are running to he's not Nic Camden, remember that."

"That's exactly why I'm getting the fuck out of here."

JACK

"What's up, man?" I greeted Edris at the bar.

"How you holdin' up, fell off the monogamy wagon yet?" he replied, laughing.

I mocked his laughing. "Everything is good with Faith. I'm good! She's been gone, nothing but a couple of days."

"She's pushing your limit then, huh?"

"Shut up," I said, play punching his shoulder. "Trust me, I'm good on that too."

"I'm poking fun at you. Where's Bryant?"

"Bryant isn't coming, so you're stuck with me. Chloe got a flat tire on the way home from school, so he went to rescue her."

Edris nodded, signaling to the bartender for more beers since he finished the one he had started before I got here.

"What's up? You look heavy today."

"Yea, heavy with a lot on my mind."

"Katrina problems?"

"What else and who else?" We shared a laugh.

"What is it now? She should be in heaven since she can brag that she set me up."

"You know she's never satisfied, and that's why I'm thinking of leaving Katrina for real."

Deep down, my heart was rejoicing, leaping like a leper outside the temple. I'd wished this for a long time, but on the surface, I had to say something else. "Why now?"

"Well, for starters, she's crazy, we both know that. But I don't think she's the one. I'm tired of dealing with her like I'm an inmate and she's my warden. How long have we been together, and her trust and control issues still run deep."

"You sound real sure for somebody who is always preaching about love and monogamy along with Bryant."

He chuckled, knowing he was going back on a few things he said to me. "I love Katrina, don't get me wrong, but I can't keep living my life the way I do with her. I'm not ready to get married, and she is. In her mind, either we get married, or we are not together at all. I'm not going to let her manipulate me into a marriage I'm not ready for, so I may as well put this sad cow relationship into the meat grinder while I can."

"Did she actually tell you marry her or else?"

"I've been with Katrina long enough. I can see all her little hints and intentions."

"You think she'll let you go so easily?"

"Trust me, I've already considered the war that will rage, but I'm prepared. And I've started looking at some condos over by you."

"If you live near me, it will be bachelor life all over again."

"No, it will not, Mr. Faithful, don't try to use my breaking up with Katrina as an excuse to do dirt. Remember a woman named Faith?"

"What's the point of being with Faith now? You've proven the theory I've had all along! You are a terrible example." I had to bust his chops.

"You have something good with her, y'all good. Besides, you have to go through being with someone to truly know if what you have together is worth it. If not, you'll always question it.

And let's be for real, Faith isn't anything like Katrina. She's not pushy or plain out of her mind; she's got a good head on her shoulders, and most importantly, she has her own life. She's not trying to build one around you. People forget that distance in a relationship is a good thing."

"Look at what you've built with Katrina. Can you really walk away?"

"It's not me you should be worried about. She's the one about to get a reality check. I've seriously thought this through. With the money I can save taking her car back, I can start over, and I've got a little stash put aside."

"Now you know that woman will cut you over that car."

"I'm not blowing smoke, Jack, I'm dead serious. Katrina better get herself together because her free ride with me is over." I never thought I'd see the day. He continued, "Keep this between the two of us for now. I know Bryant will overthink this shit to death, and I don't need him trying to influence my decision. I've made up my mind."

"When do you plan on telling Katrina, because you know the girls have their minds set on this little couple's dinner party when Faith gets back in town?"

"You say that like you want to do it. I'm getting you off the hook. I bet Katrina won't want to have shit to do with me after what I have to say."

I smiled deviously, covering my elation with a swipe down my lips and chin. "Yeah, you're right about that."

Edris and I sat at the bar for a while longer and talked about different things, but I could tell he was still thinking about Katrina and how to break out of ad-seg. I was happy to see my boy not settle or be forced into something he didn't want to do.

As our conversation circled back to Katrina, I thought about Faith and what she could be doing. I imagined her sitting at a large oak wood table with publishers, editors, and people who thought they knew what was best for her, telling her that her ideas weren't as good as theirs. Then she would come home to me, and I would give her all the comfort she needed. I imagined making love to her, and I wasn't even sure if I loved her, but I would set the mood so by the morning, when all the moaning had ended, she would love me, and I could say she fell for me first.

After Edris and I ran out of things to say, I decided to head home. I was sort of disappointed to see that only 8:32 was illuminated on the alarm clock in my bedroom, and I thought about what I could possibly do for the rest of the evening all alone. Usually in this situation, I would find someone to keep me company, but I would remain Mr. Faithful, as Edris had called me.

I couldn't sit here all night and wallow in my fantasies of Faith. Hopping back in the car, I headed over to a tiny lounge spot I always went to alone when my boys were too wrapped up to hang out. I went in, and it was the same as usual, music playing from small speakers situated in the corners of the large room. Some couples tried to show out on the minuscule dance floor in the front center of the room. I scoped the place, quite a few beautiful women to look at. This was now looking like a bad decision, but it wasn't wrong for me to look, right? Shit, how many more hours until Faith came back home? This turning over a new leaf thing wasn't easy, but I was determined to do it.

I grabbed a table in the far corner close to the dance floor and ordered a drink from a too perky waitress. Sitting back, this beautiful, tall woman caught my eye as she worked her lean and elongated body dancing with a guy who couldn't seem to keep up. She reminded me of Ciara in her 'Promise' music video. The music seemed to be following her rhythm instead of the other way around; nonetheless, the two flowed together agreeably. I had a feeling I wasn't the only man in here studying her, and the same went for the lesbian sitting at the table next to me, licking her dark-stained lips.

Before I knew it, I had watched her through two songs, as if she were performing for me. I snapped out of it when she waved at me. I was busted as she started to make her way over to me. Her hips seductively led the way. A true test of fidelity was headed towards me at a sensual speed.

"Did you enjoy my moves?"

"Yes, you are an exceptional dancer."

"J. Lo didn't seem to think so when I auditioned for her." She winked and pointed to the chair across the table from me. "May I?"

"Sure, have a seat."

"My name is Willow."

"Jack." I wasn't trying to start anything, even though the thought crossed my mind already.

"What are you doing here all alone?"

"My girlfriend is out of town, but I didn't feel like staying home alone."

Faith was doing a number on me; I'd given up the 'girlfriend' word so easily once again. Before, I would have said I'm just out and left it at that to see where things would lead.

"You must be missing her. I can hear it in your voice. How long have you been dating?"

"A few weeks, not long, but you are right, I do miss her."

"What's her name?"

"Faith, she's gorgeous. Your boyfriend is out of town, too?" I smirked at my poor joke.

"No boyfriend here, I have an ex-husband and three children, though. I scream baggage to men and scare them right off."

"Don't think of it that way, think of it as experience, and don't be down on yourself, you are an attractive woman, you will find another man. Maybe another woman from the attention you drew with those hips." I laughed, looking in the direction of the masc-presenting lesbian who was now watching us with envy in her eyes.

That brought a smile to her face. "I'm not too concerned. I'm not looking for a man, and women are totally out of the question."

"What, you don't think there's another man out there for you?"

"No, it's not that at all. If God wanted to send me another husband, he could with a snap of his fingers."

"Do you ever wish you hadn't gotten married since it ended?"

"No, I guess it's like you said, it's experience. And it gave me three beautiful sons."

I shook my head in agreement.

"Would you like to marry your gorgeous Faith?"

"The thought hadn't crossed my mind yet, I mean, it's only been a couple of weeks, and she's the first woman I've taken seriously in a long time."

"You never know. Get in touch with yourself, your mind, your heart, and they will tell you what's right for you."

Thinking with my heart had never been a go-to for me; I preferred to keep my heart in a frozen state. But Faith had already been chipping away at it. And damn, never thought of it, but ultimately did I know myself outside of sleeping with different women? Hadn't taken the time to process those thoughts either.

Willow let out a gigantic deep breath, even fluttering the lone white napkin that had been on the table to catch my drink sweat. "I'll see you around, Jack. Maybe next time with your gorgeous wife."

I lifted my hand to salute her off, her hips doing that captivating dance again as she trotted away. So much to think about from the short conversation. I looked over at the lesbian who'd been watching us. She rolled her cinnamon eyes as if I had stolen moments that belonged to her. Willow said herself that women weren't an option, so there was no need to be mad at me.

I headed home, almost in a daze because my thoughts were all over the place, but I decided to call Faith; it was only about 7:30 p.m. her time out on the West Coast. I was hoping to catch her before she probably headed out for dinner. Thought about whether or not I should tell her I missed her, let her know I was thinking about her. Even thought if I should tell her about the beautiful stranger.

She picked up. "Hey, is this the one and only Jack Spencer?"

I knew I looked stupid driving with a big goofy grin on my face. "What's up, baby?"

"You should be happy to know, I'm on my way home."

"What do you mean? I thought you weren't coming back for another day or so?"

"Wrapped up early."

"So where are you now?"

"At the airport."

"Oh, you are on your way for real?"

"On my way to you."

I knew I was grinning hard now because my jaw started to lock up right behind my ears.

"You sound like you're in the car. Where are you headed?"

"Home."

"No time out with the guys?"

"Meh. I'd rather head home, wait on you."

"I'm getting in pretty late. I have a layover in Atlanta."

"Well, at least call me and let me know when you get home."

"Alright."

We both paused. I heard the muffle of random flight numbers in the background.

"Faith."

"Yea."

"I miss you."

"I miss you too." I heard the smile in her voice, "And baby, guess what?"

"What's that?"

"I'm already making plans for us in my mind."

"Oh, is that right?"

"Yes."

"And what would these plans include?"

"Let's just say, it involves you, me, and your bedroom for about two or three days."

Damn, was she the one?

FAITH

I couldn't get back home fast enough. It was just after midnight, and I was a dog lying in a dead position, tired. I couldn't wait to shower and get the stench of cheating sweat off me. I knew as soon as I got home, I was hitting the shower.

Regret wasn't the word for what I was feeling. I already knew I didn't have to see Nic to close the toxic *situationship* we had going on, but I had flown all the way to the West Coast despite knowing that Nic was an egotistical jerk. I should have stayed here and focused on my plan. I'd laid perfect groundwork with Jack, and I was going to ruin it all trying to keep Nic in my back pocket.

I dressed up in a black tube dress and silver jewelry with Jack's favorite black suede pumps, sprayed on some Coco Noir perfume that I knew Jack loved, and headed towards his place. When I arrived, I didn't see his car, but instead of calling him, I figured he had parked in his garage. I took the elevator up to his place and touched up my makeup before I rang the doorbell. To my surprise, Edris answered the door in his boxers, and a moist chest was showing itself to me.

"Faith, um..." He shifted his body around. "Come in, I'll finish getting dressed." He ran towards the second bedroom, and I wanted more information on why Edris was here half-naked and where Jack was.

"I'm sorry for showing up unexpectedly like this, but I had no idea you were going to be here." I stood opposite the bedroom door to catch a glimpse of Edris's body again.

His cognac eyes drew me in, but my eyes lingered down to his robust pecks, his arms muscular and pronounced. He didn't have defined abs, but his stomach was still flat and sexy. His small waist gave him that perfect inverted triangle shape.

"I decided to come back early and wanted to surprise Jack." I raised my voice so he could hear me.

"I know you've been out of town; a lot has happened while you were gone. I take it you haven't talked to Katrina since you didn't know I would be here."

I tilted my head just right to peep him pulling his jeans up.

He began searching around for a shirt. "We broke up, that's why I'm here taking a shower." He came back past me to grab his shirt from the bathroom counter, as I had wedged myself in the hallway.

"Where is Jack, by the way?" We stood face to face as I leaned against the door jamb of the bathroom.

"He said he was working late." He grabbed his watch from the counter. "But he's probably on his way. It's almost eight." He smiled at me.

"I'm sorry, am I interrupting your plans?"

"I don't have plans, but I'll get out of your way, don't worry. I know you and Jack want to be alone. It's nice that you would want to surprise him like this."

If I was going to make my move, it had to be now. What better time?

"What happened with you and Katrina, if you don't mind me asking?"

"We broke up a few days ago. Nothing much to tell. No offense, but you know how your girl can be."

I chuckled. "Yes, I know. But I thought the two of you would work it out and find your forever, you know."

"It's over forever, that's all I know."

"Do you miss her, yet?"

"I feel relieved, actually, but I probably shouldn't be talking to you about this."

"Why not? I'm a good listener?"

"You're also Katrina's girl, you'll probably tell her everything I'm saying, huh?"

"No, I promise not a word, besides, Katrina and I aren't as close as you think we are. Think about it, you didn't know about me until a short time ago, so I'm not that important in her life." He was so easy. "Edris, I have something to tell you, but you can't repeat anything I tell you; it's about Jack. I know you guys are boys, but this is important. Can you promise me?"

"Only if you promise me the same because I have something to tell you, what do you think about that?"

"I like this too much, you first." I leered. From the way he was looking at me, I had a feeling we were on the same page.

He came closer to me to whisper in my ear, I assumed. "I've been thinking you are all wrong for Jack. A man like him isn't ready for you, nor can he handle you."

"Then what do you suggest I do?" I whispered back.

"Let me show you what you deserve."

"You must be reading my mind because that's exactly what I was going to say, but now isn't the right time."

He made me weak in an instant. He was more handsome and appealing to me now, maybe because he didn't have a hip attachment. He was a charming and dashing man, more in my eyes than Jack, and I had no idea that his body build was striking, reminding me of Pooch Hall. "Tomorrow night, meet me at The LJ Palm on Santana, ten o'clock sharp."

"The far side of town, good thinking!" He came even closer to me. "Are you sure this is what you want?"

I kissed his neck. "I guess we'll find out tomorrow night."

Just as the offer was put on the table and accepted, keys jingled outside the front door. Who else could it be? I darted into the living room as Edris slammed shut the bathroom door, putting our flirtatious amusement to an end.

"Faith, what are you doing here?"

"That's how you greet me?" I said, going to Jack.

He dropped his work bag. "I didn't know you were going to be here."

"I wanted to surprise you." We hugged, and as I turned him around opposite the bathroom, Edris was peeking out of the door to see if we were clear and never to be found out. "Edris let me in. I've only been here for a few minutes."

"Come to the bedroom, I got a gift for you."

"You didn't have to get me anything," I said as Jack grabbed my hand and led me to the back room.

Jack continued. "Yes, I did. You're my woman, I'm showing you I care." He reached into the drawer of the nightstand next to his side of the bed and pulled out a long red jewelry box, handing it to me.

My mouth dropped open to catch a few flies when I opened the box. I knew exactly how much this bracelet cost, rose gold, encrusted in diamonds, interlocked in curb style links. I was speechless, pushing the thoughts of my previous mental affair with Edris to the side and my deceit with Nic even further away.

Damn, Jack's feelings were getting tangled in a web of double-dealing. I had expected him to be playing the same game that I was, but we were at two different sporting events.

"Are you going to stay with me tonight?" Jack asked.

"Honey, I'm beat really, I just wanted to stop by, plus I've been missing my bed."

"But I've been missing my baby. Why don't I stay at your place, so you'll be more comfortable?"

"I guess you did miss me."

"You didn't miss me," he had a smile that said I'd better tell him yes.

"You play a hard game, Jack Spencer. Alright, let's get going. I want to talk to you anyway about some things I was thinking about while I was away."

Jack began to pack a bag, and I was hoping he wasn't expecting too much to come from tonight, especially when Edris and I were on a special assignment. I did have a conscience for what I was doing, not to mention what I had been doing, but I wasn't able to fight my impulses.

Jack followed me in his car, and I was trying to think of how to cover my tracks if he asked me a million questions about what I'd done the past couple of days. I knew to keep my stories short and tight if I wanted everything to work in my favor.

My bedroom was still a mess from packing for my sin trip. "Please excuse my mess," I said, opening the door as we arrived at my place.

We headed straight to the bedroom. He threw his bag in the chair next to my bed. "How was your trip anyway?"

"Normal, a lot of work, right now I don't care if I ever see a piece of paper, red pen, or pencil for a long time."

"How did your idea for a book of poetry go over?"

"Not great, which I expected, so I had to pitch a story."

"Oh yea? What was that?"

"A woman who seduces men to get what she wants, but one of her malicious plans goes all wrong, and everything spirals out of control. Something with a lot of twists and turns."

He approached me, grabbing me by my waist, "You make it sound so destructive." He gently nibbled my earlobe. "Where do you come up with these crazy ideas anyway?"

"A lot of different places, things I hear, things I see, anywhere and everywhere. Everything has a story behind it; it's what you choose to take from it."

"Do you think deeply about everything?"

"You sure do have a lot of questions for me," I smiled, not really wanting to hear his inspiration for this interrogation.

"I know, I thought a lot about us while you were gone, and my mind is so wrapped around you now, no matter how much I try to fight it. I've wondered if you realize how much you have changed me in this short amount of time. But there are still some things about me you have to understand.

"This entire time I've been having an internal fight with myself, and why now I feel like I'm ready to try and be in a real relationship; to have a relationship period. I'm being vulnerable with you right now, and I hope it's for a good reason."

We sat back on the bed. "This is where I've been trying to get us. Be vulnerable with me. I'm your woman, and I'm who you can let your guard down to."

"I'm glad you said that, but I have to tell you what I did while you were away." His face had an expression of hurt, which led me to think he did something that would validate my Edris craving.

"What did you do?"

"It's not so much what I did but a conversation I had. Edris and Bryant were busy, but I didn't feel like sitting in the house, so I went out to this little spot I usually go to alone."

"And you met a woman," I rushed him along.

"I did, and she told me some interesting things." I wasn't sure where this conversation was going, but I had a feeling the vulnerability had just begun. "What did she have to say?"

"She told me a lot of things, some things I don't want to think about, but that's not what I'm trying to get to. The details of the conversation aren't important. What I'm saying is that I'm happy you're a part of my life now, and I want you to know how serious I am about this; about us."

I was speechless and could do nothing but kiss him. If I allowed him to keep talking, I would feel more and more guilty about what I had done and what I was planning to do.

***

After Jack's confessional session last night, things were getting thick quickly. I needed to bump up the timeline for my plan before everything blew up in my face. The last person I needed to see was Katrina, but here I was meeting her for coffee. I shuffled back a step or two when she reached to greet me with a hug. I knew I had to make my mind completely blank for this to go smoothly. I chanted internally, show no signs, show no signs.

"How was your trip?" She asked me.

"It was okay, full of work." I looked around for a quick escape if need be. The ladies' room was only a couple of steps away, and the bar a few more, the front door too far. "How was everything here on the home front?"

"I have so much to tell you, but I'm sure Jack opened his big mouth about why Edris has been staying with him."

I looked down at my hands. "Yeah, they both sort of told me, but they didn't tell me how it all happened? Edris and I had a brief conversation while I was at Jack's last night, but he said he didn't think it was appropriate to talk to me."

"Basically, Edris left me and had the nerve to take my car in the middle of the night like a thief."

"Why would he take your car?"

"He bought my Lexus, but I emphasize *my*." I knew Edris was providing, but not like that; he drove a Lexus himself, and neither he nor Katrina drove old schools. If he was coming out of pocket for two Lexuses, then our plans to meet up could possibly work to my benefit. Just imagine the look on Katrina's dumb face if Edris had me rolling just like her.

"So, you're really going to let him go?"

"I don't need to fight for him, I gave him what he wanted, the single life, but I know he'll be back once he sees what's out there, a bunch of nothing women who will only want him because he'll throw his money around. I'm not worried. He'll be home in no time," she crossed her arms.

"Be honest with yourself, do you want him back?"

"I love Edris. I do, but it's like I feel this freedom now without him. And I'd be lying if I didn't say the loneliness is setting in. We spent so much time building this relationship to walk away so easily, but what else can you do when you are unhappy, and the other person has clearly decided that you aren't enough for them."

"You don't feel the same way that you will go out and date and see that there's nothing but crazy men out there and want to run back to Edris?"

"I'm not thinking about dating, I want to have some fun."

"You know, eventually your womanly needs will kick in."

She laughed. "I know, they are already creeping up on me."

We talked, and I asked as much as I could to find out more about Edris without coming across as a hawk. He seemed like a pretty low-maintenance man. Katrina didn't know what she was doing. Edris was the best kind of man to have. Only asked for loyalty, affection, and was a gift-giver. Expensive gifts at that. Katrina told me not just about the car, but the trips, the jewelry, the clothes, and the expensive dinners. I would have been on my best behavior, calling that man 'Daddy' if he wanted me to.

Katrina continued. "I guess there's no sense in my plan for a couple's dinner now."

"Hmph. Yea, I guess not."

She snickered. "The guys probably would have weaseled their way out of it anyway. Just like a man."

"Now, don't go hating all men because you are currently going through a breakup."

"I'm surprised you don't."

"And what's that supposed to mean?"

"I'm sorry, I shouldn't have said that."

"You've already started, so you may as well finish." I squinted my eyes, making them tight as I eyed Katrina.

"After Quinton and especially after the Nic situation, how could you not be bitter?"

I took a long draw of breath, my lungs expanding as they filled up with anger I was working to suppress. As much as I wanted to haul off and slap the fake lashes off this chick, I wasn't going to. She would be getting hers soon enough. "Well, you know, Katrina, bitterness isn't healthy. And I plan on living a long time, so I don't want to fill my mind or my heart with such a negative emotion. I think that with time, you'll get over Edris, move on, and see what I'm talking about."

"How long did it take you to get over the affairs you were having in college?"

Was this bitch serious? Her name should be changed to Past Dweller. I didn't know if she was trying to make me feel bad or draw me into her misery over losing her man, but this was blatant disrespect. "We both know those situations were a dark time for me."

"There's something about that situation that I never understood."

Keep pushing bitch!

"You seemed so surprised when Rayven said she never wanted to see you again. What did you expect after all of the shit you had pulled?"

My blood pressure was rising as my heart sped up; it was beating so fast I could barely keep up with the rhythm as it began to echo through my head.

"Still no contact with Rayven, I'm guessing?"

Show no signs, show no signs. "No, I haven't spoken to her."

"I guess she kept you blocked from everything, huh?"

"What the hell is wrong with you?" My voice cracked as my emotions began to bubble and would no doubt start to ooze from my ears soon.

"Oh, come on, I'm joking."

"Are you?"

"I think that if anyone can understand how I feel right now, it's you. I'm heartbroken."

"Doesn't seem like it, and wasn't your nickname in college Black Heart? I didn't know that hearts frozen over could feel the emotion of heartbreak." I said in rebuttal. Now I really was going to take her man.

Katrina tilted her head back, cackling like the vile sorceress she was. "I forgot about that. I guess you can start calling me that again, because I will probably never try to open up to anyone again, as I did with Edris. I wasted the last three years on that man just to end up with nothing."

"You got a Lexus out of it. I'd say that's not too bad."

"Oh, please, I wanted to spite Edris by taking the car, I know I can't afford it. I'm still paying for my damn student loans, and now I'll have to keep up with the rent that he stuck me with."

What did she want from me? Sympathy?

She continued. "You've been through enough, Faith. I truly hope Jack doesn't break your heart."

"You're right, I have been through enough, more than you'll probably actually ever know."

"Do you blame yourself?"

"For what?"

"Your broken heart, after all, you did create all of the drama."
My plan was a go.

EDRIS

I was running late to meet up with Faith, so I quickly dressed casually, throwing on some black jeans and a dark gray diamond jacquard polo shirt. I wasn't moving fast, but my heart was thudding in my chest. Even walking down to my car, sweat beaded up on my forehead. It didn't help that although it was after 9 p.m., it was airless, and a sticky 84 degrees.

I managed to slip out of the condo while Jack was in his room on the phone. It crossed my mind that he could be speaking to Faith, but I didn't want to let my mind wander there. I was risking way more than she was, but my lustful attraction to Faith was driving me towards this hotel.

From the first time she walked into Jack's living room, I thought she was sexy as hell. That cinnamon skin looked so soft; her raw umber eyes drew me in so easily. I recalled wanting to hear her whisper my name in my ear, and I hoped that she would tonight. More like screaming my name so that the people next door would complain to the front desk.

I knew my thoughts were wrong as soon as I had them, but I was so over my situation with Katrina that I wanted to admire Faith's beauty. And the day I came home to find her in my living room. I knowingly held on to Faith's soft hand to connect with her, and I don't think Katrina noticed. I was sure she had been bad-mouthing me before I walked through the door, and if she was, it didn't seem to have taken effect with Faith. I wasn't sure what all of Faith's motives were for tonight, but this was nothing but lust for me.

When I arrived at the hotel, I got a text from Faith telling me she was in room 712, and she requested that a key be given to me by the front desk attendant. I got the key with no problem and rode the elevator up to the seventh floor, running the back of my forearm across my forehead to relieve myself of the last bit of sweat. I couldn't believe how nervous I was. Then it dawned on me, I hadn't been with anyone but Katrina for the past three years. Shit! Katrina was easy to satisfy. Hell, our sex life had diminished so much that we both acted surprised whenever we ended up being intimate.

I pushed all those thoughts away as the elevator chimed to a stop. I wiped my forehead again and thought about how I should have bought deodorant with me. But maybe I could convince Faith to slide her perfectly shaped body into the shower with me. My manhood jumped at the thought. I crossed my hands in front of me as I knocked on the door to announce my arrival before using the thin white plastic to open the door.

Faith's voice called out to me, light and enticing. In a matter of seconds, she was at the doorway, swiftly pulling me inside. Candles were lit in every direction; the scent of sweet almond oil filled the room complimenting the ambient glow of the atmosphere. I was more turned on by her thought to make this more than a seedy meetup.

I took Faith in, and she was even sexier than the other times I'd seen her. Dressed in black lingerie, thin lace covered her hardened milk chocolate nipples. I licked my lips in anticipation of being able to taste them. Roll the small buds across my lips.

"I'm so glad you could make it." Seduction dripped from her copper-stained lips, "I almost thought you were going to back out on me."

"Why would I? I'm a man of my word."

"Can you give me your word that this will be worth my while?"

"You don't have to worry," I replied.

"I ordered us some champagne," she reached for my hand with comfort. "Come here and have a seat with me." She motioned for me to come sit next to her on a large chaise lounge near the large open window. The lights of the nearby hotels and city life sent a holographic glow into the room.

I noticed flowers were scattered all around, enough to make someone feel like they were at a funeral, but I didn't mind it.

"It looks good in here. Where did all these flowers come from, though?"

"They were delivered, but that's not important. I saw your ex earlier."

"That's not important either. I'm not here to talk about her, just like you are not here to talk about Jack. Tonight is about us and what we came here to do. Let's not spoil this."

"You are absolutely right," She made her way over to the small bar and mini fridge to grab glasses for both of us. She returned with the glasses, handing me one and a small tray of strawberries. "I don't know about you, but I like a bit of sweet fruit with my champagne."

I picked up one of the plump berries and held it towards Faith's flawless, glowing face. Without a word or a hint of hesitation, she slowly licked the tip of the strawberry, letting her tongue linger on the rounded edges. Damn, she was sexy.

"I made it sweeter for you."

"I want to see how sweet you taste."

She paused, "Last chance to back out. I won't be upset."

"I think it's already too late," I whispered to her.

Our lips met, pulled together so that our infatuation could finally be quenched. Her flesh pressed against mine, a sweltering heat formed rapidly, going straight to my already at attention manhood. I broke our kiss, taking the glass of champagne from Faith. I set my glass and hers on the small square table next to the lounge chair.

I attacked her lips again like a dog tasting a new treat for the first time. I inhaled her alluring scent as I tasted more of her warm tongue, still carrying the flavor of strawberries and alcohol.

Faith slid her cinnamon thigh across my lap, her curvaceous body followed as she sat on my lap. I was sure my hardened member had greeted her. She jumped a little as he poked at her, but she didn't mind; her eyes only widened. "That for me?"

"Of course."

She let out a petite moan, and I knew this was going to be mind-blowing. I seized her backside, that plump mound I'd wanted in the palms of my hands since the day she walked into Jack's place. The lace at the bottom of her camisole was the only thing between her enticing skin and my fingertips. I pulled the lingerie up, pressing my fingers into her backside. Faith moaned in my ear, pressing her breast up to my face. I lay my head into the soft heaps of flesh, her scent filling my nose again. I wanted nothing more than to rip the silk from her body and stuff her overflowing breast in my mouth, but I wanted to savor the moment. Didn't want to rush.

Faith took me by surprise when she stood up, pulling her body away from me. She dropped down to her knees and went straight for the button and zipper of my pants. I wasn't going to stop her. As far as I was concerned, she could have whatever she wanted tonight.

I lifted my body enough for her to pull my pants down, and Faith was going for it; she pulled my gray boxers and pants down all in one swoop. I loved that she was taking control. My manhood unfolded as she unleashed him.

I reached for her; it was my turn to take control. I pulled her lingerie up from the bottom, quickly slipping it over her head, revealing her bare cinnamon body. My eyes went straight for the bow of her hips as she returned to her bowed position in front of me.

We kissed again as I leaned forward to her lips, but it didn't last long. She pulled back, giving me a gentle shove to lie back on the lounge chair. The tips of her fingers trickled down my rib cage and to my thighs. The ball was back in her court. She used her right hand to stroke the length of my manhood. Her touch, seamless and sure.

I looked down, our eyes connected. Faith kept her desire-filled eyes on me as she took me into her mouth. I tilted my head back and got ready to enjoy the ride.

Shivers went up and down my body as Faith played tongue games with my fully extended friend. She took the time to roll her tongue across every inch. Much different than Katrina's straight-in-and-out approach. Faith was taking her time, and I couldn't deny the work her other hand was doing, massaging my balls. Giving me amazing eye contact when I peeked down to check out the action, she was sexy as hell, no rushing to get the job done.

I loved the attention, but I didn't want to blow too quickly, so I put my hands on Faith's shoulders, guiding her up to me. She stood up, playfully wiping her lips.

I pecked her lips as she climbed on top of me, becoming a scavenger to my neck and collarbone, her kisses strong and dominating. The warmth from between her legs slid across my manhood. I was ready to dive in.

"You ready for me?" she whispered hungrily in my ear.

"Wait, let me grab a condom."

"Condom?"

"Uh, hell yea."

"I thought you really wanted to feel me."

"Trust me, I'll feel you."

I reached for my pants she'd discarded to the floor, pulling a couple of rubbers from the pocket. I ripped the foil with my teeth and swiftly slipped into the confinement.

"Come sit on it," I told Faith as I put my hands back to her hips.

She used my shoulders to support herself as I guided her onto my hardness. The junction of her thighs pulled me into her wet depths. Faith got into a wonderful rhythm, sending waves of delight and fulfillment through my entire body as I enjoyed the view of her chest in my face.

I decided to take one of her hardened buds into my mouth. Sucking and licking as Faith's moans grew louder. I loved her outward expression, letting me know she wasn't afraid to show her enjoyment. It was refreshing to have someone into me and want to see me have a great time. No sense of selfishness, just pleasure for both to enjoy.

***

I woke up feeling weird, reaching for Faith, I only found a note instead of her soft skin. She explained she had to go and couldn't lie in her secret for too long. I wondered when she left and if I was a suspect in her disappearance. I doubted it, but still had to acknowledge the possibility. I looked at the clock, and it was 8:38 a.m., so I figured I would make use of the free room; checkout wasn't until 1, and I was sure Faith wasn't coming back for round 4. I opened the door, and she had thought to put the 'Do Not Disturb' on for me.

I decided to shower, flashbacks of the night before began to flood my mind, just as the water flowed over my body to wash away all traces of my roommate's woman. I didn't know what Faith was trying to prove last night, or maybe Jack wasn't giving it to her right, but she seemed insatiable and acted as though she was never going to stop. As good as it was, regret started to set in, but I couldn't change what was done. As I thought about it more, I didn't want to change it. It was nice to have a woman pay attention to me and do things that satisfied me for once.

Stepping out into the chill of the desolate living room area, my phone chimed back-to-back with calls from Katrina and Jack. Of course, the two people whom I wanted to avoid the most right now.

Katrina called for the third time. "Yeah, what's up?"

"Are you busy?"

"A little. Is there something I can help you with? You blowin' me up."

"I wanted to see if you were busy today, I-...I wanted to see if you wanted to have lunch or something." Her stammering was funny to me. Why would she think I wanted to see her?

Against my better judgment, I agreed. I was curious to know what she could possibly want besides lunch? Katrina never wanted something simple. "Don't bring your sarcastic, manipulative attitude with you, and it's all good. Where do you want me to meet you?"

"That little restaurant in that hotel on Santana was nice when you took me there a while back."

"The LJ Palm?" Was she watching me or what?

"Yes, that's the one. I'll be on that side of town around then."

"I guess I'll see you soon then."

I hoped Katrina wasn't coming to start no shit with me or even try to reconcile. I knew all her mind tricks, and typically they would have worked on me; that's how she got a custom

Lexus, but today was going to be different. I wasn't going for it. This breakup was no one else's fault but Katrina's, and she needed to realize that. She was too busy trying to wear the condom and the diaphragm.

But I guess I should have seen the signs from the beginning. From the day I met her, Jack told me not to talk to her, but I just had to know her name. Something about her drew me in, and we got together rather quickly. Katrina made it clear from the beginning what she wanted in a relationship and from a man. She told me she wanted to be spoiled, but I had no idea how far she would make me go. I didn't have a problem giving Katrina every material item she asked for, but it'd become more of a demand than an allowance of appreciation.

Jack and Bryant warned me innumerable times that I needed to watch what precedent I set with Katrina, but I didn't listen, never thinking she would take advantage of me. I brushed it off, especially from Jack. I never knew what Jack's real beef with Katrina was besides the fact that he thought she was just out for money, but it was none of his business how I used my money when it came to my woman.

I headed downstairs to meet Katrina. Out of the corner of my eye, I spotted Faith in the bar area. What was she still doing here? I had to make a quick decision on whether to go over to her. She could be acting like she didn't know who I was, and I wasn't in the mood for games. We both knew what we'd done was wrong, but I didn't want things to be awkward. I looked down at my watch. The risk of the two of us being seen together was too big, and Katrina would be too suspicious.

I went around the guest entrance of the restaurant to look for Katrina, and there was no sign of her. A server walked past me and asked. "Sir, are you looking for someone?"

I replied yes, and I described Katrina, and he said he hadn't seen her, so he seated me, and I made sure to be far away from the bar. Now I only had to hope she didn't run into Faith on her way to me. I doubted Faith would outright tell Katrina what we did, but at the same time, I didn't know Faith well enough or what her motives were in this tryst. She probably lived for drama like this so she could write from the experience. Either way, I would deny, deny, deny.

Katrina arrived, almost stomping over to the table in yellow wedge heels with no expression on her face. Her long white maxi dress floating behind her for more cinematic effect. I'd seen this game before; we hadn't been separated for too long. This face was her master manipulator mask. A simple revving of her engine.

I didn't get up to pull out her chair when she approached as I typically would, and that made her crack a smile.

"You know this doesn't have to be that type of lunch; we can be civil towards each other, right?" She said, pulling out the chair herself.

"Why did you want to see me?" I wanted to get straight to it.

"We've had time to calm down, and we need to talk about why you flipped on me and dipped out like I didn't even matter to you."

"You don't get it, do you? I'm tired of you, Katrina, and the way you think you can get whatever you want and control me."

"So that's it; you are going to throw away everything we've built together with no regard to my efforts to save us?"

"If you wanted to save us, you would change."

"You haven't given me a chance, that's why I'm here now."

"And you haven't asked for a chance before? I already know what you are going to say. You will be better to me, nicer to me, and more appreciative. It's impossible for you to think of anyone else but you. Maybe that's exactly it, you can't be in a relationship that doesn't revolve around you; you should just date yourself."

She put her head down and covered her mouth with her hands. "I'm trying to change that, but give me a chance."

"No, I'm done with giving you chance after chance. Katrina, I'm done, period."

FAITH

Edris came into the restaurant walking at a swift pace. I knew he saw me, but decided to keep it moving. I moved around to the other end of the bar to see what he was doing and who he could possibly be meeting, only hours after being with me, or if he felt guilty and was ignoring me. I'd thought in my mind to head home when I left our room this morning, but I wasn't ready to go home and face the mirror yet.

I'd successfully put my plan into action, but I hadn't thought of how to deal with the aftereffects or aftermath that was sure to come. I didn't know how long it would take for this rendezvous to get back to Katrina or Jack. He was the only person I felt guilty about.

I needed to think, but my thoughts were interrupted shortly after Edris was seated, when waltzing in came Katrina, joining him at the table. Just what the fuck was this?

They didn't hug or kiss or anything when she approached, but she still had a slight smile on her face, Edris not so emotional, probably trying to hide guilt. I couldn't help but watch them and their body language. It was interesting watching two people who used to share a bed, and they couldn't sit at a table and make eye contact now.

Katrina's face was distressed as they began to talk, but Edris appeared solid and unfazed by whatever she was saying. Damn, I wanted to be a fly on the table. I wanted to know, no, I needed to know what they were saying. Would Edris let the secret of our tryst slip right now? If either one of them saw me, what would they say? Shit, I needed to get out of here before this all exploded. I wasn't prepared for any of this. I only knew that I wanted Edris, and I wanted Katrina pissed off, but what now?

I turned around to have the bartender cash me out for the couple of spiked lemonades I had, but when I turned back around to stuff my debit card back in my purse, Edris was gone, and Katrina was left at the table alone. Shit! Where did he go?

I moved around to the other end of the bar to see the front door. Just in time to catch Edris bopping through the sliding doors, headed to the parking lot. His stride said that he had won the battle. My eyes quickly darted back over to Katrina, who was flagging down a server. If I was going to get out of here, it had to be now.

By the time I reached the front doors, I saw Edris peeling out of the parking lot. I quick-stepped it to my car and headed home.

My mind was swirling. Last night was exactly what I'd been hoping for. The chance to break down Katrina's world. From the looks of that meeting she just had with Edris, she didn't need my help, but why not add to her impending misery?

Katrina hadn't changed one bit from the college girl who had abandoned her so-called friend. I could still see that she would do anything to play mind games, just look at the game she tried to play with me, bringing up Rayven. Well, we were going to see how she liked it when her game was played against her.

JACK

I hadn't seen Faith in a few days, so I was excited when she accepted my invitation to stop by. When I got off work, I went to the store and picked up her favorite wine and some chocolate-covered cherries to match the mood I was trying to create. It was nice to think of Faith and know that I didn't have to do much to make her happy; she appreciated the small things. When we were together, it seemed like the mood was always right, our chemistry was great, so I didn't have to try too hard to get the juices flowing.

She would probably show up in her usual sophisticated dress with heels that made me want to lick every inch of her smooth skin. She was a lady at all times, and that was what I dug about her. I couldn't believe it, but I actually wasn't thinking about heading straight for the bedroom. I wanted to talk to her and look into her eyes. I had missed hugging her and the flowery scent of her hair when she was close to me.

The doorbell rang, and there stood my angel right on time from heaven's gates. "Hi, Beautiful."

"Hello."

She looked anxious, a vibe I'd never gotten from her before. "Please come in, I got your favorite wine."

"Thank you, that's very sweet of you."

I poured the wine, complimenting her on the exquisite dark purple dress she was wearing and sexy slingback heels that graced her feet. She gave me a slight, but forced smile as she took the flute of the glass.

"How have you been? I feel like I haven't seen you."

"I know," she said, taking a gulp when she typically sipped. "Just been busy."

"How's the writing coming?"

"Good."

"That's it?"

"Yes, same ol' same ol', you know writing isn't that exciting, so not much to report." She smirked again, tipping the glass up, finishing the last of the Moscato I'd just poured.

"Is something wrong?"

"No, what do you mean?"

"You just don't seem like your normal self. I mean, you look great, do you feel great?"

"I'm sorry, I'm just tired, I guess."

"Yea, writing may not be exciting, but it takes energy."

"That's for sure."

"Well then, we don't have to talk shop."

She was quiet, then said, "Where's your house guest?"

"Don't worry about him. He won't be interrupting us tonight."

She nodded her head, then hopped off the sofa to pour herself another glass of wine. She stood at the counter and downed the medium-sized glass.

"Faith, sweetheart, are you sure you're okay? You seem off tonight. Tell me what's going on with you?"

"I'm wondering, Jack, why me?" she inquired.

I raised an eyebrow at her question. "Why would you ask that? We've already had that conversation. Are you having second thoughts about our relationship now?" I joined her at the counter. Now I needed a refill.

"What is it about me that you are willing to change to be with me?"

I paused. "Do you remember while you were out of town, I told you I went out and met a woman I spoke to for just a couple of minutes?"

She fidgeted around, her head hung like she didn't want to make eye contact with me. "I remember."

"She said something that has stuck with me, and that's to use my heart and my mind to make decisions. That probably sounds simple, but I've never thought this way and always used snap decision-making. With you, I didn't do that. I can honestly say that I chose you with my mind and now I'm choosing you with my heart."

She finally made eye contact with me, but sorrow sat in her usually jubilant eyes, and I wasn't sure how to take her reaction to what I was saying. This was not the reaction I'd been hoping for when I was being truthful and vulnerable.

The doorbell rang, saving me from overthinking Faith's reaction. I didn't particularly want to get it, but I thought maybe it was Edris and he had misplaced his key. I shook my head, "It's probably Edris, forgot his key, I'll get rid of him."

Faith shot over to the hallway, "Um...I'm going to use the bathroom in your bedroom."

I was confused. "Ok." I turned to answer the front door.

When I looked through the peephole, I knew my life was going to get more interesting than it already was and more than what I wanted it to be. The doorbell sang out again, and this time she looked like she wasn't taking my brush off as easily. Judging by the look on her face, as far as the peephole would show me, she was ready for war. I couldn't believe the mission she was on to have her legs up again on my couch, but that was a different man she was looking for.

I'd be an idiot to open the door. I shook my head and made my way towards the hallway to check on Faith. Instead of being in my bathroom, she was sitting on the bed. Her body language was much more relaxed as she leaned back on both of her arms. She allowed my eyes to play with her skin tone. I wanted her; there was no denying that.

DING DONG, DING DONG, DING DONG. This wasn't happening! Apparently, my now stalker wasn't giving up, and I was not about to get caught up in late-night love triangle drama.

"Jack, who is that?"

"Don't worry about it, they will go away."

DING DONG, DING DONG, DING DONG. Shit!

"Is that a woman out there?" she scoffed.

I hung my head. "I'm not going to lie; it is, but she was before I even met you."

She scooted off the bed. "Then I guess I'll have to make my presence known. I'll take care of it."

I didn't know whether to stop her or not. But I learned a long time ago to never come between two women when I was the only man around, and the situation didn't call for physical sharing.

She opened the door, but no words escaped her lips. The two women stared at each other, both beautiful enough for us to go back to my bedroom and settle whatever was getting ready to happen, but I had to remember that wasn't me anymore.

My past spoke first. "I was wondering when I would find you here."

Faith's face scrunched. "I should be asking you why you are here at my man's place. What, you out for revenge?" Faith stepped into her face, and her voice became low. I could barely make out what she was saying, so I crept into the kitchen closer to the door. "I know it was you who told Nic about Jack."

"First of all, your man?" she mocked. "You can never seem to find your own man. Jack was mine first, honey. And you damn right I told Nic about you and Jack. He needed to know the liar you still are."

"You're so stupid. He's the one still playing you, but you're back over here worried about what Jack is doing with me."

"I'm stupid?" Rayven's head flipped back, her neck jutting out like a bird. "You're the one still trying to hold on to a man that was never yours and grasping at my leftovers."

I had to be the man who messed with women who knew each other. And who the hell was Nic? And just what the hell did Rayven mean by her leftovers?

"You need to excuse yourself." Faith didn't back down, raising her tone.

"I'm not going anywhere. I should kick your teeth in for continuing to sleep with Nic, but I'm here to tell Jack the truth about you. I'm sure you've told him all kinds of lies trying to make yourself sound classy and much better than you really are, when I know and you know, you're a Grade A Slut Bag."

"My man knows everything about me he needs to, and you are not going to kick anything around here. Like I said before, you need to excuse yourself before I call the police and they excuse you for me."

Faith obviously had a secret or two she was keeping. The muscles in my jaw tightened, and I unbuttoned the top button on my shirt. She wanted me to be honest, but she couldn't return the favor. I was the idiot who had fallen for her fake ass facade, and I don't know that I could ever forgive myself for this. Change, who needed it. Change was a lie we sold ourselves to make us believe that we could be better people. Bullshit!

"Just remember karma has an address bitch!" Rayven slammed her hand against the door and yelled, "Jack, ask your *woman* where she was last week." She stormed back down the hallway; Faith slammed the door.

I came around the corner looking directly into Faith's eyes, and she matched my intensity. "So, I guess we both still have a lot of getting to know each other to do."

She put her face in her hands. I took that as a sign of fate intervening before I fell any harder for her. I knew this relationship was too good to be true, and I felt my old self coming back around.

"So, should you start, or should I?" I was eager to get into this argument.

"Yea, I'll start," her head popped up like a mechanical toy on a Putt Putt course. "How do you know Rayven?"

"Oh no, the more important question is, did you go see your ex, whom you told me about? The one who treated you like dirt?"

She hesitated.

"Tell me the truth, Faith, before I kick you out of here."

Tears welled up in her eyes. "I want to tell you, but I know you'll probably never want to see me again."

"If you don't tell me the truth, you're right, I won't."

She took a deep breath, "Nic used to date Rayven as well."

"And what does that have to do with you?"

She wiped her eyes.

I was getting tired of her dragging out responding to my direct questions. "Faith, tell me the truth right now, or we're over." I barked.

"Ok." She sniffled. "He cheated on her with me for years, and it's just been a vicious cycle of bullshit since then."

"Is this who you were with last week? You being gone for work was a complete lie?"

She shook her head up and down.

My hands began to shake, my teeth about to bear down on my tongue. I leaned on the counter for support. I snickered, "You talk a real good game, and you had me going these last couple of weeks." I went to the sofa and grabbed her purse, handing it to her. "You can leave now."

"Jack, wait..."

"There's nothing for me to wait on, I've seen who you really are, and I've seen enough. You can leave now."

"Wait, I don't want us to end like this."

"It's too late. You deserve an EGOT for the act you've put on with me."

"I'm sorry." She whispered.

"You can save the sorry. I meant everything I said about changing for you, but everything about you is a lie."

"You don't understand. I went to cut things off with Nic."

"You don't think you should have done that before getting involved with me?"

"You're right, I should have. I don't know what I was thinking, but please. Please, don't end things like this."

"You obviously have a history of not giving two shits about anyone's feelings, and no one can trust you, so why should I? I've already played the fool for you; I'm not doing it again."

I walked over to the front door, opening it for Faith to make her exit. She wiped her eyes and sniffled. The dramatics continued. Purely cinematic.

She stood on the other side of the door and turned to face me. "I really am sorry. This isn't how I wanted things to go."

"Goodbye, Faith." I shut the door.

I went back into the kitchen, my fist clenched so tight I could feel each nail of my fingers digging into my palm. Winding my arm back, I slapped the wine glasses off the counter and into the stainless-steel fridge. Glass and liquid exploded on impact, and I didn't care.

I punched the side of my head right on the temple, three times, reciting: stupid, stupid, stupid. How could I be such an idiot? Ignoring all my intuition. I bet I'd never do it again. It was becoming painstakingly obvious to me that I was meant to be alone. This couple bullshit and soulmate garbage weren't for me.

Faith played me like a jug in a juke joint, the word 'imbecile' plastered across the front of my jug. As aggravated as I was, I still wanted the truth. I didn't trust that Faith had told me everything, but I knew who would.

I rapidly searched through my phone for Rayven's number. Of course, she had no problem reappearing, especially on the premise of making Faith look worse than she already did. Rayven was back within 25 minutes, and she was not dressed for the occasion.

"I was hoping you'd kick that ho back to the gutter where you found her." She was dressed in a skimpy black sheer dress, her black underwear clearly visible. She wasn't shy at all. She thrust her body into mine, pushing both of us into the condo.

"Rayven, this isn't that type of call."

"Look at the time on the clock. Why else would you call me when clearly Faith is gone?"

"I didn't call you for that, so calm down. I called you so you could tell me something about Faith I don't already know."

"What is there to tell? She's the conniving daughter of the devil." She leaned into me, attempting to steal a kiss.

"Rayven, seriously, stop it. I want to know what really happened between you, Faith, and this Nic guy."

She put her index and middle fingers to her lips, "Oh, you still haven't figured it out." She chuckled, but I didn't see anything laughable.

"Then tell me what I don't know."

"I'm the fourth friend from college that Faith ripped off. Katrina and Chloe were the smart ones who left Faith out in the cold when she had lost her damn mind, using drugs and stealing money from us. And Ms. Faith has a long history of touching what doesn't belong to her. The final straw for Katrina was when Faith started sleeping with a couple of our college professors before she was kicked out of school. The girl was out of control back then, and she's out of control now."

This was getting more fathomless by the moment, and exhaustion was taking over my mind. I couldn't believe I had fallen for this shit. As much as I wanted to place the blame on Katrina for even bringing Faith back around, I could only blame myself for getting involved with her.

"Where does this Nic guy fit into the picture?"

"Damn, baby, you really know how to kill a mood with density."

"What?"

"Jack, come on, put it together. Nic, the man I busted Faith with the night we met."

I wanted to scream, *What the fuck,* but my lips were sealed shut, and my brain was in overdrive, finally connecting all the breadcrumbs that were left visible, especially for me. Goddammit, Jack, you were an idiot.

"You know what would really get back at her?" Rayven approached me again, placing her hands on my chest. "You and me rekindling what she interrupted." She smiled deviously.

"You must be out of your mind to believe that I would sleep with you right now. You and Faith are already fighting over one man; I won't be the next."

EDRIS

I woke up paranoid as hell. Sweat pooled around my entire body. The white sheets of the bed were victim to my guilty feelings. I checked back into The LJ Palm, not wanting to go back to Jack's place. I couldn't believe I risked my friendship, too busy having a vendetta against Katrina and feeding into my want for physical release.

My phone buzzed against the nightstand next to the bed. It was Jack. Of course it was. I checked my call log, and he had called me about five times, and I had several missed calls and texts from Bryant as well. What the hell was going on? Were they both trying to hunt me down to take me out?

I didn't know how to proceed, but my phone went off again with a call from Bryant, so obviously something was up. "Yo."

"Where are you? Both Jack and I have been blowing' you up."

"Well, it is like two in the morning."

"And your ass has been living here, but somehow you're not here. Jack is going crazy. You need to get over here ASAP."

"What is going on?"

"He broke things off with Faith."

My stomach sank to my ankles. "What do you mean they...they broke up? Why?"

"Some shit about her fucking another dude. He's not speaking in complete sentences. Just get your ass over here." He hung up the phone.

Faith fucked another dude, what the hell? I jumped out of bed and threw on my shirt, grabbed my sweatpants from the floor, and stumbled to put them on while snatching my car keys.

I had no clue what I was walking into as I made my way up 95 through Oakland Park. I kept reviewing Bryant's words in my mind over and over, specifically, *some dude*. If they knew it was me, they would say so, right? I didn't think Bryant would let me walk into something blindly; he was the peacemaker of our little group. But that still didn't tell me what Jack knew.

I hopped out of the car and trotted into the building to catch the elevator. I was sweating all over again. I told myself. Come on, Edris, get your shit together. I took a deep breath. It was simple; keep your mouth shut.

My damn hand shook as I pulled my key out to open the door. When I walked in, Bryant approached me, shaking his head. "Where were you anyway?"

"Just out."

Jack came stomping from his bedroom. "Please tell me you weren't with Katrina."

"Hell no." I twisted my face in disgust. "Look, where I was doesn't matter; what the hell is going on that you guys are blowing me up like this? What's the deal with Faith?"

"This shit is crazy," Jack exclaimed. "I found out that Rayven, the chick I met a while back when we were out, she's the chick that all the girls were friends with back in college that Faith screwed over."

"What do you mean screwed over?"

"Apparently, I ain't the first dude these two have fought over. I'm just the latest."

Bryant and I looked at each other, confused, and both of us were growing agitated.

"Rayven came by here again earlier, and I listened while she and Faith went back and forth, shooting insults at each other. At first, I realized Rayven also went to college with Chloe and Katrina, along with Faith. Apparently, Rayven and Faith went one way, and y'all's chicks the other.

"Ex-chick," I interjected.

Jack said, "You know what I mean." He continued, "Rayven told me, last week, when Faith said that she was out of town for work, she was really with some cat named Nic, who's Rayven's ex-boyfriend."

Shit! Was I in the clear?

Bryant said, "Why wouldn't the girls say something about all of this?"

I didn't have a response for that. I didn't expect Katrina to tell me the truth about much of anything. We weren't the best at communicating about our relationship in the present, let alone the friendships she had back in college. Bryant was spoiled by having Chloe be so open with him, but I had a feeling this lack of information wouldn't sit well with him.

"I don't think that Chloe and Katrina know about this Nic guy, but that's not even important. Forget that." Jack paced back and forth in front of the TV. "Faith played the shit out of me."

"Now hold on, Jack, because I have a feeling where this conversation is going. Don't try to use this situation as ammunition to go backwards. I know this didn't pan out the way you thought it would or the way you wanted it to, but don't allow Faith's mistakes and bad decisions to take you back. She just wasn't the one." Bryant tried to reason with our friend.

"I've already accepted it; there's no such thing as a *one* for me."

"You shouldn't say that. You never know what God has in store for you."

I remained quiet, not wanting to bring any attention to myself or rock the teetering boat. I don't know that I've ever seen Jack this way. I hadn't realized the depth of his feelings for Faith; now I really felt like an asshole.

Bryant turned his attention to me, "Why are you so quiet?"

I shrugged my shoulders. "I'm not sure what to say. Faith took all of us for a ride with this fake persona she decided to show us."

This woman was apparently getting all over the city. Jack, her ex, me, and, at this point, who knows how long her list was. I didn't want to say, but I thought of the possibility that Faith was with someone else right now.

Jack suddenly stopped his pacing. "You know exactly who's going to pay for this shit." He pointed towards me. My throat jumped up almost through my nose. "Katrina's ass."

"Ok, now hold on," Bryant said. "What does she have to do with all of this?"

"Seriously! She's the one who brought this chick through my front door. Hell, she never even asked me if I was okay with this ho being invited to my place."

"You weren't saying all that when you were trying to get with her. You're just mad right now, sit down." Bryant attempted to calm Jack.

I wasn't surprised at all that Jack felt this way. This could be traced right back to Katrina. Most negative situations in our lives tended to stem from her. Shit, look at me. Damn near homeless and screwed over my best friend. If Katrina had acted right, I wouldn't have left her ass, and if she had focused on us instead of trying to set Jack up, we all could have kept living our lives without even knowing of Faith's existence.

"Jack, what are you going to do now?" Bryant asked calmly.

Jack finally sat down on the couch, but his legs shook uncontrollably. "There's nothing I can do, and that's what's really bothering me." his head hung low. "I appreciate y'all. I'm sorry I dragged you over here so late. Go, get back home to Chloe."

Bryant stood up, the two of them dapping each other up. "Yea, I should get going before Chloe gets too worried. You're going to be all right, man?"

"I'm always alright."

Bryant turned to me, we shook hands, but I couldn't bring myself to look in his eyes. I was disgusted with myself, and like Jack, I wanted answers from Faith.

***

I returned to the hotel in the morning to get my things to go back to Jack's. I didn't want to, but I wasn't seeing much of a choice. Even though I'd insisted on getting a room to give Jack some space, he said I was talking nonsense, and there was no reason for me to leave. Besides, he didn't want to be alone.

I sat on the edge of the bed with my phone in my hands, biting my lips. I managed to press the dial button to call Faith. I needed to know if I was just another on her 'to-do' list and if Katrina had put her up to all of this.

Katrina trying to convince me that she had changed and that I should give her another chance was already maddening enough, but if I found out she had a hand in all of this destruction Faith was causing, then I was sure we were completely over, and I never wanted to see Katrina again.

"Edris," Faith answered.

"Faith, I need to see you."

"You need me?"

"I'm not playing with you. I know what you did."

"What are you talking about?"

"Faith, cut the dumb act! I know all about Rayven and that you've been fucking around with another dude. What is wrong with you? Why would you drag me into this shit?"

"Drag you?! Boy, please, you were sniffing around me. You were the one so unhappy with Katrina that you wanted me from the moment we saw each other."

"Sniffing around you, come on, you were the one on me in your own man's place. And I use *your own man* very loosely, considering you're trying to be with every man in the city."

"Really, you want to go there?"

"Did you do all of this on purpose? What's your game?"

She grew quiet. No snappy comeback this time. Guilt was resonating. Faith had only been around for a minute, and she had managed to implode our entire group. At this point, I was worried she'd blow the whistle to Jack about us, or even worse, to Katrina. I didn't have the capacity to deal with another whirlwind backlash from her.

"Faith, I don't know what your plan was from the jump, but you know it's best if you leave all of us alone."

"Oh, please, you're just worried about Jack and your precious Katrina finding out about us."

"You're not?"

She exhaled, "Look, you don't have to worry about me saying anything. I'm sure I already look bad enough in Jack's eyes, and the last thing I need is another fallout with Katrina and Chloe."

I was relieved, but could I actually trust her? "Promise me you'll stay away."

"I can't do that, Edris."

"Why not?"

"What would that look like to Katrina and Chloe?"

"You think they aren't going to find out about you still being with that other guy?"

"I know they will, but you let me worry about that. I'll keep your little secret."

CHLOE

I marched back and forth across our tiny living room, waiting for Bryant to come back. I knew something was going down between Jack and Faith, and I needed to know everything as soon as Bryant came back through the front door. I was restless and would be until he clued me in.

I decided to give my tired legs a break, but as soon as I was going to sit down, I heard Bryant's keys jingling, and I met him right at the door.

"What's going on?"

"Sweetheart, let me get inside. What are you doing up anyway?"

"Do you think that you jump up out of bed at two something in the morning and I'm not going to be worried? Tell me what's going on."

"Long story short, your girl and Jack broke up."

"Why? I thought things were going well."

"Let me ask you a question. Who is Rayven?"

My mouth dropped. That was the last question I expected him to ask. And the last person's name I'd thought I'd ever hear again. I guess I had to come clean for Bryant to tell me what was going on.

"Rayven went to college with all of us."

"Just like Faith, you ladies never mentioned her."

"I know." I wasn't sure where this was going.

"Faith told Jack that her falling out with Rayven was the same situation that caused you and Katrina to stop speaking to her. Is that true?"

"I guess if you want to put it that way, but what does that have to do with now?"

"Evidently, Faith hasn't changed much, and she's been hanging with Jack and a guy named Nic who is apparently also involved with Rayven."

"Hold on." I closed my eyes for a split second, holding up my right hand. "What do you mean, Rayven messed around with Jack?"

"Exactly what I said."

"How does Jack even know Rayven?"

"Same way Jack knows every other woman in this city."

What in the world were the odds of that? I didn't know Rayven was still in the city. Last I knew, she was in New York. Of all the men in the city, it had to be Jack. Yet another man, she and Faith both gravitated towards. These women were too much alike for their own good.

"Well, baby, there's nothing we can do tonight. Nothing we can really do at all. Let's get some sleep."

I followed behind Bryant to the bedroom as he cradled my hand in his. I couldn't believe this was happening all over again. Faith waltzes back into our lives, and now everything is a dramatic, tangled mess. But, I guess that had always been Faith's story, a theatrical tangled mess.

As I lay in bed with Bryant, watching his chest rise and fall, I wondered how I'd been blessed to find this incredible man. Bryant never played any games with me, and I appreciated that. I always tried to fulfill every need he had to do my part for the happiness of our relationship.

Of course, I wish that all my friends could be this way and experience the joy that I feel lying in Bryant's arms, but I knew they couldn't if they lived in the world of vendettas, guilt, mistrust, and anger.

I thought that maybe I could help them, but I knew Bryant wouldn't take too kindly, as he's always telling me to mind my business, but he didn't understand. I knew words had power, and I would start with Faith.

***

"So, you haven't changed a bit, huh?" I called Faith.

"I take it you know."

"Yes, I know about you and Jack, and I know about you and Nic and Rayven. Seriously! What is it with the two of you? The county ain't big enough for y'all to find your own men?"

"How was I supposed to know that Jack and Rayven fooled around? That doesn't even matter at this point. What did you call me for, to make me feel worse?"

"No," I remained stern. "I called you because I'm worried about you. This is the same behavior you had in college, and let's be for real. We are all too grown to be acting like this. I don't want to watch you go down a dark path again."

"So, you called to give me the *grow-up* speech?"

"Why do you think that I'm trying to chastise you? If anything, my question is, don't you think you deserve better in life? Living with a vendetta is no way to live. Chasing behind a man who can't be faithful to anyone is no way to live. Acting out and isolating yourself from people who care about you is no way to live. You can't tell me you don't want better than that."

"I messed up, Chloe. I messed up bad."

"Where did you think all of this lying would get you anyway?"

"I was genuinely starting to feel for Jack, and I blew it."

"Unfortunately, I must be honest, I think you did. I'm not sure that this can be repaired."

"Well, can't you talk to Jack for me or talk to Bryant and have him talk to Jack?"

"Faith, trust me, Bryant won't help. Maybe I can talk to Jack, but you must tell me one more thing."

"What's that?"

"Have you lied about anything else? You must come clean right now if so."

After a long pause, she stated, "No. No, I haven't."

***

Surprised I hadn't heard a peep from Katrina, I thought for sure she'd be blowin' me up to discuss all of the drama going on, especially since it centered around Faith. But it didn't occur to me that with her being out of the loop with Edris, she may not know. I debated whether I should call to probe and see what she knew.

I decided to call, but not for the specific purpose of telling her about our horror of a college reunion. I wondered how she was dealing with her breakup now that more time had passed.

"Hey, Chloe." Her tone hushed.

"Why are you whispering?"

She paused, "You won't believe it, but I'm with Edris."

"Where?" My eyebrows furrowed.

"At our place."

I wanted to fall out of the kitchen chair. "You're back to *our place*?"

"I mean, we had sex this morning."

"I miss you sex, I just need some sex, or let's work this out sex?"

"Does it matter?"

"In your case, absolutely. But that still doesn't explain why you're whispering."

"Edris is still sleeping."

She was too blissful. She must not know. I wasn't going to ruin this moment by inserting my two cents. "You can call me later."

"Let's meet up for lunch."

"Sure."

She definitely didn't know. If Edris had told Katrina about this earlier this morning, she would have been tearing down the city looking for Faith and maybe even Rayven, too. She was way too cheery right now. Whatever was going on between her and Edris surely put a pep in her step.

Hours later, Katrina came trotting into our usual spot with a big, wide grin on her face. "You won't believe the day I'm having."

"Bet I can guess." I smiled back through a clenched jaw.

"Last night, well, this morning, was amazing."

I hadn't seen Katrina this bright in a minute; it was almost unsettling.

"Get to it. How did Edris end up at your place?"

"He called me. Said he wanted to see me. I told him to come over, we said we missed each other, we made love, it was wonderful, and now I'm here with you."

This didn't sound like *our place* had been reestablished to me, more like I need to get off. I didn't want my friend getting her heart broken for the second time, even though she tried to play it off the first time. From what she was describing, it sounded like Edris just went for what was familiar, and he didn't have the intention of rekindling anything.

"I didn't realize how much I actually missed him."

"Rewind back a little for me. What happened to being done with each other, hating each other, wanting to move on?"

"He still loves me. I told you."

"Did he say that?"

"I mean, we still have a lot to talk about. Some minor issues to work through."

My eyebrows squished together. "Some minor issues?"

"I think Edris and I can be like you and Bryant; I know we can."

"You shouldn't try to duplicate someone else's relationship. You and Edris aren't the same people as Bryant and me." I almost felt insulted at the notion.

"That doesn't mean we can't be just as happy. I knew Edris was meant to be my husband."

"Now hold on, slow down. If you and Edris are getting back together, I don't think you should jump right into the marriage talk again."

"Why not?"

"Come on, Katrina, you can't expect to leap right back into the same point of your relationship. You need to slow down, take the time to understand how the two of you ended up at a breaking point in the first place. And more importantly, the two of you need to understand what each other needs from the relationship to make sure you're not making the same mistakes repeatedly. Did you talk through these things with Edris?"

"Well, no, but if he didn't want to get back with me, why did he want to see me?"

"Is that a real question?"

"Wait, you think he just wanted to fuck?"

I lifted my eyebrows.

Katrina shrank to the size of a pea in her chair, "That bastard used me?"

"Hold on, he may not have, I just want you to be realistic about what's happening between the two of you. Don't get all flustered and go into ready-to-attack mode. That's part of what got you to this place."

She exhaled, "You're right. I won't keep making the same mistake. I'm going to vow to be better to Edris."

"Ok, what does *better* actually look like?"

Katrina's eyes dropped. "What do you mean?"

"Girl, think about it. Think about what you're saying and what you want to happen with Edris. You can't just say words and not put action behind them."

Katrina's lips crumpled together. She knew what I meant, but she wasn't going to admit that she didn't know how to respond, or more so, what actions to take with Edris. Oftentimes, I thought Katrina wanted me to figure her relationship out for her, but I couldn't, and I wouldn't.

Katrina changed the subject. "Have you spoken to Faith?"

Every bit of moisture in my mouth dried up in a matter of seconds. "Why do you ask that?"

"Last time I spoke to her, she didn't seem so happy with me."

"Well, what did you say to her?"

Katrina rolled her eyes, "Maybe I wasn't kind, now that I think back."

"Katrina, what did you say?"

"I may or may not have mentioned Quinton."

I could only drop by face and shake my head into my hands. I long wiped my face. "Why in the world would you do that?"

"I was upset, ok. It burns me up that she's into Jack and things are going well with them. I wasn't expecting that shit at all. I thought she'd be another on his list and tossed aside."

"Well, I wouldn't be too sure about that." I sort of mumbled, but I knew Katrina could hear me.

"What are you talking about? Jack kicked her to the curb already?" Katrina's devious face lit up.

"Ah, I don't even want to tell you."

"Oh, it's on the table now. Spill."

I exhaled. "Faith has apparently been with Jack and another dude on the side."

Katrina's mouth dropped open; she looked like a prehistoric shark gulping small guppies.

"That's not even the end of it." I shook my head.

"Spill, girl!"

"The side dude is some guy Rayven also messes with."

"Shut up! No damn way!" Katrina beamed with this information about drama.

"I know, it's all so crazy and ridiculous really." I continued to shake my head. "One million men in this city and these two can't seem to find their own."

"So what now?"

"I did talk to Faith, and she feels bad. You were right, she was into Jack. She feels as though she ruined it, and she wants him back."

"No way."

"What, go ahead and say it."

"Well, what did the woman expect when she's still playing the same old games? Apparently, I had every right to say what I said to her."

"I don't know that I would agree with that."

"What then? You think she and Jack should be together?"

"For all the dirt Jack has done, he should be a bit more forgiving, especially if he was feeling Faith as much as he was telling Bryant that he was."

Katrina giggled. "I was right all along. She hasn't changed."

I hated the way Katrina was taking all of this as a joke when I was sure all of this was a cry of pain from Faith, and there was no doubt in my mind that this mess of a situation Faith had created would be a setback for Jack. He wouldn't admit it, but he was already fragile enough, and the first woman he decided to take his time with does this, I'm not sure how I'd react myself.

What I did know is. All of us needed to grow up when it came to our relationships. I was relieved this wasn't a problem between Bryant and me, but our counterparts seemed bent on pretending to be in great relationships while hiding behind veils and deep-rooted lies in order to appear normal instead of just being normal. Let's face it, relationships take work, and it seemed like everyone around me wasn't willing to do the work.

I wanted to help, and I think I knew exactly how. I had a feeling Bryant wouldn't be too happy with me, but I wanted him to see that we could show others how to love each other because of how we carried ourselves and how we dealt with our own relationship. We would be great coaches, and that's exactly what we were going to be.

EDRIS

What was I thinking?! I shouldn't have given Katrina any type of inclination that we were getting back together, and I knew those were her exact thoughts when I fell back into her web by spending last night with her.

I hated myself for crawling back over to what was familiar instead of taking my ass back to Jack's. I wanted badly to feel like I had some control over my life, but what control I thought I did have, I'd just given back to Katrina.

Bryant rang my phone, saying he and Jack were going to shoot some pool, and I should come later tonight and join them. I was hesitant, knowing I was still carrying the Faith secret and now this shit with Katrina. And I was sure in no time at all, Bryant would be hearing from Chloe about me being with Katrina. And who knows what rampage Jack would go on since he was probably still ready to blame everything going on with Faith on Katrina.

I had no room to ask any questions; I would only be setting myself up to let my secret breed in the light, and that was something I definitely didn't want to do. Either way, I needed to set Katrina straight.

***

"Thank you for coming."

"Sure."

I called Katrina and asked her to meet me at Luff's on East Palmetto Park, which was one of her favorite restaurants. I thought maybe she would keep her composure since we were in public, and she'd never want to be banned from this place.

"How was your day?"

"Do we really have to do the pleasantries?"

"Why not?"

"Look, I asked you here to talk. Katrina, listen..."

"Wait, before you say anything, I have a surprise for you." Her eyes were sensuous, the same look she had given me last night when we hooked up.

Those were words I'd never heard her say before.

She motioned to the server who had seated us. He nodded his head and swiftly made his way to the kitchen. In what seemed like a split second, he set a big glass of ice cream overflowing with whipped cream on the table. Katrina's eyes beamed, but I was confused.

"What is this about?"

"You don't remember?"

Rubbing my chin, I swallowed hard.

"You brought me here on like our third date, and we ordered this apple pie milkshake," she giggled. "You ate so much of it; we went back to my place, and I rubbed your belly all night because you ate too much."

I laughed, "Ah, damn, I had forgotten about that."

She handed me a spoon. "When you said to meet here, it was the first thing I thought about."

I smiled; I couldn't believe she remembered that.

"Do you remember the time we were supposed to be going to the Waterside Shoppes and we got lost and ended up in the Everglades?" she poked fun as she licked whipped cream from her spoon.

"How could I forget? It was pouring rain, the GPS stopped working, and we both had–and still have– a terrible sense of direction. I was sure we were going to get eaten."

"Yea, we pulled over and waited for the rain to pass out at that *Texas Chainsaw Massacre* looking rest stop."

I dipped my spoon back into the thick shake. "Yea," my voice went low. "We made love in the backseat of my Tahoe."

Her eyes slowly raised to meet mine. "We did."

Damn, we did have good times together. I guess buried deep in our gloom were memories that we hadn't stopped to think back on. There were good times, but how could we possibly get those feelings back?

"Edris, listen, I know I've been a pain in the ass to deal with, and I'm sincerely sorry for that. I'd be lying if I didn't say that I wanted to make things work with you. I didn't think I could miss anyone this much, but I miss you more than I can describe."

My lips wouldn't move. The communication between my brain and my lips was nonexistent.

"Please give me another chance. I promise I'll be the woman you fell in love with. You have to be patient with me."

Shit, what do I say? Do I flip the table and say hell no? Do I act like she hadn't disrespected me for the past two years? Do I forget that she wanted to give me an ultimatum of marry her or else? And how long would it be before she was back on that train?

"Katrina, I'm not sure that it's that easy or simple."

"I'll do whatever you want. I just want you back home with me." Her eyes turned into puppy puddles. A look I'd never been able to deny.

I always wondered if the saying, love conquered all was true, and I guess I had to keep making this journey with her to find out. I couldn't pretend I didn't love her and that I didn't think about her.

"Edris, please," she begged, rubbing her fingers gently across my hand on the table.

I shook my head yes.

***

Walking into the bar, I paused in the entryway to look for Jack and Bryant. Bryant's frantic hand flew up over by pool table 16 near the restrooms in the back. We didn't frequent this place very often, and I remembered why. I thought it was illegal to vape inside businesses, but as I made my way through the thick clouds, I guessed this place was the exception.

"You're running late again," Bryant said, shaking my hand. "Where are you coming from?"

"You won't believe where I'm coming from. Where's Jack?"

"In the john, he's been throwing them back already. I'm sure he's trying to drown himself and the drama."

"I've never known him to drink like that."

"We've also never seen him actually heartbroken."

We both knew this had to do with Faith, but Jack would never admit how much this situation was affecting him. He'd fallen deeply for this woman, and it was more evident by his actions. I wondered if he would ever trust another woman again, or me, for that matter. I just had to keep my trap shut.

Jack emerged from the bathroom. He gave me a head nod, then headed for the bar to grab another drink before coming back to the pool table. "What's up, man? You've got woman problems too; knock back a few with me." He handed me a beer.

"You'd better be careful, looks like you've already had quite a few."

"Oh, I'm just diving in."

We were silent for a moment, not sure how to approach the situation.

Bryant decided to put the attention on me. "Edris, have you talked to Katrina?"

I couldn't avoid a straight-on question. "Yeah, we've talked."

"What happened?" Bryant pushed.

"You know we talked, and I guess we are going to work things out."

"Meaning you gave in and got back with her!" Jack stood back on his heels.

"It's not giving in; it's working on a relationship."

"Why do you always let that girl walk over you? Not too long ago, you were ready to finally let the ship sail; you should have stayed on that path. Let Katrina sail away and wave goodbye as she disappears into the distance forever."

"You can stop right there, okay; I already know the spiel."

"I can't believe this." Jack shook his head, taking another gulp from the long-neck bottle.

"Come on, it's not even that serious. I'm sorry you still have issues with Katrina, and you're also dealing with your own shit, but I realized I don't want to be alone forever or out here playing games with multiple women."

"Go ahead and be with Katrina. Apparently, you can't leave each other alone for a reason, so go ahead. I'll be in the front row at your wedding, alone."

Bryant decided to contribute. "Jack, you may not want to hear this, but have you considered giving Faith another chance?"

"I can't get the girl out of my head, but look at the shit she pulled." He rubbed his arm as if to soothe himself.

"And look at the shit you've pulled over the years." Bryant countered.

"I know," he said sullenly.

"You need to be honest with yourself about how you feel for Faith. If you're truly into her, give her another chance. Maybe the two of you can work together to fix how you view relationships and how you function in them."

Jack pouted like a child before taking another swig of his drink. His face tells the story of drinking and thinking. From my recent experience of drinking and thinking, I wasn't sure this was a good idea. Drunk reasoning wasn't exactly the best reasoning.

Jack turned to me, "Why are you so willing to give Katrina another chance, seriously?"

I wasn't sure of the answer to that question. Loneliness was never a reason to get with or stay with someone, but that was my truth right now. I was afraid of being alone. I didn't want to start all over, and there was Katrina. "I can't deny that I love her."

He brushed me off. "That love shit."

Bryant said. "Love does make you do some strange things."

"Chloe has that love power shit over you, too," Jack said, pointing at Bryant.

"This has nothing to do with power. Chloe and I work because we both work together instead of against each other or trying to one-up each other. There's mutual respect, and even when we do disagree, we sit down like mature adults and talk through what's going on. We operate from a standpoint of always coexisting peacefully. You guys need to think more about communication as problem-solving instead of trying to be right."

Bryant was right, and I could see why he and Chloe were always the calm ones. Maybe I had contributed to Katrina's behavior by not communicating with her properly. I should have kept my cool more often and tried to be more understanding of her feelings, but Katrina had to come with the same energy. Communication couldn't be a one-way street.

Bryant turned his attention to me. "So, what are you thinking? Can you make it work with Katrina?"

"We have more talking to do, but yea, I think we can."

"And what about you?" He turned to Jack. "Are you willing to hear Faith out?"

"You're right, she and I have done some of the same things. I owe it to her and myself."

A slight smile came to my face.

Jack didn't like it. "Just what are you smiling about?"

"Look at us being grown men."

THE COUPLE'S DINNER

PART TWO
FAITH

Walking up to Hotel St. Michel, I didn't know what to expect. Well, that wasn't the complete truth. I expected everyone to be there. Chloe, Bryant, Edris, Katrina, and Jack. I even mentally prepared myself for if Rayven would be invited. At this point, it felt inevitable that our paths would cross again in some sort of anomalous way. Although I was prepared for Rayven, I would have to turn tail and run if, for some reason, Nic was here. But all of this was Chloe's doing, and I didn't think she'd take it that far.

I was dressed in an LBD and put on my favorite Gianvito Rossi mirrored slingback heels to meet everyone and see what Chloe had up her sleeve. Curiosity killed me as I thought about what Jack would say about seeing me again and if he would even speak to me. On top of that, this would be the first time that Edris and I would be in the same room holding onto our secret.

From what I assembled from Chloe's message gathering us all here, Edris and Katrina had rekindled their relationship. Seemingly, Edris was keeping the secret rather well. But why the hell was he back with her so damn fast? We shared one night, and I knew that was all it would be, but seeing him back with Katrina so rapidly made my pulse go into hyperdrive.

I walked through the black, ornately decorated doors of the restaurant. The hostess asked what party I was joining and swiftly escorted me back to a private room where Bryant and Chloe were already seated. Chloe stood to greet me with a hug, and Bryant nodded his head. I nodded back without words. I wasn't sure what that meant.

I sat down at the round linen-clothed table lined with soft glow candles set for seven and wondered who that additional seat may be for. As prepared as I was for Rayven, I prayed it wasn't her.

Soon enough, Jack came walking in, escorted by the same hostess. He stopped for a second, looking directly into my eyes. The expression on his face was softer than I imagined it would be when we saw each other again. It was like he had compassion for me in his eyes.

He was dressed suavely, sexy. His burnished bronze cap-toe dress shoes were polished, and navy blue slacks fit his physique just right. His black dress shirt buttoned just to the middle of his chest; his matching blue suit jacket swayed with his movement.

He licked his lips as he approached me. "Hello, Faith."

"Hi, Jack."

He exhaled. "I'm glad you're here."

"Really?"

"Do you mind if I sit next to you?"

"No, of course not."

Was he serious? He didn't seem mad at all and wanted to sit next to me. What was that about? Did Chloe say something to him? Could I have another chance?

I wanted to start asking Jack questions, but Katrina and Edris arrived hand in hand. Katrina was wearing a red bustier dress that hugged the curves of her breasts and hips. Edris held her by the waist in a dark gray suit similar to Jack's. They stopped short of the table as if posing for pictures on an invisible red carpet. I rolled my eyes internally. Were they the "it" couple now?

They greeted everyone; I noticed Edris's obvious attempt not to make eye contact with me; I didn't sweat it. I wasn't here for that. They sat down across from Jack and me, just right for me and Katrina to be face-to-face. Looking at her now, my whole revenge plan didn't even seem worth it anymore. She'd gotten on my nerves so bad, but look at where she was sitting. Next to a man who would evidently do anything for her and saw no wrong in her. And where was I sitting? In a cloud of clusterfuck confusion.

A happy-go-lucky server popped around the table to take everyone's drink order. Everyone but Chloe and Bryant chose an alcoholic beverage. I figured we were all on the same page, thinking we were going to need alcohol to get through this dinner. I had already started with a pre-shot of Patrón before coming here.

Once the server walked away, Chloe spoke up. "Thanks, everyone, for coming. Bryant and I thought that we should all get together, put everything on the table, and hopefully walk away with clear minds, consciences, and hearts."

Bryant chimed in. "We've all been through a lot over the past few weeks, and it's time to let it all go."

Everyone was still and silent. I wondered if we were all thinking about the same thing again. How perfect Chloe and Bryant tried to be. It was enough to make you wish you didn't even want a relationship because you knew it would never be like theirs.

"Does anyone have something constructive they'd like to say?" Chloe asked.

"I'll start," Katrina spoke up.

She looked directly at me. "Faith, I'm sorry."

I turned into the mind-blown emoji as my right eye twitched. "Why are you apologizing to me?"

"I owe you an apology for the last conversation we had. I was way too aggressive, and I'm sorry for that. I was playing a game with you that wasn't right."

"And what was your game, Katrina?"

She smiled deceitfully. "I was hurt. I was upset over losing Edris, and I took it out on you. I know I said some things that I shouldn't have."

"Why don't you tell everyone what you said to me?"

She reached to hold Edris's hand that was resting on the edge of the table. "What was said wasn't important or relevant; that's why I'm apologizing now."

Chloe said, "Faith, can you accept Katrina's apology?"

"Sure. I mean, why not? I came back because I wanted the past to be the past, so why not start that process with me?" I forced myself to smile, squinting my eyes.

Chloe silently clapped her hands together. The kumbaya moment she'd waited years for was here. I heard what Katrina was saying, but I knew she was putting on a show for Edris. Katrina was acting differently, but I didn't believe for a second that she was sorry. And Edris's dumbass was sitting right next to her, holding her hand as if everything was all good.

Happy-Go-Lucky came back to take everyone's food order, but my mind went to my rendezvous at LJ Palm and the way Edris had taken his frustration out on my body. And I hadn't minded his ravishing way at all. His sex had been much different than Nic's and Jack's, like a middle ground between rutty and resilient.

Katrina continued once the bouncy server was gone again. "Faith, you have to see our hesitation in you being back around."

"What does that mean? You invited me over to Jack's in the first place. And let's be for real, you had your own plan designed before I even got there. Is that not true? And then your ass got jealous when you saw that Jack and I were actually a good fit."

She smirked again. "Jealous, I definitely wasn't."

"Then why were you so focused on what Jack was doing and who he was doing instead of your own relationship that was clearly troubled before I even came back into the picture?"

"Now, ladies, hold on," Chloe said in a tone of warning. But she knew it was the question on all our minds. And I was sure that question had been lingering since before I entered this circle of domestic dysfunction.

"Chloe, don't try to stick up for her. I swear, since college, you've always come to this girl's rescue, but not anyone else's." I was huffy.

"Faith, don't do that." Chloe retorted. "I don't rescue Katrina; I just understand her better than anyone else."

"Oh, me of all people know how close the two of you are. I'm surprised you even have men and can function apart."

"Ok," Bryant spoke up gruffly. "You will not talk to my better half that way. I've remained quiet, but what you will not do is be disrespectful to me and definitely not Chloe. Especially, when all she's trying to do is help by gathering us all here together anyway."

"This is really between us," I said, my irritation growing. "We've had the same issues since college, and I don't know why I'm surprised or why I expected now to be any different from then."

"Can I ask a question?" Jack spoke up, and everyone shifted. "This is for you, Faith. To me, it seems like you are the one who is caught up in the past and always wants to talk about it, but you're also the one who says they want to move on from it? Now, which one is it, because you can't do both?"

His words pierced me. I expected that question from Chloe or Katrina, but hearing it from Jack's mouth gave me a different realization. He was right. I couldn't let the past go, as much as I wanted to.

Life hadn't panned out the way I thought it should, but what could I really complain about? I did end up finishing college like I wanted to. I have a successful writing career, a home, and a car. But I was alone. I looked around the table. Chloe, holding

Bryant's hand, and Katrina, still clinging to Edris's hand. Rayven was probably with Nic right now, and I was alone.

I looked over at Jack. His eyes were still steady as he looked into mine. I wondered if he was reading my mind.

"Jack, you're right," I admitted. "And, unfortunately, I don't have an explanation. I wish I did."

"I want to understand why you would do the things you did. Do you not care about anyone or anything? Or do you harbor negative feelings?"

"I don't know if I can answer any of those questions either."

"Faith," Chloe said softly. "I apologize for my part in how you feel about the past. I never meant to make you feel like I didn't have your back. Can you accept my apology?"

"Yes, Chloe, I can. And I appreciate you saying that. Can you forgive me for the wrong that I did against you?"

"I did, a long time ago, but I appreciate the humility in your apology."

Katrina smacked her lips and folded her arms.

Bryant said. "Katrina, is there something you'd like to say?"

"It's so easy for Faith to be cool with Chloe, but when it comes to me, it's a completely different story."

"Don't address me like I'm not in the room. And I didn't react to you any differently than I did, Chloe."

"Seriously?! Come on." Katrina's eyes shot around the table. "You all saw the extra."

I sneered, "I know you are not the one talking about extra. Everything about you is extra." I raised my voice.

"Don't start that shit with me, Faith."

"You started with me. As usual, everything is fine and going smoothly until you butt your nose into what's going on. That was a moment between Chloe and me that had nothing to do with you, but you just had to say something. What do you do when the attention isn't on you?"

"Faith, please, let's be for real about who's the attention whore here."

"Attention whore! We goin' wit' the name callin'?" I'd been holding back, but I was ready now. "You stupid bitch!"

"Who are you talking to?"

"You, dummy. No one else in this room is the jerk you are."

"What the hell is wrong with you?"

"Act like you don't know."

"You were invited here, back into our lives, and this is how you talk to me."

"Oh, please, quit trying to play the good Samaritan. We all know you ain't shit Katrina."

"Faith, you're so disrespectful."

I smirked. "You're right." I stood up from the table. "You're absolutely right, Katrina, I am disrespectful. Disrespectful ol' Faith. That's why I slept with Edris."

Stillness surrounded us, but it didn't last long. Glass crashed into the plant-lined wall behind me. I flipped my feet out of my heels and climbed onto the table. I lunged my body towards Katrina's reaching for her 24-inch chestnut brown hair. I kicked plates of mushroom risotto, linguine, and asparagus. Nothing was going to get in my way; she was finished. My fists swung furiously at her head. Her hands were attempting to cover her face.

Someone wanted to keep us apart, but rage had taken over. I didn't care, and I wasn't letting up. I kept swinging. I heard Chloe's high-pitched screams in the background. I think Jack was screeching for me to stop, and Edris could only drop F-bombs.

Everything went blurry. I didn't care. All I wanted was to knock Katrina's head off her shoulders. I seized the opportunity. For years, I'd wanted to get my hands on her, and I wasn't letting go. I didn't care if I had to take the roof off this ancient hotel. I was going to make her bleed.

I was still swinging until I realized Bryant had grabbed me and was rushing me out of the private area, into the main area of the restaurant, and towards the exit. I tried to regain my composure, but I knew I looked like a complete fool standing outside on the sidewalk with no shoes on. My breath was uneven, but my eyesight was coming back into focus.

"Faith, Faith…" Bryant's foreign but familiar voice faded in and out. "Faith, say something."

"What?"

His face scrunched. "Faith, do you know what just happened?"

"Hell yea, I tried to beat Katrina's ass. And she's had it coming for a long time." My breathing continued to be labored as I regained my sense of reality.

Chloe came rushing through the front doors, my shoes in her hands. She shoved them towards me into my chest. "What is wrong with you? Why would you do that?"

"We both know she needed her ass whooped a long time ago."

"You decide this is the place to do it?"

"You heard the bullshit she was spewing."

"Faith," Chloe huffed. "This is ridiculous. You never should have taken it there."

Jack came through the doors, his look of compassion replaced with disgust and vexation.

He stopped in front of me, his index and thumb squeezing his pursed lips. "Is there anyone you won't sleep with?" He squinted his eyes.

I realized what I'd blurted out. *Shit!* He started to walk away. "Jack, wait, no, please, let me explain." I stepped on a sharp pebble in my effort to catch up to him.

He swiftly turned back around. "Explain what?!" he yelled. "You're despicable. I can't believe I came here thinking that we could have another chance together. You turned out to be exactly who I thought you were."

Tears began to fill my eyes. As much as I wanted Jack to stay, for him to give that chance he was willing to give, I knew there were no words I could string together to make this better. He could never trust me. At this rate, *I* could never trust *me*.

If I thought I'd destroyed my life before, it was completely demolished now. Annihilating every hope for a normal life and a normal relationship.

Chloe said, "I guess this was a complete waste."

"I'm sorry, Chloe." Tears rolled down my cheeks.

"Are you really? I mean, come on, you're a grown woman, and you let some little irrelevant comments take you there? And what the hell were you thinking, hopping into bed with Edris? Katrina was right, you haven't changed at all, and we're still paying for it." She was done with me; it was written all over her face. "You need to look inside of yourself and figure out where all your anger is coming from and deal with the trauma. Seriously, Faith, you can't expect anyone to be on your side if you keep holding on to what doesn't matter and acting as though you have not one moral bone in your body."

She turned and walked away. Bryant reached for her hand. Even in complete chaos, they managed to connect and find calm with each other. She leaned into him, and he placed his arm around her. They were unshakable, and that was the bond we all were chasing.

KATRINA

"What the fuck, Edris?" My voice cracked as I tried to hold back inevitable tears as I stood up from the table, smoothing down my dress. "How could you? Of all damn people. How the fuck could you mess with Faith?"

My face was sore from Faith's demented attack. I couldn't believe she'd jumped over the table like a wild person with no damn sense or manners. I couldn't even defend myself for Edris, Bryant, and Jack pulling us apart. I rummaged through my purse to find a mirror to check my face.

I was more pissed at Edris, "So, what was this, payback?"

He looked me in my eyes but couldn't stutter his way to an explanation. But what explanation could he possibly give? He let me walk into this dinner like an absolute fool.

He continued to be speechless.

I screamed. "Say something!"

"No... no... that...that wasn't my intention at all, Katrina."

"Then why the hell did you let me walk in here thinking that you were with me and only me?"

"I am with you."

"Me and apparently her. And you're not even denying it. So, it's true?"

"Katrina, it's really not how you think."

"How I think!" He was trying to play me for sure. "You stuck your dick in her, and we hadn't been broken up that long. That's exactly what happened. And then you had the nerve to come back into our bed as if everything was all good."

No response.

"How could you, when you know the history I have with this woman, and you let me beg you to get back with me, knowing what you did. When did you plan on telling me, Edris? And your answer better not be never." I pressed my fingers into my right cheekbone; it was starting to swell.

Edris hung his head, sliding his hands into his pockets, "I know I should have told you before tonight, but I didn't think that Faith was going to be here."

"You think I'm dumb, don't you?"

"No, Baby, I don't."

"Now, I'm Baby? When's the last time you called me that? Don't try to play me, shit, you've already done enough of that. I did so much blaming myself for how our relationship was, and all of this time, you were lying in bed with that chick. Why would you do this to me?"

"I wasn't intentionally trying to hurt you."

"That sounds like a crock of bull. And you know it."

"I'm sorry."

"You're not. If you were, you would have told me the truth." I grabbed my purse from the chair. "I want you out, and this time, this is it."

"Katrina," he called after me.

There were no words to get me to turn back around. I quickly strided through the dining room, taking every precaution not to make eye contact with any of the other patrons who no doubt heard every bit of our commotion. I slumped my shoulders down as far as possible and shielded my face with my hands as I made my way to the exit.

EDRIS

"Katrina!"

I didn't want her to walk away, but what did I expect her to do? My secret was out there now. Out for an entire restaurant to judge. I was such an idiot.

I followed Katrina through the dining room. "Katrina, please wait."

She ignored me, continuing to exit through the front doors.

"Katrina, just listen to me for a second." I finally caught up with her on the empty front sidewalk.

She whipped around. "For what? So, you can lie to me some more. You are not the man I thought you were, clearly. Besides the fact that you ruined any chance of us figuring out our situation, I bet you've lost your friendship with Jack. I may have had ill intentions when I set Jack and Faith up, but I can admit that. You fucked your best friend's woman. A woman he actually was feelin'." She walked up to me to meet me face-to-face. "I hope Jack never forgives you."

Shit! Jack!

Katrina turned on her heels towards the parking lot. She was right. I was left on this curb, alone. I ruined the only relationships I had. Katrina made it clear; she didn't want me near the apartment, and I should be concerned that Jack was in the bushes waiting for me. I decided to high-tail it to my car.

I was at a loss. I didn't know why I expected Faith to keep her damn mouth shut. She may not have cared to save her friendship with Katrina or her relationship with Jack, but she was imploding my life. I hated the day she walked into Jack's house. I knew then she was going to cause problems between all of us, and here it was.

My phone rang through the Bluetooth of the car. Everyone I knew was probably mad at me, but I pushed the call button anyway. "Yea."

"Edris, man, what the hell?" Bryant's voice came through loud and clear.

"I already know what you're going to say."

"You should have thought about what everyone was going to say before you went and did all this damn dirt."

"I know, I know."

"Please tell me Faith is lying. Please tell me you weren't with this woman."

I was done lying. "It's true."

Bryant was silent.

"Bryant, you there?"

"Jack is going to murder you."

"He wasn't with her anymore."

"You smiled in the man's face when he told you how upset he was over this woman." he paused. "Hold on. Were you with her the night we couldn't find you, and was blowing you up?"

"Does that really matter at this point? I regret the day Katrina even introduced Faith to all of us."

"You can't be serious."

"Everything was fine before Faith came along."

"There's no possible way you are serious right now. You are dumb as hell if you really think all of this started with Faith. Now, no, I don't agree with every action she's taken since she's been around, but you cannot possibly blame her for the demise of your relationship with Katrina, you ruining your friendship with Jack, or the fact that you couldn't control who you chose to do your dirt with."

Bryant was right. I had no one to blame but myself. In trying to blame Faith, I was being a coward. I did decide to lie down with her for reasons that weren't even worth it. And although my relationship with Katrina was already on the outs, I never should have done anything to jeopardize my friendship with Jack.

"What are you going to do?" Bryant's voice echoed through the car.

"There's nothing I can do. I've destroyed everything."

"You need to talk to Jack."

"There's no way I'm going to talk to Jack right now."

"Well, you need to do it sooner rather than later. And you'd better have an outstanding explanation than the one you're trying to pass off now. What did you say to Katrina?"

"I told her the truth, and she kicked my ass out."

"Did you think this was never going to come out and you could keep living your life? I'm just trying to understand your rationale."

"I don't know."

I was already feeling ashamed enough. I knew Bryant was trying to help, but this wasn't what I needed right now. If anything, I needed to figure out where I was going to lay my head tonight and hope that Katrina hadn't burned all my things by morning as I headed towards "our" place.

CHLOE

"Well, what did Edris say?" I prodded Bryant as I took off my dress.

Bryant shook his head. "Nothing that will bring clarity to this whole mess."

"I can't believe this. It's like college all over again." I sat at the small vanity table in our bedroom in only my underwear to take my makeup off.

"I'm sorry to say, babe, but I'm starting to feel myself as though you and Katrina made the right decision in leaving Faith behind back in college. Re-inviting her into your lives now hasn't been worth it. And I wish, babe, I wish, that you had stayed out of it."

"Seriously? That's what you have to say right now. I had nothing to do with Faith or Edris's actions. There's no way you can put this on me. I did stay out of it. I only brought everyone together to put everything to rest. How was I supposed to know the major secret Faith and Edris were carrying?"

Bryant sat down on the bed behind me. "I'm sorry, you're right. No, you're not to blame for any of this. I'm just confused. I don't understand what's going on that everyone feels the need to lie and be deceitful with each other. And more than anything, I'm worried about Jack. I was already worried before about how he was going to react to Faith fooling around with that other guy, but now she's adding salt to the wound with this whole Edris thing."

"Faith did so much preaching about how she'd changed, and I believed her. I wanted for her and Jack to work things out despite everything, but I guess that's a raggedy raft on choppy waters now."

Bryant grabbed my hand to cradle it in his. "I know that Jack did want to work things out, but now I can't see him having the same feelings. I'm doubting that he'll ever give another woman a chance."

"I hate that for Jack. He could be such a great man."

"But when you've been hurt so much, why try anymore?"

"Will you talk to him?"

He exhaled. "I don't know if I can find the words this time, sweetheart."

I exhaled. "Let's not give it anymore energy tonight."

"You're right. There's nothing we can do anyway."

"My boys will have to figure this out on their own."

Bryant was right. I wanted to feel guilty, but if it wasn't for this dinner, no one would have ever found the truth.

JACK

Here I was, pacing all over again. I was sure a gouge was being created in my new carpet. I could wrap my bare hands around Edris's neck for this shit. He'd never betrayed me like this, and why would he do it now? Of all people–Faith? Maybe he wanted to get back at Katrina. But why get at me in the process? And I let him stay at my place.

My temples pounded. The day I came home, and Faith was here...that bitch nigga! How dare he? And he knew firsthand how I felt about that woman.

Fuckin' Faith Watson! She was setting a record for playing me. And I went to that restaurant with the intention of seeing if we could start over. I wondered if she would have told me what happened if we had the conversation of rekindling.

What was this woman's deal? Did she feel like she had to have real-life experiences to write her books? I remembered her book being full of drama and backwards relationships, but I thought it was purely fiction. She made it apparent that her art imitates life, but I wasn't up for being one of her projects for inspiration.

I was done with Faith. And I was done with Edris.

FAITH

TWO YEARS LATER

"A love lost. Love tarnished. All in the name of deceit. Designed lies for comfort. Designed lies for recovered hearts. But lies help whom? Lies help love? How could they? Lies create designs. Designs of shells. The shells of who we are."

Snaps erupted from the crowded cafe as I finished my short poem. I'd been nervous all day about getting up on the stage, but after years of procrastination, I decided it was time. I was happy to see the crowd responding so well. This had been a great place to try out material that would be coming out in my collection of poetry, but my publisher finally decided to put it on the shelf. I could only hope this book would shoot me back to the top of the bestseller's list, getting the same response as my previous novel.

I made my way through the crowd of mixed mocha to chocolate to honey faces, to the back, where Mr. Tower handed me a hot cup of chamomile tea. "Thanks, Mr. T." I winked at him.

"You did great tonight. I'm glad to see you finally getting up there to share instead of just hosting," his voice gruff but reassuring.

"Thank you. I appreciate you saying that. And I appreciate you letting me continue to host."

"Your voice has a home here for as long as you want." He smiled at me.

"Thank you, T. Do you mind if I get this to go?"

"Sure, pretty lady."

After grabbing my to-go tea, I headed home, and the only thing I was thinking about was lying in my bed, but I was caught off guard when I received a wedding invitation in my mailbox.

"You are cordially invited to the holy matrimony of Bryant Fabor and Chloe Raben..." Seriously?!

I threw the black and gold thick stock card and envelope on the kitchen island and scoffed. Chloe contacted me a few times. She never mentioned Katrina or trying to get the two of us back in the same room together, but I never responded. And I never expected to receive an invite to her wedding. I was sure Jack, Katrina, and Edris would be in attendance. I wasn't up for another reunion.

I wondered, as I ran a hot bath in the garden tub of my master bedroom, why Chloe had continued to reach out to me. So much time had passed that I couldn't believe I was still on her mind. Has there been trouble in the world of the perfect friendship? What if she and Katrina were no longer friends, and I just so happened to be the branch Chloe reached for? Either way, I wasn't too keen on accepting this invitation.

***

As I walked into the coffee shop the next morning, I bumped into a man coming through the heavy glass doors. "Oh, sir, I am so sorry. I'm so clumsy, please forgive me." I looked up to find a familiar face.

"Faith?" he said questioningly as he licked coffee from his fingers.

"Jack."

"It's been a long time, right?" He smiled at me as if all sins had been washed away.

"Yes, it has been a long time." Shit, he looked amazing.

"Well, you look great." he paused, taking a moment to look me up and down. "Radiant even."

I knew I was blushing. "Thank you. You look great as well."

"Hey, are you coming to Bryant and Chloe's wedding? Bryant told me Chloe invited you."

I cringed, "Um...I'm not too sure about that."

"Listen, you should come. They wouldn't have invited you if they didn't want you there. I have to run, but think about it."

"Maybe."

He nodded his head in reassurance and waved goodbye.

I walked away smiling. He looked so good. Better than I remembered from the night I played Flo Jo over a dining table. His eyes shone with happiness to see me, instead of disappointment and regret. I couldn't quite remember the last time we kissed, but I was reminiscing about his lips touching mine again. His strong hands took over my body. I wouldn't mind any of that or anything else he wanted to do.

Unfortunately, I was smack in the middle of a drought and hadn't been intimate with anyone in what seemed like a decade. It hadn't been that long, but I hadn't found anyone who could satisfy the yearning I had for passionate companionship and affection. I'd been out on a few dates, but nothing major; barely any second dates. It was tiring dumbing myself down to attempt to create a bond that was about as sturdy as a pile of blocks stacked by a two-year-old. My fears were coming true. I wasn't going to meet anyone else. And after seeing Jack just now, I knew I still wanted him.

Now I was intrigued about going to the wedding. I could see Jack again and see if it was true, whether time heals all wounds. After all this time, I still wanted his attention. I spent weeks after the incident at the restaurant trying to contact him, but he never reached out to me as I figured he wouldn't. Judging by his ear-to-ear smile from today, my hope for another chance had been renewed.

But what lingered in the background was my aversion to seeing Katrina again or Edris, for that matter. Who knew if they had been as forgiving as Chloe, Bryant, and Jack? I didn't even know if they were still together. If they were, then why couldn't I have hope for Jack and me?

Unfortunately, my attendance at the wedding ran the risk of all eyes being on me instead of Chloe, and no doubt Katrina and Edris's eyes would be shooting flaming darts at me from their stance up front next to their best friends. I knew if I did decide to go, I'd have to be prepared to have my shield and guard up.

It was time to call Chloe. I was sure she'd catch me up and help me feel out if I should voluntarily sacrifice myself to the lion's den. I sat down at a small rectangular table in the back corner of the coffee shop and pulled out my phone to call Chloe.

"Faith Watson," she exclaimed. "You are still alive." I could hear the smile in her voice.

"Yes, I'm alive and well."

"That's good to know, considering I tried getting a hold of you, and it seems like a lifetime has gone by."

"I know, I know."

"How have you been?"

"I've been good. Still writing. My new book will be coming out soon. A couple of new books, actually."

"That's amazing. You've apparently been a busy woman, writing your heart out."

"Exactly."

"I assume you got my wedding invitation?"

"I in fact did."

"So…?"

"Chloe, I'm happy for you and Bryant, but I'm not sure that my coming is a great idea."

"Listen to me, everyone has moved on, and I want you there."

"I just ran into Jack a few minutes ago, and he did suggest that I should come."

"Oh, really. See, I told you, everyone has moved on. So, will you come?"

I knew I was going to say yes. I needed to see Jack again. "Yes, I will be there."

EDRIS

I popped out of my new SQ5 and briskly walked up to the billiards club; the sky was getting ready to open with a downpour, and I didn't want my new white sneakers getting wet. Vain, but on my mind.

I swung the glass doors open and set foot into the dimly but fluorescently lit room. There was a bit of a crowd, but everyone seemed more interested in getting a drink from the oversized cedar bar than shooting pool at the 10 tables equally spread about to fill up the open space. The guys and I hadn't hung out in some time, Bryant was busy planning his upcoming wedding, and Jack was enjoying married life himself since he and Celeste tied the knot about 6 months ago.

I was the solo dolo one now, but it suited me just fine. After everything happened with Faith, Katrina and I knew we needed time apart. And time apart showed us that our lives together had run their course. The time had come for us to move on. Single life was cool, though. I'd dated a few women, but I was starting to feel like Jack; no woman had been worth my time.

As for Jack and me, once he linked back up with Celeste, it was like life started all over for him, and nothing about the previous world mattered. I was happy for my boy, even though I thought he and Celeste were settling for each other. But who was I to question his relationship decisions? I stayed out of it, and I stayed away from Celeste. Jack had forgiven me, but I'd never put myself in a position again to have my friend not trust me and risk losing our friendship. That was a dumbass mistake that still haunted me, even with his forgiveness.

I squeezed my way to the bar to order a quick beer. I noticed a stunning woman sitting on one of the high-back swivel stools, her coffee-black hair tousled in loose, wavy curls framing her delicate neckline.

The bartender quickly poured a beer for me and slid it across the aged wood top bar. I decided to hold my position, deciphering if I should speak to her. Turns out, I wouldn't have to.

"Excuse me, do you know what time it is?" She swiveled the stool towards me, and I could make out the green, round cut emerald pendant hanging gracefully from her gold chain down to her rounded breast.

I checked my watch. "About a quarter to 9."

"Thank you." She smiled brightly. "Weird question to ask nowadays, right?"

I chuckled, "Yea, a little bit."

"I left my phone at work, but I was rushing here to meet my brother on time, and he's not even here."

I smirked.

She turned further, now completely facing me. Her long legs uncrossed and recrossed in dark jeans; her pink toenails showed through open-toed high-heeled sandals. I noticed she sported a sleeve of tattoos; I admired the artwork uncovered by her sleeveless top. A phoenix took over her upper arm, various flowers filled in the crease of her elbow, leading down to an ornate arm cuff that ended just below her wrist. I straightened up my posture and raised an eyebrow.

"I'm Gabriella."

"Gabriella, it's nice to meet you. I'm Edris."

"Nice to meet you too. Forgive me if I'm bothering you. I just moved down here and don't know a lot of people yet."

"Oh, really, where are you from?"

"A small town in Ohio, even if I told you the name, you'd never find it on the map." She had an adorable giggle.

"Well, since you don't know a lot of people yet, I'd be happy to keep you company until your brother arrives. Pending, he won't pull up and try to beat me down for talking to you."

"Ah, you don't think you could take him?" She giggled again, infectiously. Licking her cherry-stained lips.

"Not the fighting type."

"Oh, then what type are you?" She inquired, her lips curling as she sized me up.

Gabriella was captivating, her voice provocative and absorbing. I could listen to her talk for hours. My eyes were drawn to her champagne eyes as she talked. Whenever she blinked, I took the small opportunity to admire her golden skin. I was curious about the pendant on her necklace. I'd never seen anything quite like it. When I asked, she began to tell me about her family business, and it was the reason why she had relocated from Ohio.

Her family owned a jewelry company, and she moved to help open and run their latest store. I was immersed in her before I knew it, and I didn't want our conversation to end.

"Damn, I'm sorry, I'm just rambling away."

"No worries." I smiled.

"I'm sorry, but would you mind if I used your phone to try to contact my brother. He should have been here by now."

"Sure, of course." I reached into my back pocket to retrieve my phone. "You actually know his phone off the top of your head."

She giggled again. "Easy to remember when we've both had the same number since high school."

I nodded.

As much as I wanted her company to remain with me, I realized my friends were late as well. I peeked over to the front entrance. I spotted Jack walking in, looking confused, no doubt trying to spot a familiar face. I threw my hand up, signaling him over. He nodded his head, making his way in my direction.

Jack greeted me. "What's good, man? Sorry, I'm running late."

"No problem, Bryant isn't even here yet. I was just having a beer."

"Cool," he waved to the bartender, pointing to my drink to request his own.

I turned my attention back to Gabriella as she finished up her phone call. "Looks like my brother isn't going to make it." She said, pressing the red dot. "Thank you, Mr. Edris, for keeping me company. I guess I'd better head back to the store to get my phone."

I wasn't going to miss my chance. "I'd love to keep you company again sometime."

"In that case." My phone was still unlocked. She dialed her number in and sent a call to the number. "I guess we'll be in touch."

"Absolutely."

She waved goodbye.

Jack said. "Who was that?"

"I just met her," I said, eyeing her as she made her way to the front door.

Bryant walked up to join us, passing right by Gabriella. "What are y'all looking at?"

"I think I just met my next woman."

"You're next woman?" Bryant said. "For real? Do you really want another woman you met in a bar?"

"Give him credit," Jack said, slapping me on the back. "This is at least a pool hall." He tipped his beer glass up to his lips.

They could talk shit all they wanted. I could already feel that Gabriella was different. Her energy was too vibrant, something that was drawing me in. "Whatever. Y'all just saying that because for once I'm the single one. The two of you have women at home waiting for you."

Jack cackled. "You sound like me not too long ago."

"My point exactly."

Bryant spotted a table opening up, and we rapidly descended on it like vultures before anyone else could try to move into our territory.

Jack asked Bryant how wedding planning was coming as we racked the solid and striped balls up.

"It's going. Chloe is, of course, driving herself crazy with every little detail. I try to help, but I know this day will be all about her."

Jack exhaled as he popped his stick to start the game off. "Can't say that I miss those days."

"Oh, I do need to tell y'all something, though, about the wedding."

I raised my hands in defense. "Hey, I already bought the expensive ass tux; tell Chloe to change her mind back."

Bryant chuckled. "It's not that."

"What's up then?" Jack inquired.

"I'm going to be straight up and say, Chloe invited Faith to the wedding, and it's looking like she's going to be there."

I knew my face was twisted in disgust. Utterly speechless and surprised. I looked over at Jack, who I thought would share my expression, but he only shook his head and took another shot.

"Who's there doesn't matter." Bryant continued. "As long as Chloe and I are there and I have my boys by my side, everything else is irrelevant."

"Are you serious?" I questioned.

"I'm dead serious."

"And Jack, you have nothing to say?"

"Why would I? The past is the past. And I actually saw Faith a few days ago."

"What?" I exclaimed.

"Yea," he leaned onto his stick as Bryant took his shot. "Just bumped into her at a coffee shop. She told me she'd gotten an invitation, and I told her she should come."

I didn't understand a damn thing that was going on. "Why would you tell her that?"

"Because none of this has anything to do with us. All that shit, that apparently still bothers you, is in the past. Faith is Chloe's friend, and this is Chloe's wedding; if she wants her friend there, then so be it. Besides, just because she's there doesn't mean we have to talk to her."

Shit, when did Jack become the voice of reason?

He continued, "Edris, you shouldn't be worried. By the way, that gorgeous woman just handed you her number, you should be set."

"Jack is right," Bryant said. "Everyone has moved on, obviously, and if you haven't, you need to. Stop giving all that old stuff so much energy."

The guys were right and wrong. They were right that it was all in the past, but they were wrong to assume how much energy I was giving it, as Bryant had dubbed it. I wasn't concerned about Faith, but I found it extremely odd that she was even invited in the first place. Of course, I understood that Faith was a long-time friend of Chloe, but why would she invite her into the same vicinity as Katrina, and on a day when you don't want any drama? But Jack was right about one thing: we didn't have to socialize with her. And, how great would it be to show up with the stunning Gabriella on my arm? I had work to do. I hoped she hadn't given me the wrong number.

***

"Hey, Gabriella, this is Edris."

"Hey, what's going on?"

"I was thinking about you. How are you doing?"

"I'm good. I can't lie, I was looking forward to your call."

That sultry, radiant voice grabbed me by my shirt collar. I wanted to go through the phone to be close to her.

A few days had passed since I'd met Gabriella. I wanted to call her the same night, but didn't want to come off thirsty. I didn't know what she was expecting, and I didn't want to assume either.

"Looking forward to my call, eh?"

She giggled. "Yea I was. What's on your agenda for this evening?"

"Taking you to dinner if your agenda is clear."

"Pick me up at 7:30." She was direct. I liked it.

She gave me her address, and I had less than two hours to get dressed and get over to her place, which was almost 45 minutes away. It's been a long time since I picked a woman up for a date. I wondered if it was the comfort Gabriella felt with me that she was willing to invite me to her house to pick her up, and this was our first time out. Shit, should I be worried?

Seems like all women these days think every man is a serial killer and wants to skin them, so they wouldn't even mention what side of town they lived on. But I knew my intentions were good.

When I drove into her neighborhood, I was impressed. I found her address and was amazed at the architecture of her house. The Spanish-style home was stucco, but beautifully crafted with a high-pitched tiled roof, and a large half-round glass and wrought iron door sat in the middle of a short-arched corridor. I was nervous, but I rang the doorbell, which played a jingle, as opposed to the standard ding-dong. Based on these digs, Gabriella had me thinking that I was in the wrong business.

Gabriella waved through the glass as she approached the door. I heard her put an alarm code in before opening the door and flashing her perfect smile at me. "I'm so glad you could make it. Please, come in."

"Thank you." I entered the high-ceiling entryway. "Your home is beautiful."

"Thank you. I'm still moving things around and settling, so hopefully, it will start to feel like home soon."

"You look beautiful as well." I smiled at her.

"Thank you. You clean up nicely yourself."

"You ready to roll?"

"Let's do it." She reset the alarm, then reached for my hand, leading me back out through the front door.

I escorted Gabriella down the flagstone driveway, opening her door to my car for her to slide into. Her black tube dress moved up her thigh a bit as she settled into the seat. I tried not to let my mind wander about what touching her thighs would feel like. For the first time, I noticed another tattoo, a butterfly on her right ankle.

I hopped into the driver's seat and started up the engine. "Do you like Jamaican food?"

She gasped. "It's one of my favorites."

"I knew I liked you." I winked at her.

I took the scenic route to the restaurant. I didn't want Gabriella to stop talking. She was so giggly and cutesy, it was attractive. She came across as one of those people who was always in a good mood. There were no awkward pauses or uncomfortable silences. It felt great to be around someone who could carry on a conversation about anything.

She was intelligent and well-rounded; I could tell she was understanding and loved her family. She shared a little about her brother and why she worked so hard for her family's business. I could tell she had pride in what her father had started. I was more impressed that her family owned most of the few black-owned jewelry stores across the country. Made me wonder if her father would look at me like a peasant if I ever got to meet him. But let's slow down.

We sat in the restaurant for hours, even after I paid for our dinner and continued to talk. Her vibe was so different, I could see myself staying up all night to talk to her. We talked about everything, from goals to work, to clothes, to cars, and books. Gabriella was enjoying life, and that came across in her thoughts on various topics. Her carefree, no-stress, and intelligent way of thinking turned me on.

Unfortunately, time wasn't on our side, and we were shooed out of the restaurant at closing time, but I didn't want the date to end. We returned to her place, and I walked her up to the door.

"Edris, I had a good time with you, and hopefully we can do this again."

"I feel the same way." I put my hand on her face under her chin. "Are you busy tomorrow?"

She went up on her tiptoes and kissed me.

"Does that answer your question?"

"How's lunch for you?"

"Perfect."

She'd given me a quick peck, but I wanted to taste her tongue. I leaned down for the real kiss. She didn't seem to mind. Gabriella raised her left arm, placing it on my shoulder, bringing her closer to me. As our tongues played, my body temperature rose and my manhood right along with it. I pulled away.

She stepped back. Her giggle was quieter and more reserved this time. "I'm sorry." She ran three fingers across her full and shapely lips.

"Why are you apologizing?"

She bit her bottom lip. "I like you a lot."

"I like you too. A lot."

She turned to unlock the front door. "Tomorrow then?" she said over her shoulder.

"Sure thing."

JACK

I watched my wife in the mirror, her reflection visible from the bed. She was either unaware of my eyes being glued to her body or trying to send me a subtle but straightforward signal. She'd been upset with me over the last few days, saying I hadn't been as attentive to her as I should be, but she knew work was taking every piece of my energy. Business had grown almost 30 percent, and I was struggling to keep up myself, let alone keep my team up to par. I guess she had been waiting for me to show her she was number one in my life despite my work schedule.

She flipped the light switch in the bathroom off and came into the bedroom dressed in a silk negligee that draped her body perfectly.

"Baby, you put that on for me?"

"I'm surprised you noticed." She said, slipping her body in between our new teal colored bed sheets.

"Don't be that way," I said, kissing her cheek. "I know I've been busy lately and I apologize for not spending more time with you and paying more attention to you, but I'm trying right now."

She huffed. I hated it when she was like this. It was childish and annoying. She obviously had something to say, so why didn't she just say it? I was doing what she wanted, but she still wasn't happy. This wasn't the married life I'd imagined, and for us to only be 6 months in, I was pretty nervous about the decision I'd made.

After all the drama went down with Faith, I tracked Celeste down and begged for her forgiveness and to see me as a changed man. It definitely took some doing, but after weeks of old-school R&B begging, I finally got Celeste to give me another chance and start over with me.

"Celeste, talk to me."

"I don't have anything to say."

"I don't get you." I lay back on my pillow, looking up at the ceiling. "What do you want from me?"

She sat up to face me and to look down on me. "I want you to genuinely want to spend time with me."

"It's ridiculous that you think that I don't. Yes, I know I've been working a lot, I've acknowledged that."

"You need to take some time off."

"Celeste, seriously. I took three weeks off after our wedding, and you know I just landed the biggest client of my career. I can't collect commission and take another vacation. And someone has to keep this roof over our heads. Remember, it wasn't my idea to move to St. Andrews."

"And you didn't object either."

I blew my breath. "Celeste, I'm not trying to fight with you. I'm really not. I was trying to give you the attention you've been asking for."

I turned my back to her, she returned to her lying down position, and shortly after turned her back to me. This had become our norm whenever Celeste didn't get what she wanted, and typically, I would chase her across the mattress, but I wasn't up for it tonight. She could stew in her thoughts.

My thoughts turned to Faith. I had every intent on telling Celeste that Faith would be at the wedding, but a good time hadn't presented itself. Celeste had made it painstakingly clear that she didn't like Faith and hoped she never bumped into her. But, from my run-in with Faith, it was proven this city wasn't that big.

Faith looked great when I saw her at the coffee shop. Of course, I had always found her attractive, but she was luminous that day. Her eyes were smoldering when she looked at me. She hadn't crossed my mind in some time, but I wondered if she had that look because she finally found a fulfilling relationship, or maybe she was happy to see me. Her smile was nervous and surprised, but also genuine. I couldn't help but think that she had changed her mind about her invitation to the wedding because of seeing me.

She would no doubt be dressed impeccably, and I looked forward to seeing her again. Maybe not the right thought to have as I lay in bed next to my wife, but it was the truth.

I tried not to spend too much time thinking about Faith, but it would be a bold-faced lie to say I hadn't thought of if things had worked out between us. If she hadn't designed lies to be so underhanded, then maybe things would have been different. Maybe things could have been how I envisioned before coming to know of her relentless animosity towards Katrina.

Could it have been possible for her to be lying next to me right now? Would I have been secure enough in our relationship to put a ring on her finger? Would I still have changed into who I am now? Changed for the better or the worse? Even after all this time, so many questions surrounded the pocket-sized time Faith and I had spent together.

I tossed and turned all night, even with my eyes closed, sleep evaded me, but came and went as it pleased. Luckily, it was the weekend, so I slept in a bit before the smell of maple sausage aroused my senses.

I wiped the crust from my eyes, headed to the bathroom to splash some water on my face, and brushed my teeth before I headed down the ash wood and glass L-shaped stairs that led into the kitchen. Celeste was still dressed in her negligee as she scrambled eggs at the oversized 6-burner stove.

I pulled out one of the leather gray, tall-backed chairs from the island to sit down. "Good morning."

"Good morning, Jack." She said flatly.

"Smells good in here."

She handed me a plate. "Plans for today?"

"I have a few runs to make, not too much."

"I thought that we could have a date tonight. Maybe go down to Ocean Blvd., get something to eat."

"That would be nice, baby."

She came and sat on the chair next to me with a small plate of food, planting a kiss on my cheek. So, she wasn't mad at me anymore? I was too exhausted to think too deeply about what was going on with Celeste this morning. I wish that she would pick a lane and stay in it. Preferably, the one where I didn't have to apologize for making a living.

We ate breakfast in awkward silence since I didn't know how to react to Celeste's proposal of a date tonight. If this breakfast was awkward, what would tonight be like?

I thanked my wife for breakfast, put my dishes in the sink, and headed back upstairs to get dressed. As I stood in the substantial shared closet, my mind wandered back to Faith again. Since I saw her face again, she was ruling my thoughts. I wanted to know if she had been thinking of me the way I had been thinking of her.

***

I should have been heading home to shower and change my clothes to take Celeste out, but I was in the car, headed to the little cafe by Young Circle Park, where I hoped to find Faith still hosting her poetry night. I knew I had no business going this way or even thinking of seeing Faith again, but I couldn't get her off my mind. I had to see her again. I designed a lie and told my wife I was working late; I was on a tight midnight deadline, and I promised to make up our date to her.

I walked into the small space. I could barely get inside the door. I quickly spotted Faith off to the side of the remodeled little stage. She was nodding her head to a caramel brotha on stage spitting spoken word about the designed lies of the government. A topic I was sure never got old in this forum.

To my luck, Faith called for a break between performers. I swiftly moved through the crowd and over to Faith as she leaned against the bar. I called out to her to get her attention.

"Jack," her face jumbled, "what are you doing here?"

"I came to find you."

"Find me for what?"

"I wanted to see you again."

The wrinkles of confusion softened on her face, her lips curling up into a smile. "I can't believe you came here to find me."

"I'm glad I did."

"Come on," she reached for my hand. "Let's go in the back for a second."

I wasn't going to say no, I'd come all the way down here.

"So, I heard you decided to come to the wedding."

"I did."

"I was hoping you would."

She smiled. "Was that a part of you wanting to see me again?"

"It was, but I guess I couldn't wait another couple of weeks."

Silence lingered between us, but it was comfortable. She continued to hold onto my hand; the spark between us was still there. Her thumb gently sliding over mine. She wanted to see me again, too.

I knew I was playing the most dangerous game of all. This time, the stakes were much higher. Celeste wasn't just another woman on my list. She was my wife now. I'd made vows to her. I couldn't remember every little thing I said on our wedding day, but I knew I had made a promise to be faithful. I could easily turn back now. Seeing Faith right now wasn't a crime, but from the way our eyes were locked, I wasn't sure I'd be able to go back. I willed my feet to move, but my limbs weren't cooperating.

I still wanted Faith. As much as I tried to deny her, not think about her, here I was wanting to sit her on top of this booth and remind her how she used to become a thunderstorm whenever we were intimate.

She finally dropped her hand from mine, "I should get back." She began to walk away.

I blurted out. "How much longer will you be here?"

She turned back to face me. "We have a couple more poets."

"Can I stick around? See you after."

She didn't look surprised by my admission of wanting to spend more time with her. She nestled her fingers between mine. "Would you like to come to my place?"

***

Faith and I had an unresolved chapter. At least, that's what I told myself as I headed for her house. My wife texted me a sad face and a tear emoji that I wasn't home yet.

When I pulled into the driveway, the house was completely dark. Maybe Faith had changed her mind. Just as I thought about backing out of the driveway and going home to my wife, the porch light clicked on. I got out of the car, and she rapidly opened the front door.

"Glad you made it." She greeted me in a silk floor-length robe, the cleavage of her breast poking out of the middle. Her delicate fingers cradled a glass of red wine.

"Had to," I put my hands around my back to remove my wedding ring. Faith never seemed to notice it, or she didn't care.

"Please come in." She turned her body to allow me to follow her inside.

All her African décor had been replaced with Asian, and the feel was entirely different. "Your place looks good."

"Thank you. I go through phases. Would you like a glass of wine?"

"No, thank you."

"Did you tell anyone you were coming here?"

"Should I have?"

"No, I don't have plans to kill you or anything."

"What plans do you have?"

She put her wine glass down on the side table and turned to face me. She put her arms on my shoulders, her fingers delicately placed on the back of my neck. Damn, she smelled good. I put my hands on the back of her silk robe, knowing her skin was just as soft, but I refrained from going right for touching her all over her body like I truly wanted to.

"I've wanted you here with me for so long. But I was afraid of the hate you may have still harbored towards me."

"The past is the past."

"In that case, shall we take this to the bedroom?"

"Thought you would never ask."

She pulled me by my hands towards the stairs. We couldn't even make it up the stairs before Faith's lips pressed to mine, and her tongue was ready to explore me. She was hungry for me, and I wanted her just the same.

I fell back onto the side of the bed thanks to a friendly shove from Faith. She stepped back to give me a show. She loosened her robe; I unbuttoned the first two buttons of my shirt. Faith slowly let the black robe fall from her shoulders, revealing a white lace teddy. The delicate fabric looped around her neck and flowed down in strips across her nipples, the sides of her breast exposed as well as her smooth sternum. The white lace circled her waist and created the sexiest *V* down to her playground. She turned around to show me her exposed back and the tiniest string that held the entire piece together that went between her ass cheeks.

"Are you sure about this?" she leaned down between my legs.

"I'm here, aren't I?"

"Had to ask, only to be polite, you're not getting away from me this time."

I motioned for her to straddle my lap. Her thighs brushed against mine as she got comfortable. Her eyes, deeply connected to mine. I was enthralled as the scent of rosehip took over my nose, even more enticed by watching her lick her lips before she reconnected them to mine.

As we kissed, I closed my eyes and let my hands see the curves of her body. Her skin was just as velvety as I remembered. I worked my way from her thighs, up the curve of her ass, across the valley of her back, stopping to relish the broadness of her hips.

Faith sat up, forcing me to lean back on the bed using my elbows to prop myself up. Using her hands, she pushed me back, forcing me to lie straight back on the bed as she continued to straddle me. Her forceful touch became gentle as she rubbed my shoulders, down my collar, her fingers finding their way into my shirt. She caressed around my collarbone, making her way down to begin unbuttoning the rest of my shirt. Her exploring hands wasted no time peeling me out of my jeans and boxers. She moved down off the bed to snatch them from my body and throw them to the floor.

It wasn't too late, I could still turn back, but I looked Faith in her raw umber eyes as she climbed back on top of me, and I knew I didn't want to leave. This felt too right and like exactly what I'd been missing from my world. It was like when *The Wizard of Oz* turned to color. I hadn't realized how clouded and gray life had been. With each stroke of Faith's fingers, my world was getting brighter and brighter.

She leaned down to kiss me. Our intensity grew as her hands made their way over my head, and I planted mine on the cups of her ass. I didn't remember her backside being this plump. I liked it, turned me on. I could feel her womanhood getting just as hot as I was as she began to rub her southern lips against my hardness. It was clear neither one of us wanted to move from this spot.

"I've missed you," she whispered in my ear.

"I never stopped thinking about you."

She took my dick into the palm of her hand, rubbing the head against her lips coated in sweet sap. Her touch was hot, but in a way that only made me want her more. I knew what she was about to do, but I didn't want her to go there yet. I needed her lips locked to mine. I loved the way our tongues played hide and seek.

"You look so good," I told her.

"Jack, come on, don't tease me."

I simpered. "Who's the one on top?"

She smiled widely. "You know what I mean. I need you inside of me right now. And I mean right now."

She didn't have to say anymore. She didn't know how bad I wanted to be deep inside of her. I flipped Faith to the mattress, and she let out a groan, more filled with pleasure than anything else. I wasted no more time sliding into her wet opening.

"Hold up!" She completely halted. "I haven't seen you in how long? You need to put a rubber on."

I dropped my head back against the bed. "Damn girl. You say that now."

"Bathroom. Drawer next to the sink." She got down from on top of me. "Hurry up." She patted me on my bare bottom as I went to the bathroom.

I huffed my breath and scurried to the dark bathroom. I shuffled around in the drawer until I felt the foil packs. Faith wasn't wrong, but she obviously had this planned; she couldn't have put these in a more convenient place.

I hurried back to the bed, slipping the condom on as I walked. "Now come here." I pushed her up onto the bed, lifting her cinnamon legs.

I found that wet spot again, I'd been craving, and slipped in with no problem. Faith took a deep breath. I could feel her pussy squeeze me tight, sucking me into her. She was pure perfection.

Her moans grew as I got comfortable and picked up my pace. "Damn, Jack."

"Oh, you sayin' my name already, baby."

"Oh yes."

"Say it again."

"Jack, yes."

She was melodic, making me even harder. I couldn't remember the last time I'd heard my name in this way.

"Don't stop, baby. I want to feel all of you."

"You want it all." I continued my exploration of her wetness. I could feel it coating me. Pulling me deeper inside of her.

"Yes," she groaned, her fingertips starting to press into my lower back.

There was definitely no going back now. I was literally deep into a place I shouldn't be, but the pleasure was undeniable. I wondered if I had walked away too soon and made the mistake of marrying the wrong woman.

Out of my thoughts, Faith switched positions, pushing her left leg up and over my shoulder. I was able to push even deeper inside of her, her moans blooming into more euphoria.

She sang, "Ooh, baby, that's my spot."

I never wanted to leave this spot. Her thick thigh pressed into me as her leg gripped me. I could feel her pussy tightening around me, but I was only getting started.

I pulled out.

"Where you goin'?" she said, reaching for my shoulders.

"Don't worry, I just want to talk to her for a second."

Faith smiled, biting her bottom lip. One hand went to her mouth, her index finger on her lips, her other hand on top of my freshly cut hair.

I kissed down to her navel, stopped to savor the space between her navel and the V of her precious sweet sap. I wanted to take my time, but I was hungry for Faith. I scooped her legs up, holding her by her plentiful thighs. I pushed her legs up and back. I wanted her lips completely exposed to me, and I wanted to use my tongue to explore every part of this place.

Kissing her lips before diving in, I lapped and sucked at the center of her sweet spot. She seemed to love the combination as her body tensed every time I switched up my tongue movements. I loved it too; it turned me on to know that she was at this heightened pleasure because of me.

I didn't want to stop, but before I knew it, Faith was grasping at my head and telling me that she was going to cum. I couldn't wait.

"Damn," she breathed heavily. "You licked me just right, baby." She sat up, leaning down to plant a kiss on my lips wet from her juices.

"Turn over, we're not done yet."

KATRINA

"Chloe, look at these."

"Please, girl, I don't want to trip and fall on my face down the aisle."

"Yea, right, I've seen you work heels this high in the club."

She laughed, and it was great to see my friend excited about her upcoming big day. Chloe and Bryant were finally going to get married, and I couldn't believe it had taken this long, but the past two years had been a bit different for all of us.

After Faith's exit from the reunion, Edris and I were over, of course, and I was devastated. I thought for sure Edris and Jack's friendship was decimated, but after Jack got back with Celeste, he didn't seem to care about anything Edris had done.

That sort of left me out of the picture. Since Edris and I weren't together anymore, there weren't any football parties, basketball parties, dinners, or anything that involved all of us being a group. I didn't expect that there would be, but it had been an adjustment. Now, most of the time, I was alone. And I knew my alone time would only increase once Chloe and Bryant were married.

"What did you do last night after you left my place?" Chloe asked as she riffled through some shoe boxes looking for her size.

"Same thing I do every night. Go home, eat cannoli ice cream, and fall asleep watching old 90's shows."

"Katrina." Chloe shook her head. "You have got to get a life."

I knew where this conversation was going. What life did she expect me to have? I got up every morning, went to school, taught my students, and came back home to grade papers. I was a real adult.

"I thought we were going to talk about you. This is *your* time after all."

She stood up with one white stiletto heel shoe on. The shoe was gorgeous, too. Satin lined with an intricate lace design. "Everything has been about me lately with the wedding coming up. I want to know how you are doing."

"Chloe, I'm fine. I really wish you'd stop worrying about me."

"Alright, alright. Well, what do you think about these?"

"Perfection. Get them. You should get some slippers too, for the reception."

"You're right."

I smiled.

"So, I have to tell you something about the wedding, but I don't want you to flip out or be upset with me."

"Just shoot it straight. What is it?"

"I invited Faith to the wedding, and she said she'd come."

My face turned hot, but I didn't want to show it or admit it. "It's your day."

"What does that mean?"

"If you want the devil there herself, that's on you."

"Stop calling her that."

"Well..."

"You can't tell me that you're still blaming her for stuff that happened so long ago."

"No, I'm not. I don't understand why you need her there or even want her there."

Chloe placed the shoes back in the box. "I'm going to ask you this and don't blow up on me."

"I didn't blow up when you told me about the devil."

Her eyes lowered to tell me to stop it. "Have you talked to your therapist about Faith and everything that happened?'

I exhaled. Exhaled hard. "She's come up, in passing."

"In passing, huh. Well, maybe you should stop passing up the subject and let your therapist help you deal with what you're obviously still harboring against this woman."

"I'm not harboring anything."

"You apparently are, Katrina. The mere mention of her name and you get flushed with what's clearly pent-up anger."

I started going to therapy about a year ago, and while it had helped me deal with some things in my past, I'd been partial to pushing anything that had to do with Faith or Edris to the deepest recesses of my mind. I wasn't interested in revisiting the most painful part of my life.

I sincerely loved Edris, and I thought that we were back to-gether for good until Faith decided to embarrass all of us in the middle of a restaurant. As much as I loved Edris and wanted us to have a life together, I couldn't forgive him for being with Faith. That, I couldn't handle.

"Just think about it. You've come such a long way over the past year, and I think if your therapist has helped bring you into a better mindset with everything else, then why not this?"

I rolled my eyes. She knew I wasn't interested in this topic. "Since you invited her, I hope you have a plan to keep us apart."

"Come on, we are all grown. I'm not going to be playing secu-rity between the two of you on my special day."

I shrugged my shoulders.

After Chloe finally picked out her wedding shoes, I was ready to head home and crack open my cannoli ice cream. I wanted to get into my comfort zone and forget about having to see Faith again soon.

I didn't know how I felt about Chloe bringing up my therapy. We hadn't spoken extensively about it, although she knew about my time with my therapist, Dr. Alice, and I wanted to keep it that way. I wasn't exactly trying to broadcast that I was seeing a therapist.

Therapy was deeply personal to me. And I wanted to deal with my attitude and how I viewed relationships to better my life. I didn't want to keep going down the same road over and over again since it was obviously getting me nowhere.

After I ended things with Edris, I spent time thinking about everything that happened, even before Faith came into the picture. As much as Chloe tried to warn me about my behavior, pushing Edris away, I didn't want to see it or do anything about it. I had no one to blame but myself. I still didn't think that gave Edris free reign to sleep with Faith, but it happened, and history couldn't be changed.

I knew, going forward, I didn't want to run anyone else out of my life that could potentially bless me with more happiness than what I imagined with Edris. And that's what I focused on in therapy.

Dr. Alice was cool. She was a young black woman shedding a different light on mental health. She'd come to my school to assist with a school-based therapy program the school implemented, and after a conversation in the lunchroom, I decided to reach out to her for some help.

I liked talking to Dr. Alice because she was so easy-going and down to earth, and with her being a black woman just like me, she understood everything I was going through and saw the world much the same as I did.

She opened my eyes to not having to react to everything said or done to me. I saw how destructive my self-centeredness had been, and I saw how my time at college had truly affected me, even though I never wanted to admit it.

Although I shared with Dr. Alice parts of my college experience, I thought maybe Chloe was right, and it was time for me to face how our circle of friends played a part in my shutting down my emotions to only experiencing the negative ones.

For a while, Dr. Alice has been trying to convince me how healing and reparative writing can be. She'd been instructing me to start a journal and bring it with me to sessions, but I hadn't started, and I was unsure if I ever wanted to. Even when I thought that it was a good idea, my mind kept going to the fact that Faith was a writer, and I was pretty sure this was the same way she had gotten started. And I didn't want to do anything remotely on the same course as her.

Dr. Alice also had the bright idea of me getting back into the dating game. I'd been alone for the past two years, but I still couldn't fathom being with another man. Not because I was still hung up on Edris, I wasn't sure I was ready to put my heart back out there. And let's be for real, who was ready for me?

I looked around my dispirited apartment and decided, even if I didn't go out with the purpose of looking for a man, I still needed to get out of the apartment. Sitting on the couch, eating ice cream, and watching *Living Single* wasn't the way to go. I got up off the couch, cleaned myself up, and got gorgeous.

I settled on going to the Hot Tamale, remembering the last time I was there for a party, and it was stacked with beautiful brown skin tones in each and every shade. I worked my way over to the bar and ordered a drink. I never thought this would be my life. I should be married by now, or at least on the way, not out alone, hoping someone would take pity on me and ask me to dance. I should be at home having a romantic dinner with my man, sipping champagne.

Some trap music mixed with bounce was blaring across the lounge, and everyone seemed to be vibing to it. In the middle of the dance floor was a woman moving her hips as if no one existed here but her. She was reminiscent of Debbie Allen mixed with Mya and Ciara.

Once the mix ended, she fanned herself and made her way to the bar by me. "You're a very good dancer." I leaned over to say to her. "I've never been bold enough to dance alone."

"Thank you. I just flow with the music and don't worry about what everyone else is doing."

"How do you have that confidence?"

"Every woman has it, takes the right situation to pull it out." She ordered a drink from the burly bartender who looked like he should have been the bouncer. "You sound like a woman who's stepping out for the first time in a long while."

"I guess you could put it that way."

"You're a pretty woman, I'm sure you could snatch up any man in this place if you really wanted to."

"Pretty has nothing to do with it.

"You're right about that. Pretty don't keep a man."

"I can't even decide if I want a man right now."

"Why do you say that?"

"Been through enough with them."

"You can't let the past affect your future that much. You must control your happiness. Whether it's with a man in your life or not."

She was right.

"There's definitely not enough time in the world to wait for another human to bring you happiness."

"What are you, a relationship counselor?"

"More like a woman with experience."

This woman appeared out of the sweat and fog of an adult lounge and was making complete sense to me.

"My name is Katrina." I extended my hand.

"Willow, nice to meet you." She bobbed her head to the dancehall beat that the DJ had switched up to as she sipped her drink. "If you don't mind me saying, you sound like me shortly after my divorce."

"Oh, so you were tired of men as well?"

"So over them that I didn't care if I ever saw another one for as long as I lived."

"How did you get over it?"

"I started focusing on me."

"Don't we all already do that?"

She laughed. "Not in a selfish way. But I focused on spending time rediscovering myself, learning new things. Anything that sparked my interest, I'd explore. I started going to yoga classes, and I joined a book club. I traveled solo dolo and sincerely spent time enjoying things for myself. I stepped out of my comfort zone and did anything I wanted. Life is too short to wait for someone to do things with."

I shook my head in agreement.

"Doing things for yourself isn't selfish, it's making sure that you keep your mind and your body and your soul healthy to deal with the stresses of being a woman day in and day out."

EDRIS

Lately, I'd been spending so much time with Gabriella that I hadn't seen Jack or Bryant. Bryant would at least shoot me a text to see what was up with me, but Jack had been silent as hell over the past week or so. At first, I didn't think about it too much. I figured he was living peacefully and still honeymooning with Celeste.

"Aye, you talked to Jack?" Bryant said, leaning over the pool table to break the balls as we met to catch up.

"I was going to ask you the same thing."

"I hit him up about coming out with us tonight, but he didn't even respond. When's the last time you heard from him anyway?"

"I can't say that it was recent."

"I don't know whether or not to be concerned."

I shrugged. "He's probably just busy with married life. You're about to know how that goes."

Bryant's dark lips held a smirk. "I guess so."

"Things probably won't change too much for you and Chloe. It's like y'all already been married for like six years anyway."

"As nice as that thought is, I can't completely agree with it."

"Why would you say that?"

"I'm pretty sure things will change. Expectations will change. It's a whole different level of commitment, man."

I knew Bryant always took his relationship with Chloe seriously, but I could hear in his voice the conviction he had of how saying I do will change his life. But his relationship with Chloe had always been so solid that there was no doubt in my mind their marriage would follow the same standard.

People didn't have relationships like theirs anymore. I could see us going to a 50th wedding anniversary party for those two. Seeing them dance and look in each other's eyes the same way they do now. I had a feeling nothing would ever change between them.

I hoped to find that. If Gabriella was the one, I wasn't sure, but I was willing to put in the effort with her to see. We'd been having a great time getting to know each other, but I wasn't interested in rushing things or trying to force myself into a Chloe and Bryant situation. Things with Gabriella were day by day.

"How's the wedding planning coming?"

"Seems like it will never be done. I'll tell you, though, I am ready to get it done and over with."

"I'm sure the day will be here and gone before you know it," I said, making a bad scratch move.

Bryant chuckled. "How are things going with Gabriella?"

"Good, things are good. She's a pretty cool chick. I like everything about her."

"You've been keeping her a secret. Tell me about her."

I snickered. "She's not a secret. I've just been taking my time. Getting to know her, spending time finding out the little things about her."

"What does she do?"

"Her family owns a jewelry store business and just opened a store here that she's running."

"Geeze, her people into diamonds and gems."

I laughed. "Yea, she took me past the store once. Her grand opening is in a few days; you can roll with me if you want. Good chance for you to meet her."

"I'm there, but I'm leaving Chloe at home. I don't need her thinking that more jewelry besides that wedding ring is coming her way."

"Ha. Don't be like that. Bring wifey, she's going to be by your side for the rest of your life anyway."

"You're right about that. And guess what?" He grinned at me. "I wouldn't have it any other way.

***

I always felt a sense of relief when I pulled into Gabriella's driveway. I couldn't wait to wrap my arms around her and plant kisses on her cheeks. Her skin was always soft, inviting my lips to taste it in any way that I could. She was so open to my affection that I'd come to enjoy that I could give it to her without worry of her rejection or being unappreciative. A kiss to her shoulder always got the job done.

I trotted up to the door to ring the bell, but she was already there waiting for me. She opened her arms to embrace me as I walked through the door. She was gorgeous, dressed in a black sheer sleeved shirt and Seven Jeans with black stilettos, so simple, but so sexy.

"Did you change your hair?"

She ran her fingers over the freshly cut bangs. "Yea, I did, you're the only man I've been around who notices things like that." She smiled, and I knew I'd won some points. "I'm happy you could stop by. I've missed you."

"I missed you too. I couldn't wait to see you."

We hugged for a few moments; Gabriella's rose perfume overtook my nostrils, but made me feel comfortable. I hoped that she found the same comfort in my arms.

"Come in. I was putting some things away in the kitchen." She guided me through the entryway and passed the formal dining room, decorated in white and tan decor with accents of black.

The entry to the kitchen was wide and spacious, giving way to an open, fully equipped kitchen, complete with a see-through fridge. "All of this kitchen, do you cook?"

"Sometimes, mostly when I crave something specific. But the majority of the time, you know me, it's fresh fruits, veggies, fish. I like to keep it simple."

"I know you like to get down on some jerk chicken. Don't play." I teased her.

"You are right about that." She said as she stacked containers of fresh berries into the fridge. "I have some calls I need to return. Take a look through the house. I won't be long."

She was open to allowing me to go through every room in her home, so she clearly had nothing to hide. As she headed down a short hallway off the kitchen, I wandered into the living room, her flat screen bigger than mine. Bryant and Jack weren't going to believe how cool this woman was. In all the time I'd been hanging out with Gabriella, I hadn't spent much time at her home, so it was interesting to see more of her personal style. And I was happy she felt comfortable enough to let me in her space.

She leaned around the wall from the hallway, pulling her phone from her mouth. She whispered, "Go upstairs, check out the rest."

I headed up the angled staircase and saw the makings of a mini library. Books were stacked everywhere, along with book-cases still needing to be assembled. I picked up one of the books from the small table next to a wingback chair; it was about business finance.

Across the hall was a bedroom where another flat screen hung on the wall opposite a huge oak canopy bed. I thought it was a California King, but it had to be custom because it seemed much bigger. I placed my hand on the black and gold comforter.

"You like it?" She asked, standing in the doorway.

"I'd never get up."

"It is hard to get up in the morning sometimes. But lucky for me, I can operate on my own schedule."

I smiled. "I saw your library across the way."

"Yea, still a work in progress, but it's coming along. Much like the rest of the house."

"The house looks great to me."

She approached me, wrapping her arms around my neck, and my hands moved to her waist. She spoke soothingly into my ear. "You look good to me."

I didn't waste time talking. I kissed her. Her lips were toasty and delicate. I could feel the velvet of her lipstick; our tongues played, building up to a simmering passion.

Gabriella slowed down, releasing my tongue and putting her head down. "I'm sorry."

"Why are you apologizing, sweetheart?"

"Are we moving too fast?"

"I can't speak for you, but I'm ok. If you're not, please let me know."

"I just...I feel so comfortable with you."

"I feel comfortable with you, too, but I don't want you to question anything that may or may not happen between us. I want you to be sure in any decision you make."

Her eyes reconnected with mine. "Thank you for saying that."

I reached for her hands and brought them down between us. "We can move at any pace you want," I reassured her. "Listen, why don't I cook for you tonight. We can snuggle up on the couch and watch a movie."

Her brilliant smile returned. "I'd like that."

We went back down to the kitchen hand in hand. It didn't take us long to decide on shrimp with rice and fresh spinach. Gabriella pulled out some pans and cooking utensils for me to use before she settled in at the large, dark wood four-seat island. She propped her chin on her wrist and watched my every move.

"You almost look like you know what you're doing." She laughed at me as I almost lost a shrimp to the sink as I peeled it.

I had to laugh at myself.

"Edris, who taught you how to cook?"

"Kind of had to learn on my own. You know, when you move out of mom's house, you realize what skills you should have paid more attention to."

"That's for sure. What is your favorite thing to cook?"

"Nobody can mess with my BBQ skills."

She giggled. "Oh, yea, then you're in luck. Look out there on the patio."

I peeked through the window over the sink and saw a stainless-steel grill.

"Complete with burners."

"Oh, you think you doin' something."

"Hey, we can fire it up whenever and see who can really get down."

"You're on, little woman."

As I cooked, I glanced over at Gabriella, and she wasn't breaking her watchful eye. When our eyes would meet, we'd giggle like teenagers, but not speak. We were building a connection, and I liked it. I wanted us to continue to bond and get to know each other at a progressive pace.

"How's the grand opening for the store coming along?"

She sighed. "Sore topic."

"Sorry."

"No, it's just stressful, as you can imagine. It's a new business, so there's a lot to do. It's like a never-ending list of things to do."

I finished up the food and started making a plate for Gabriella. "Well, if there's anything I can do to help, let me know. Until then, don't even think about it. I'm sorry I even brought it up." I handed her a plate of steaming food.

"Thank you. This looks great."

I sat down at the island next to her. "I'm so interested to get to know more about you."

"Like what?"

"Everything. I mean, why are you the way you are? You're such perfection."

She laughed. "Now don't say that. I am by no means perfect. But I could as easily say the same thing about you. All you've shown me is kindness; you're sweet, understanding, caring. Got a little smarts and swag to you. I find myself wondering why you're single."

I smirked at her compliments. "I've been taking my time with dating. I was in a long-term relationship that didn't go well, that also didn't end well, and it's taken me some time to be willing to put myself back out there."

"I can understand that. It's good you took the time to be sure that you were ready. So many people hop from situation to situation and then act surprised when they either get their heart broken or end up in a relationship they have no business in."

"You said that you've been single for some time yourself, right?"

"Yes," she exhaled harshly. "Unfortunately, my situation was traumatic to me, and it took me a long time to get over it and, like you said, put myself back out there."

"Do you want to tell me about it?"

She looked me deeply in my eyes. I could tell she was searching for trust. "You don't have to if it makes you uncomfortable."

"No, it's ok. I want you to know."

"Take your time then," I said, sitting next to her with my plate of food.

"I was in love with the man I believed would be mine for the rest of my life. Our story started like a fairy tale. I met him in high school, my senior year, and even though we went to different schools, we were inseparable. We ended up going to college together, and he asked me to marry him. We got married three months later, and six months after that, I was pregnant with my baby girl." She paused as the memories of her past clouded her eyes.

"Take your time, Gabriella." I reached for her hand.

She composed herself. "I had a beautiful daughter, and my fairy tale turned into a nightmare. My now ex-husband is in prison for killing my daughter."

I was speechless. What could I say? There were no words to fill the void in the heart of a parent with no child. All I could do was put my arms around her and kiss her forehead. I wasn't prepared at all for this, so all I could do was offer her solace.

"I'm sorry. I shouldn't have pushed you to talk about this."

She sat up from my arms, wiping her eyes. "No, it's okay. I wanted to tell you."

"I can't say that I have any idea of how you feel because I don't, but I am so sorry."

"It's been four years now since my daughter was murdered, and I can't lie, it does hurt every day knowing that I never got to watch my baby grow up, but I had to come to a point where I kept my life moving forward."

Gabriella was showing me another part of her that I couldn't help but be attracted to. This vulnerability and real human emotion made her even more beautiful to me.

"You're amazing. And I'm not just saying that. I don't know too many people who have the spirit you do and have been through what you have. It's amazing to watch, and I'm so happy I've gotten the opportunity to even be around you."

A slight smile came to her lips. "Thank you. I appreciate you saying that." She gave me a peck on the cheek. "I hope you stay around for a while, Edris."

CHLOE

I sat in the big bay window of the new house that Bryant and I had just purchased. I never thought I'd be buying a new house and paying for a wedding at the same time, but since I'd taken a new teaching job at a private school out in Spring Gardens, the raise had been much appreciated and put to good use.

I loved our new home. It wasn't quite our dream place, but we'd been able to make some upgrades that made the place more of our own. The ranch-style house had 3 bedrooms and 2 bathrooms, which were well-suited for our plans for a couple of kids. Hopefully, a boy and a girl to satisfy us both.

I heard Bryant coming down the long hallway from the bedroom before he joined me in the front living room. "What's up, baby? Why are you sitting here like you're waiting for your lost puppy to come home?"

I rolled my eyes at him. "I'm not."

"Then what's up? Why do you look so sad? We're getting married in two days. You should be jumping up and down."

"I know." I smiled. "Trust me, I am thrilled. I can't wait to be your wife. Officially, since you know, I already have been."

He laughed, kissing me on the cheek. "I know. Nothing like official, huh?"

"You know it."

"Have you talked to Katrina today?"

"I did this morning. She was pretty excited to let me know that she's going to be bringing a date to the wedding."

"Oh, okay, who is this guy? Do you know?"

"She met him at the coffee shop close to her place. I guess they've been hanging out and she's really into him."

"Good for her. Then I guess it won't be so bad when she sees Edris with Gabriella," he raised his eyebrows.

"I'm hoping everyone will just chill and remember that the day is not about any of them."

"We know, baby, it's all about you."

I playfully pushed Bryant's shoulder. "It is not. It's about us." I leaned into him to kiss his lips.

"Yes, it is."

"Everything is so different now. I didn't imagine life would be like this when we got married."

"What do you mean by that?"

"Seriously? Come on. Think about it. Jack is married to Celeste. How is it that Jack got married first?" I laughed at the thought. "Katrina and Edris are both with new people. I didn't see that coming. I guess even after all this time, I was still holding onto the hope that the two of them would get back together, but I can see why that wouldn't be the case, and I am happy they have been able to find new people."

"It is an interesting shift in dynamic, but I'm sure everyone will be just fine all together again. Everyone will remember why we are all together and leave their BS at the doorstep."

"What's up with Jack and Edris? Do you think they will have a problem seeing Faith again?"

"Now, why would you ask that? You've already invited the woman."

"Because it's real now. It's easy to say you don't care until you have to face the situation head-on."

"Jack is married to Celeste now, and Edris has moved on with Gabriella, and they are happy together. I'm more interested in Edris and Katrina seeing each other again. What do you think about that?"

"It's the same thing you just said. Edris has moved on with Gabriella, and Katrina is bringing this guy, Johany. Everyone will be so into their dates; they won't have time to look at each other."

"If you say so."

"What are you worried about?"

"Nothing. Everything will go as planned. I'm speaking it forward now."

I stood up to plant kisses all over my future husband's face. Before I knew it, he was pulling me forward and onto his lap.

"I love you, Chloe."

"I love you more."

"Not possible," he laughed, kissing me. "You know I can't wait to fill this house with babies."

"We have to fill the entire house?" I giggled.

Bryant shrugged. "We'll start with three and work our way up."

"What happened to a boy for me and a girl for you?"

"They comin' and then twins and triplets."

My eyes ballooned up. "Now I know you're on something."

Bryant laughed heartily, "Ok, I may be overdoing it on the count, but I do mean it when I say that I can't wait to have children with you. You're going to be a phenomenal mom."

"Thank you, baby. I know you're going to be an awesome dad."

THE WEDDING

KATRINA

I rushed up the stairs of the church to the dressing area, where Chloe was putting on her dress. I must have run up and down these stairs at least 105 times, getting whatever Chloe could think of. This time, it was her lipstick because she couldn't wear what the makeup artist had brought for her. Before that, it was her headpiece, before that, she needed water, and before that, I can't even remember. I was dizzy and needed water myself. I was beginning to think I would never put my own dress on. I'd have to hobble down the aisle in my distressed jeans, t-shirt, and one heel.

On one of my innumerable trips, I caught a glimpse of Edris arriving. He wasn't dressed in his tux yet, but he still looked good. I closed my eyes, took a deep breath, and made my way back up the steps, thinking of Johany. I couldn't wait for him to arrive later for the reception. I'd begged him to come to the wedding, but he had to work and couldn't get off duty at the firehouse in time, but promised he would be off in time to meet me at the reception.

I wanted Edris to see me with Johany, but what difference would it really make? Edris and I hadn't spoken in a long time; it was apparent he no longer thought about me. Not even enough to see if I was still breathing.

However, I was interested in seeing Faith again. While the two of us hadn't spoken either, I'd seen the release of her new book and wondered if she decided to take the tell-all approach or hide behind made-up characters. Chloe begged me not to start anything with Faith when I saw her. I questioned why she would think I would, and she only gave me the evil eye.

She needed to trust me; I wasn't interested in starting anything, and even if I was, I knew better than to do it here. If Chloe was truly worried, then she shouldn't have invited Faith in the first place. We both knew she was the one who liked to start shit at inappropriate times.

I was more interested in the show of Edris and Jack seeing Faith again. Their friendship seemed to have survived her shenanigans, but since I was now out of the loop, so to speak, I didn't know if that was entirely true. Chloe told me they still hung out every Thursday night after work, but Bryant also told her that Jack had been sort of weird and off over the last couple of weeks, but no one knew why.

I knocked on the door to Chloe's dressing room. "Hey, girl."

"Hey." She could barely turn around with all the tulle that made up her princess-cut gown. The makeup artist was putting on the finishing touches as Chloe's mom sat in a chair next to the mirror, admiring her soon-to-be wedded daughter.

I approached my best friend and saw how beaming and radiant she looked. "Chloe." That was all I could bring myself to say. I was going to cry.

"Do I look okay?"

"You look more than okay. You're gorgeous."

"Really? You don't think my makeup is too much."

"Chloe, it's your wedding day. No such thing as too much."

"I'm so nervous."

"You shouldn't be."

"Why would you say that?"

I laughed, taking her hand into mine. "You're already the man's wife. This is just the ceremonial part. You've already been in the role, honey."

We both laughed. Even Chloe's mom joined in, "I told you, babygirl."

"Katrina, have you seen Bryant? Is he here? He stopped responding to my text, and it's driving me crazy."

"Yes, he's here. He's getting dressed. Stop worrying so much."

"Okay, yes, you're right. I've got to breathe. Everything is going to be just fine today."

"It absolutely will be. Now, I've got to get dressed, or I'm going to ruin all the wedding pictures."

EDRIS

I parked in the side lot of the church, turning the ignition of the car off. "You sure you're ready for this?"

"Yes, why wouldn't I be?"

"Today is a big day."

"I know."

"You nervous?"

"I'm not the one getting married."

I laughed, joking with Gabriella. She'd only met Bryant and Chloe once at the grand opening party for her store, but she hadn't met Jack and Celeste or been subjected to Katrina yet. And it pained me to come clean and tell her the truth about what happened between me, Katrina, and Faith. As much as I wanted to keep the truth about my negligence from Gabriella, I wasn't going to let her walk into this situation blindly.

"Are you nervous?" she asked me.

"No, why would you say that?"

"You know why. When is the last time you've seen Katrina?"

"I don't know, but I'm not concerned about seeing her at all."

"And what about Faith?"

"No concern there either. Neither one of them matters. All that matters today is getting my boy down the aisle and hitched and having my gorgeous lady on my arm." I leaned across the seat and kissed her on the cheek.

"You're right."

"Seriously, though, I'm glad you're here with me."

"I wouldn't want to be anywhere else."

Gabriella and I were going strong, getting to know each other on a deeper level, and I was beginning to see a future with her, and maybe I would be the last of the crew to tie the knot. I never thought I'd want to think about doing it after Katrina's many ultimatums, but Gabriella was changing my mind.

As I made my way into the church carrying my tux in a dress bag over my arm, I saw Katrina scurry up the back stairs. I don't know if she's avoiding me, but if we didn't speak to each other all day, I think I would be fine with that. But how realistic was I being? Besides, I had no ill will towards Katrina.

I headed into the men's dressing area, where Bryant and Jack were already fully suited.

"Man, you are late!" Bryant wasted no time laying into me.

"I'm here. I'm here."

"You'd better get dressed; we have to go out there soon." Jack hurried me along.

"I know, I know."

It took me no time at all to get into full wedding gear and finish polishing off the shiniest patent leather shoes I'd ever seen. This was definitely Chloe's doing; if it was up to Bryant, we'd all be in sneakers. But I'd sacrifice for the sake of the beautiful bride.

I envied Bryant a little bit with his impending step into another level of commitment with Chloe. They stood together when all of us lost our minds. Even faced the death of Bryant's mother together. Nothing seemed to break them, and here they were. I wanted that. And I hoped I could have it with Gabriella, but I knew only time would tell. I couldn't rush into it like I believed Jack did.

Jack seemed to be in good spirits today, but I still found it odd that we hadn't seen him in a few weeks. Now wasn't the time to get into where he'd been hiding, but I knew something wasn't right with him.

I didn't want to assume things with Celeste weren't great, but it was usually woman problems that sent him into hibernation. I wanted to know what was up, but I didn't know if Jack would want to confide in me. We had been cool, but it wasn't a secret that our friendship hadn't been the same. I wasn't sure how he would take me questioning him or even be open to talking to me about what's going on.

I finished getting dressed and headed back into the main area with the guys. It sounded like I was walking in at the right moment.

"I didn't think you were about to make it today," Bryant said to Jack.

"Why would you say that? What makes you think I would miss this day for the world?"

"You've been a little MIA lately."

Jack hung his head. "Yea, I know, man, a lot going on at home."

"Between you and Celeste?"

"Man," he brushed Bryant off. "We don't need to get into it now. It's your day."

Bryant looked at his watch. "You're right." He exhaled. "It's time to get out there."

FAITH

Sitting in the church, listening to Bryant and Chloe confess their undying love for each other. My stomach churned. The more time went on, the more I drowned out what was being said. My attention was fully on Jack. His, no doubt, custom suit fit his body just right, and as good as he looked, I was only focused on the last time I saw his toned body and the way it had been intertwined with mine. He looked too damn good; I wanted him as soon as this ceremony was over.

I wanted to feel his lips hungrily sliding across my skin, his tongue flickering across the points of my body he knew would excite me the most. Both his lips and tongue awakened my center as he pulled my southern lips apart and tasted the dewy flesh. I quivered at the thought of our reconnecting again. I had to slow my thoughts down before I burst into flames in the Lord's House.

Once Chloe completed her I do, the two were announced as one, and they scurried off into their new lives together under a rain of white and pink flowers. It was official. Bryant and Chloe were husband and wife.

The wedding reception was to follow and was at a venue about 20 minutes from the church. As I exited the sanctuary to head to my car, I saw Edris standing at the front doors with a woman. I couldn't decide if I should say something or not. I thought, forget it, it would either be awkward now or later at the reception. Let's just get to it.

"Edris." I greeted him as I approached.

"Faith, hello, how are you?"

"Well, thank you. And yourself?"

"I'm great." He turned to look at the woman standing next to him. He reached for her hand, "This is my girlfriend Gabriella."

"Hello," her voice soft and unsuspecting of me.

"Gabriella, I'm Faith. Nice to meet you."

"Nice to meet you, too. Will you be heading to the reception?"

"Yes, I'll see you both over there." I spotted Jack right outside the door and decided to make my move while I could.

As soon as I reached the door, I felt a touch to my arm, disrupting my mission. "Faith."

I recognized the voice and knew who it was before I even turned around. "Katrina." I was right.

I turned to find Katrina in her blush pink off-the-shoulder bridesmaid's dress. She actually looked quite beautiful; her chestnut brown hair had been chopped into a Toni Braxton-like pixie that suited her quite well.

"Chloe told me you'd be coming."

"Yes, when she extended the invitation, I was a bit surprised, but here I am."

"Hmph. Are you here alone?"

Really? Same old Katrina. Low blows. "Yes, I am. And you? I just met Edris's girlfriend."

"Yea, she seems nice. If you're coming to the reception, you can meet my other half, Jahony."

"Oh, sure. I'd love to meet him. I'll see you guys over there." I waved goodbye.

I didn't need Katrina or Edris, for that matter, rubbing in my face their new lives with new people. Yes, I was single, but hopefully I wouldn't be by the end of the night. Katrina and Edris could try to rub whatever they wanted into my face, but by the end of the night, Jack would be back with me.

As I hit 95, I thought about Edris being so quick to introduce me to his girlfriend and Katrina being so quick to say that she had someone in her life. It was as if they really wanted each other to know and not necessarily me. I had a feeling the two of them hadn't spoken to each other all day.

I wasn't concerned about anyone and what they wanted to prove to each other. My mind was on one mission, making sure Jack came home with me and we re-established what should have never ended in the first place.

JACK

I wiped buckets of sweat from my underarms in the restroom of the reception venue. I'd taken off nearly my entire tux. What the hell was I thinking of going back to Faith, knowing full well she was coming to this wedding and my wife would be here?

Celeste and I were already having a tough time, and the two of them in the same room was an idiot move on my part. I was supposed to be married so I wouldn't have to put myself in these types of situations again, but here I was.

I'd spent so much time looking down on Faith for the stunt she pulled, and I went right back to pulling the ultimate coup with her. I fell to my own desire because I was in an unhappy moment in my marriage. That wasn't right at all, and Celeste didn't deserve that, and really, neither did Faith.

I exhaled, looking at myself in the mirror over the mounted floating sink vanity. My arms shook as I put my weight onto them. I knew I had to keep Celeste and Faith apart. But Chloe and Bryant decided to go with a small, intimate reception for family and close friends only, so there weren't a lot of bodies to put in between them.

I redressed and walked out of the men's room.

"Hey, you okay?" Celeste was standing waiting for me right outside the door.

"Yea, yea, yea." I rigorously shook my head up and down.

"You sure?"

"Yes, Celeste, that's what I said."

She hung her head and took off walking in front of me.

I wasn't trying to be short with her, but my nerves were getting the best of me. I rushed my footsteps to catch up with Celeste as she entered the main room to find our table. I caught up to her and reached for her hand, but she snatched away.

Things between Celeste and me were far from okay, but I wanted my marriage to work, and I knew if Celeste, more than likely, even saw me talking to Faith, I had no chance of making things better any time soon.

Celeste was fully aware of who Faith was, but I hadn't told her the entire truth, and I hadn't told her that I had just with Faith a couple of weeks ago. I preferred to take that secret to my grave.

Edris came bobbing up to the table to tell me that it was time for us to toast the bride and groom. I was thankful I wrote my toast down on a small note card, like my wife suggested, because there was no way I could formulate complete thoughts right now.

I walked up to the front table where Bryant and Chloe were seated together in large plush high-back chairs at a table for two. My legs were still shaking, fingers flipping the small card from hand to hand.

I picked up the microphone from the table, shooting a small smile to the couple who grinned back at me. They had no idea the rollercoaster of marriage they were in for. But, on the other hand, it was Bryant and Chloe. If anyone could navigate this crazy dimension, it would be them. They'd managed to do it thus far.

I was wobbly. "Good...good evening, everybody. We're here. Here to honor this amazing couple." I looked back at Bryant, who raised his glass to me. "I'm happy to be here celebrating with the two of you. If anyone can take on the journey of what the holy matrimony of marriage is, it is these two right here. I've watched over the years as the two of you came together and synced in perfect harmony. Oftentimes showing me the way. You two are the epitome of love and the peace it can bring."

As I read the notecard, peace stood out to me. My stomach was in knots as I continued to spew out the words written on the card. I thought I'd found peace with Celeste, but catching Faith out of the corner of my eyes winking at me, the facade of peace I thought I had was quickly shattering.

The mic was slipping from my sweaty hand. Edris ended my toast as he patted me on the back. Thank you, my boy to the rescue.

"Jack, thank you so much," he said, almost pushing me out of the way.

As I walked to my table to join Celeste, Edris's speech ran through my ears like wind in a wide tunnel. I zoned completely out. My mind wandered to Faith and what she could be thinking right now. Was she upset that I was avoiding her? Should I just face her? But what would that look like to Celeste?

Edris wrapped up his speech, and everyone began to clap. I missed every word. My mind couldn't keep up with what was going on around me. I wanted to leave and remove myself from the entire situation, but I knew that wasn't an option.

The DJ turned up the music, and I saw Edris heading my way. "I'm surprised. You said some pretty encouraging words there, my friend."

"Yea, I tried my best."

"You killed it. No worries."

He started to walk off, but I reached for his shoulder. "Hey. Did you talk to Faith?"

"Yea, I saw her over at the church. Introduced her to Gabriella and pretty much kept it moving. Why?"

"Um. Just wondered."

He gave me a weird side eye and went to greet some of Bryant's family. I sat down next to Celeste.

"Such nice words for a man who doesn't seem as interested in his own wife."

"What does that mean?"

"Exactly what I said. When will we sync to our perfect harmony?"

"Do you want to get into that right now?"

"Why not? This is as good a time as any. Love is in the air, right?" Her words seared against my ears.

I felt a soft touch on my shoulder.

"Jack."

I knew that voice. That sultry, seductive voice had been leaping across my mind day in and day out. I turned to face head-on what I had been trying to avoid. "Faith."

"Good to see you. I wanted to say hello over at the church, but you ran out so quickly. It's been a minute."

"It has. It's nice to see you too." I didn't want to be rude, but I attempted to turn my back.

She stepped back on her stiletto heel. "That's all you have to say to me. Nice to see you."

"Excuse me." Celeste extended her hand to Faith. "Hi. I'm Celeste."

Faith slowly took her hand. "Ok. Nice to meet you." Faith was confused. "Jack, why haven't you called me?"

"Yes, Jack, why haven't you called her?" Celeste leaned into me, awaiting my response.

"I'm sorry, who are you?" Faith inquired.

Celeste scoffed. "I'm Jack's wife."

Faith took two steps back. Celeste's words were an uppercut to Faith's gut. I could see her chest rise and fall in her off-the-shoulder high-low dress. Her breath quickened with the discovery of my real life. I didn't know what to say or what to expect next. I thought, who would swing on who first?

Faith stuttered out her words. "Jack, this is your wife? Your wife, you're married?"

"Six months," Celeste spoke up.

Faith's lips tightened, and her nose scrunched up. She began to nod her head. I knew what that meant, and it wasn't good. I didn't need to be the reason Bryant and Chloe's wedding was ruined.

"Faith, please, can we go outside and talk?"

Celeste punched me in my shoulder. "Go outside and talk for what?"

Faith's eyebrow lifted. "Yes, Jack, talk for what?" She turned her attention to Celeste. "Why don't you talk to your wife and tell her how much of a liar you are. Or does she already know that?"

"And what exactly has my husband lied about?"

"You should ask him." Faith turned on her heels to leave.

"Faith, wait. Don't leave." I followed behind her.

Celeste shouted. "Jack, what are you doing?"

I didn't know if she was following me, and I didn't care. I had to catch up with Faith. "Faith, wait, please." I caught up to her at the front door. "Please, talk to me."

"Sounds like you should be talking to your wife."

"Yes, you should be." Celeste's voice flowed into my ears from behind me. "What the hell is going on, Jack?"

Of course, I would find myself in the exact situation I was trying to avoid. My efforts proved to be futile. I was an idiot for thinking this would work out just fine. Having Celeste and Faith together couldn't have had a good outcome. I was an idiot. There was no way I could fix this mistake.

"Jack, answer me," Celeste demanded.

"Celeste, this is Faith."

"We're past that part. I know who she is, and she obviously didn't even know I existed. Why is that?"

"We hadn't spoken in a while."

"Jack, don't keep lying to her." Faith scolded me.

"Lying to me about what?" Celeste punched me in my now stinging shoulder again.

I couldn't bring myself to tell Celeste the truth. I knew I lied to her, and I knew I selfishly lied to Faith. There was no doubt about it. I was busted, and there was nothing I could deny. By the look on Faith's face, she was ready and willing to tell my wife the truth if I didn't.

"Jack, spit it out. Now!" Celeste commanded.

I stuttered, unable to formulate the words.

"He slept with me a couple of weeks ago." Faith had diarrhea of the mouth and beat me to the truth.

In a flash of wind, Celeste's hand came across my face. Her palm slamming against my cheek sent an echo back through the entire reception hall. My jaw stung like a million wasps all charged me at once. I couldn't blame her. I deserved whatever she wanted to do to me.

Celeste spoke through tears. "Tell me she's lying."

I looked at Faith, still holding my face.

"He's lying." Faith hissed to Celeste.

"Excuse me, but I'm talking to my husband." She quickly turned her attention back to me. "Jack, don't lie to me. Did you sleep with her?"

I could only shake my head yes.

Celeste flung her hand back. I braced for another impact, but she changed her mind. She inhaled deeply and twisted her body to go back inside.

I turned to Faith. "What the hell is wrong with you? Why would you do that?"

"Don't turn this on me. You lied. Why didn't you tell me that you're married?" she put her hand up. "The better question is why were you in my poetry cafe, why were you in my face, why were you at my home, why were you in my bed?"

"Faith. I wasn't trying to deceive you."

She scoffed.

"I mean it. I'm sorry."

"I can't believe I came here to try and get back with you."

"What?"

"You heard me. I came here thinking that what we shared was real and that something was still there between us. Obviously, I'm the idiot in this situation."

"No, you're not. I'm sorry. I didn't mean any of this to happen this way."

"Then what did you set out to do, Jack? Explain that to me."

"I don't know, but not this."

"Why did you come looking for me? And don't give me some *I don't know* answer, because you do."

I shrugged my shoulders. "I guess that day I saw you in the coffee shop, I looked at you, and I realized how much I missed you. How much I still wanted you."

"You're married!" She shouted.

I heard the click of heavy heels coming my direction. I turned around to see Celeste stomping towards us. "You weren't worried about that when you had my husband in your bed. Oh, I'm sorry, my ex-husband."

Celeste brushed past me without a second look. Ex-husband! "Celeste, where are you going?" I followed behind her up the sidewalk leading to the parking lot.

"I'm going home to pack up my shit."

"Baby, please."

"It's too late for please. You've made it comprehensively clear that you don't give a damn about this marriage, so why should I?"

"I drove us here, so where are you even walking to?"

She laughed. "You think I need you to get home." She continued walking down the sidewalk to a rideshare car. "You should go talk to her so you can have somewhere to sleep tonight."

There was nothing I could say to keep Celeste here. She was too angry with me, and she had every right to be. And I didn't want to risk another slap to the face.

I walked back to the front of the venue, where Faith was still standing.

"I messed up."

She crossed her arms. "Yea, you did."

"Faith, I know, I don't need you to rub it in."

"Don't act like you don't owe me an apology."

"I did apologize to you."

"You said some other things." Her eyes met mine, and I was taken aback by the compassion in them as she looked at me.

"I said a lot."

"You said you missed me, you still wanted me."

I didn't know how to respond. Any anger she may have had didn't seem to exist anymore, but why? Why wasn't she still enraged with me and looking at me as if she didn't care about the situation I had created?

"Did you mean what you said, Jack?"

"Yes, I meant it. I haven't stopped thinking about you."

"Did you miss me because we happened to run into each other?"

"No, I never stopped thinking about you."

"Then why didn't you reach out to me?"

I paused, deciding if I should tell the truth. It was time for me to. "I wanted to stay mad at you instead of confronting how I really felt for you. My hurt was more important than anything else. I didn't want to forgive you."

"Then what changed when you decided to hunt me down?"

"I saw you in that coffee shop, and it felt like some sort of fateful moment to me. Once I saw you, nothing about the past mattered. I just wanted you."

"So, you're still the same old Jack. Sees what he wants and drops everything to get it. No matter who he hurts."

Same old me? Maybe I hadn't changed. I tried to convince myself I was someone else by becoming Celeste's husband. I had only fooled myself all this time. Marrying Celeste was a mistake. All my cards built on a shifty foundation were crashing down, and I had nothing to do but blame myself.

"Jack, say something, what are you thinking?"

"I'm such an asshole, and apparently that will never change."

"The question remains, why? Why do you make the decisions you make? I had to ask myself the same question after everything happened between us and the poor decisions I'd previously made in my own life."

I hung my head, unsure if I could even answer the question of why. "I don't know that I can think of that, Faith."

"It's not a quick answer you blurt out. You need to look inside yourself and figure it out. You keep making the same mistakes repeatedly because you've ignored why you rationalize your thoughts the way you do."

"I guess I'll have nothing but time to do that since my wife is probably well into packing her things by now."

"Then go stop her." She said in a low voice.

I faced Faith head-on. Touching her arm. "What if that's not what I want?"

Her eyes slowly met mine. "What is it that you want, Jack?"

Fire burned back at me when I looked into Faith's eyes. This was the chemistry I'd been missing. I settled by marrying Celeste, and now what was real was staring me back in my face. "I've always wanted you."

"You shoved me right out of the door."

"Out of embarrassment, anger, I didn't know what to do or say back then, but my feelings for you never went away."

"Then why didn't you reach out to me before you decided to get married?"

"Time went on. I figured you went on."

"Do you love her?"

"My feelings for you always lingered in the background."

Faith took in a deep breath and exhaled. "I can't take getting jerked around, Jack. I need to know that you're not just feeding me bullshit lines. The only reason I even came here today was to talk to you."

"Why did you want to talk to me?"

"Is that a for real question?"

"You couldn't tell from when we reconnected how much I wanted you."

Damn, she was for real.

"Jack, I thought I lost you forever and lost out on something that could have changed my entire life, and then when I saw you again in that coffee shop, I thought it was fate finally twisting in my favor, too."

I couldn't take it anymore. "Come here."

I pulled Faith's arm, her body collapsing into mine. I used my index finger to lift her chin and bring her lips to mine. I needed to feel that instant chemistry and spark we'd always had. As soon as her flesh met mine, we melted into each other. She didn't fight me or pull away. We both wanted this.

A soft moan escaped her lips, and she had me. Just like before. All the lies didn't matter anymore. I wanted Faith. She'd come into my life in an unexpected way, but she'd been exactly what I needed to change my mindset.

I knew I was wrong for what I'd done to Celeste, and I was sure she would let me hear it once I got home, but it was time for us to be honest with each other and realize that our marriage wasn't right, and it never would be as long as my thoughts and feelings always went back to Faith.

It was time for me to grow up, stop being immature with my feelings, reckless in my actions, and see that the woman right in front of me could help me through it all. No more lies.

Photo By: Tyrone Mitchell of A1.image

About the Author

Carmen Elle is a novelist from Columbus, Ohio, where she crafts stories rooted in real-world dynamics with just enough escapism to keep readers on the edge of their seats. Through witty and insightful storytelling, Carmen writes for those who aren't afraid to talk back to the TV. Her work dives into the complexities of relationships, identity, and the choices that define us, offering a fresh perspective for readers who crave both authenticity and a captivating escape.